He was commanding, powerful.

"I don't know who you think you are, Derek de Molay, but you need to leave now. Immediately." She turned her back on him. Her cheeks were so hot they could have burned toast to a crisp.

He crowded in next to her, elbowing aside the patron seated in the next chair.

"Listen to me, Rachel Duncan." He leaned in close, speaking to her as if they were the only two people in Chicago. "I've been sent here to gather information and I don't have time to waste." His eyes got wide and then they narrowed into a concentrated stare. His expression was suddenly grave. "I *have* to talk to you. Something in your life is very wrong—"

She'd been staring at him, speechless at his temerity. She finally came to herself. She was used to men trying to overpower and intimidate with their masculinity and she knew how to deal with that sort of thing. Yet, here she sat.

There was something compellin
this man that h
her mesmerize

By Margaret and Lizz Weis

WARRIOR ANGEL

WARRIOR ANGEL

MARGARET AND LIZZ
WEIS

AVON BOOKS
An Imprint of HarperCollins*Publishers*

AVON BOOKS
An Imprint of HarperCollins*Publishers*
10 East 53rd Street
New York, New York 10022-5299

ISBN: 978-0-06-083325-1
ISBN-10: 0-06-083325-4
www.avonromance.com

First Avon Books paperback printing: March 2007

Printed in the U.S.A.

10 9 8 7 6 5 4 3 2 1

To my friends,
Beth, Kim and Kate,
who have forever changed me for the better.

Lizz

Acknowledgments

We would like to gratefully acknowledge the book *Leg the Spread: A Woman's Adventures Inside the Trillion-Dollar Boy's Club of Commodities Trading* by Cari Lynn (Broadway Publishers, October 2005). If you enjoyed reading about Rachel and her life in the pit and would like to learn more about this fascinating subject, we urge you to read this book.

Margaret and Lizz

Long is the way
And hard, that out of hell leads up to light.

John Milton, *Paradise Lost*, (1667)
Bk. 2, 1. 404

Prologue

He sat in the antechamber, waiting to be taken into their presence.

He remembered another time he had sat waiting like this. It was October 13, 1307. He had been a living man, locked in a prison cell, waiting to be escorted to the Chamber of Advocacy to answer for his crimes. But he was not a criminal. He had not picked a pocket or cut someone's throat. His crime was that he was a knight in the holy order of the Knights Templar.

Judging by the name of the place to which he was being taken—Chamber of Advocacy—one might have assumed he and the Inquisitors would be sitting down to hold some type of polite discourse. He would be asked questions which, as a knight, he was bound to answer truthfully.

Far from it.

Three days they spent torturing him, using every means possible—and some of them were hideously creative—to force him to confess to crimes he had never committed. They brought him as near death as they dared, then restored him to life. Sometimes, using such techniques, the tormentors went too far and their prisoners died, their hearts giving out under the cruel abuse. Derek was then young and strong, proud and courageous, and he had lived a long time, enduring unspeakable torment, until death brought him final, blessed release.

Derek had not, as had so many of his comrades, broken down and confessed to the crimes the Inquisitors maintained he had committed. He had done none of these terrible things. They wanted him to say that the Order was interested only in accumulating wealth, that its knights were traitors and cowards, thieves and murderers, sinners who had renounced God and worshipped the devil. Derek had refuted all of these charges, though they broke his bones and seared his flesh. He was a true knight and he believed his fellows to be true knights. He had remained faithful unto death to a cause in which he believed with all his heart and soul. He died with his faith in God unshaken.

It was after death that Derek started to ask questions.

After his death, his soul went to the twilight realm of Purgatory, where he waited to be judged worthy of admittance to the Blessed Realm. In

Purgatory, Derek saw Truth, as all men and women see Truth when their days on Earth are accomplished. He saw Truth and the young knight, now one of God's angels, was shocked and angered.

Derek saw the Knights of the Templar fall into the dust. The knights were not brought down by Lucifer and his Dark Angels who were the knights' sworn, eternal enemies, but by the machinations of corrupt and clever men. Derek saw some of his comrades wilt at merely the thought of torture and eagerly confess to terrible crimes in order to save their own skins. He saw the Knights Templar end up in ruin and disgrace, their noble deeds of heroism and valor forgotten.

Derek saw all this and he could not believe it. He himself had never done such horrible deeds. He did not believe that his comrades could do them. There could be only one answer. God had forsaken the Templars. God had forgotten those who died in His Name, defending His pilgrims.

Waiting in Purgatory, Derek received another summons. He was brought before the archangels who were considering his admittance into the Blessed Realm of Heaven. He watched other angels go before him. They dropped to their knees in reverence, begged forgiveness for their sins, and were welcomed into God's presence with understanding. The archangels embraced them and carried them into a beautiful eternity.

When it was Derek's turn, he did not kneel. He did not confess his sins. He stood tall and proud, a true knight, and confronted the Angels of Light in anger.

"You saw the suffering I was made to endure," he told them. "I kept faith with God. Why did God forsake me?"

"No mortal can fathom the mind of God," the archangel told him gently. "Know that He loves you."

"Love!" Derek cried, anger swelling inside him. "Where was His love for me when I was being tortured for my faith? What does He know of love?"

"What do you know of love, Derek?" asked the archangel.

Derek thought the question flippant. He was a warrior, a holy knight who had chosen valor and glory in battle above love. Love made a man weak, caused his sword arm to falter in the midst of a fight.

"Did you fight evil for God's glory, Derek, or for your own? Did you truly put your faith in God or in men? Was your sacrifice made for love of God and your fellow men or out of false pride in yourself? You must ask yourself these questions, Derek," the archangel said to him and his tone was not angry, but soft with sorrow. "You cannot enter the Blessed Realm with a heart full of rage."

"I do not want to enter," said Derek defiantly, but even as he spoke, he saw the glittering gates closing against him, shutting him out. He was tempted for a moment to beg forgiveness, but he was too proud. And he was too angry.

"I would still serve God," he told the archangels. "For I am a true knight and I would yet fight for His cause."

"You will be sent back to Purgatory, Derek," said the archangels. "There you will join the brave soldiers who wage eternal war against Lucifer and the Angels of Darkness who seek to undermine Heaven and bring mankind to ruin and destruction. It is our hope and prayer that you will come at last to understanding."

Derek hoped so, too, though he did not think it possible. God was the one who had to be made to understand. Derek accepted the angel's judgment and returned to Purgatory.

Derek was accoutered in the shining armor given to God's holy warriors. He held in his hands a sword of flame and carried a shield of honor and righteousness. He joined other men and women in the battle to drive back the archfiends of Hell, who came creeping and slithering up from the fiery depths, trying to destroy the angels who waged eternal war against them, protecting humanity as best they could from the forces of evil.

Unfortunately, the forces of darkness are powerful and men—and sometimes angels—are weak.

One day, as Derek was resting on the field of battle, weary from the day's fighting, the Dark Angels came to him. He was used to seeing them in their demonic form, their faces hideous and twisted with hatred and envy; their limbs contorted, their skin burnt and charred. He did not at first recognize these for what they were, for they wore pleasing forms. He soon came to know them, however.

"Derek," they said to him in sultry voices, "we see the anger inside you. Come join with us. You do not belong here, fighting God's battles when He cares nothing for you. He is merely using you. Join our war and help us overthrow God and set King Lucifer in His place. You will stand in the place of honor beside Lucifer's throne and be one of his commanders."

"My quarrel is between myself and God. I may have lost my faith in Him, but I still believe in good and in righteousness. I would never consider joining the cause of evil," Derek told them. "I died a man of honor and I will remain true to myself."

"The time will come when you will be sorry, Derek," the archfiends warned him. "God has forsaken you once. He will do so again."

Derek drew his sword and, at the sight of the blazing white fire, the archfiends vanished.

Derek remained in Purgatory for centuries, fighting alongside his comrades, other souls not yet ready to enter Heaven. He was proud of his work. His flaming sword and shining shield kept the Darkness at bay. If, sometimes, after a terrible battle, he recalled his glimpse of the beauty and peace of the Blessed Realm and he found himself longing to go there to rest, he would remember his own torment and his heart would harden. He fought on.

And then this day, in a new century just begun,

a century numbered 2000, came the summons. The Angels of Light wanted to speak to him concerning a special assignment.

Derek proudly put on the white tabard marked with the red cross of the Order of Knights of the Templar over his shining armor, and left the battlefield to answer the summons.

One

As he paced about the antechamber to Heaven, waiting impatiently for the angels to summon him into their presence, Derek could look out the doors into the twilight world of Purgatory. The realm existed in a perpetual red haze, for the sun never rose here, the sun never set. As there was no day, there was no night. Purgatory was a battlefield, where some of those souls who were not deemed ready to enter Heaven continued to serve God by voluntarily helping to fight the eternal battle against the Dark Angel, Lucifer, and his archfiends.

The battles were terrible, for the archfiends fought with weapons of hideous make and design. Derek bore the scars of his many wounds proudly. He was a valiant soldier and, due to his valor, he was rewarded by being given the honor of commanding a legion of holy warriors. His deeds of courage were legendary among the warrior-angels of Purgatory. Undoubtedly this was why he'd been summoned to appear before his superiors. The archangels must have some special assignment for him.

He had heard rumors that the battle between good and evil had not been going all that well of late. Some even whispered that the Angels of Light were losing the war. Certainly, the archfiends and their demons who fought the holy warriors in Purgatory were becoming more confident, more aggressive. They attacked in greater numbers and it was all Derek and his warriors could do to shove them back into the Veil of Darkness from whence they sprang.

Rumor had it that the Dark Angels had developed a new tactic. They were fighting the battle on two fronts. They continued to try to take Heaven by storm, to overwhelm and destroy the holy warrior-angels and seize Heaven by force. In addition, however, they were attempting to defeat Heaven through more subtle ploys and schemes.

Derek had never before listened to such rumors. A true knight paid no heed to gossip mongers. Dark rumors such as these undermined the morale of his troops. As the battles they fought grew more and more difficult and dangerous every day, Derek could not help but wonder if there might not be some truth in what his comrades were saying.

He was thinking of this and thinking, too, that he should be out on the field with his men, not cooling his heels in some fancy antechamber, when he heard voices. Derek ceased his pacing. The voices were coming from the realm of his superiors. He could hear them through the gate that was only partially closed.

The cherubim are the "gate-keepers" of the Realm of Heaven, responsible for opening and closing the astral gates that divide one realm from another. They are also heavenly messengers and in this instance, a cherub, a bright and ambitious young angel named Sampson, had been sent onto the field of battle to fetch Derek and, in his excitement, had apparently failed to close and seal the gate.

Derek frowned and shook his head. Sampson was a Moorish prince, who had died during the twelfth century when he wandered off into the desert and became lost. Sampson had always longed to be a holy warrior. He was continually coming to Derek, begging him to allow him to enter the ranks of the soldiers of Purgatory. The cherubim was eager and enthusiastic and his courage was unquestioned, but he had a tendency to be scatterbrained and undisciplined. Forgetting to shut the astral gate between the realms was a prime example.

Derek was not one to eavesdrop, for he considered the practice dishonorable and beneath him. He could not help overhearing the conversation his superiors were holding, however. He could hear the two archangels speaking clearly.

He was about to interrupt them, inform them that the astral gate had been left open, and offer to shut the door for them, when he realized that they were discussing him.

"Are you certain Sir Derek de Molay is the right man for this, William?" The angel speaking was the Archangel Michael, the Supreme Commander of the forces of Purgatory. Derek did not know the other angel, the one called William.

"He was a Knight Templar, Archangel," this William angel replied. "He died a martyr defending his faith. He is a gallant warrior who has served with distinction through the centuries. Sir Derek is known for his courage, his strength, and fortitude—"

"He is also known for his rebellious and hotheaded nature," the Archangel Michael said grimly. "De Molay is one of the few souls who has actually chosen to remain in Purgatory rather than repent his sins and gain admittance to Heaven."

William brushed it off. "Yes, I know all about his battle with God. Had a few battles with the old boy myself in my day—"

"Angel William," the Archangel rebuked. "We do not speak of the Heavenly Father as 'the old boy.' "

"Oh, He understands," said William with enthusiasm. "God and I are great friends. He's a hell of a backgammon player."

"What did you say, William?" Michael asked, shocked.

"Oops. I beg your pardon, Archangel. I mean to say: God is a *very good* backgammon player."

Derek smiled to himself and forgot all about the fact that he was listening to a conversation he should not have been. He wondered where they'd dredged up Angel William.

"I have to admit that de Molay's independent spirit is what led us to choose him for this task," said Archangel Michael. "Though I still have my doubts."

"It makes him human," said William enthusiastically. "Trust me, he will blend in nicely. I should know. I was on Earth myself once."

"Yes, indeed," said Archangel Michael in frozen tones. "We all know how well *that* turned out. We are not accustomed to having to post bail for one of our own. It was quite upsetting."

"All a mistake," said William. "I went into that Chicago speakeasy to try to persuade this extremely nice but very naive young Kansas farm girl who was dancing there that she would never make it big and to go back home. I was *not* informed that Eliot Ness was planning to raid the place that very night."

"You were caught playing roulette," said the archangel accusingly.

"I had to act my part, didn't I?" Michael defended himself. "And I saved the girl. She went back to Kansas and got married and had twelve children." He sighed. "I don't think she ever forgave me."

"This isn't about you, William, in case you've forgotten," said Michael sternly. "We're discussing de Molay and our plans for him."

Derek scowled. He didn't like the way this conversation was tending. This sounded like one of God's plans to try to teach the obdurate knight yet another lesson in humility and love, patience, mercy, and compassion.

He thought back to the time when he'd been a living man and failed to obey his superior's order to retreat during a desperate battle. The truth was that the fool man had panicked and, if Derek had obeyed his command, the battle would have been lost. As it was, Derek and his men ignored the order and held their position. They kept the enemy from breaking through the lines, and eventually reinforcements arrived to save the day. Derek had been in the right and his superior in the wrong, yet the high command had wanted Derek to apologize—a lesson in obedience. He refused and the matter had finally been settled by a joust between the two knights, during which Derek had knocked the man from his horse.

And then had come the Inquisition.

"Where was God's mercy and compassion for me and my martyred comrades?" Derek muttered.

"You are right, Archangel," William said contritely, "back to Sir Derek. I've been told you want someone whom you know is not a traitor. Someone who hasn't succumbed to temptation. Someone who hasn't been drawn to their side by promises of freedom and power and glory, not to mention the dice and women and gin—oh, I do so love a gimlet now and then . . ."

"Dice? Women? Please try to keep your mind on the subject at hand, William," Michael stated coldly.

"You don't get out much, do you, Archangel?" William said, shaking his head. "A pity. Anyway, I can assure you that Sir Derek de Molay's loyalty is above suspicion."

"None of the warrior angels are above suspicion," returned Michael in dire tones.

"Sir Derek remained loyal to the Knights after three days of torment," William argued defensively. "His body was broken, his flesh flayed from his bones. He was disemboweled while he was yet alive, forced to watch and suffer as they tore his living organs from his body—"

Derek grit his teeth and closed his eyes. His fists clenched. He could still remember vividly every agonizing moment.

"I have to admit that de Molay would be among the last of those I would suspect of having betrayed us," Michael was saying. "Yet there is no denying the fact that some of our warrior-angels shut their eyes and permitted powerful Dark Angels to slip out of Hell and make their way to Earth. And we know that Derek has been approached by the Dark Angels in the past—"

Derek realized suddenly what he was doing. He had no right to be spying on his superiors. But they had no right to be saying such things about him. He flung the gate open with such force that it slammed against the sides of the heavenly barrier with a loud boom. He strode proudly and angrily inside.

Archangel Michael's expression grew severe. "Were you eavesdropping on us, de Molay?"

"I would never do anything so dishonorable, Archangel," Derek said with quiet dignity. "You neglected to shut the gate and I could not help but overhear your words. For all I know, you wanted me to overhear them."

"Sir Derek," said William, beaming at him. "I've heard a lot about you. So good to meet you at last."

William was a benign, elderly angel, rather chubby, whose robes were a bit rumpled, his wings a bit tattered. Yet his face was cheerful, his smile engaging. He appeared to be enjoying himself immensely. By contrast, Archangel Michael was one of those who took himself and his duties very seriously. He was tall and thin, his expression stern and severe. His robes were immaculate, every feather in his wings in place.

"The cherubim must have left the gate open," said Michael, glowering. "He will be reprimanded—"

"No, no, Archangel," said William hastily. "It wasn't Sampson. Good boy, Sampson. It was me, I'm afraid. Always going about leaving gates open, lights on . . ."

Archangel Michael cast William an ice-glare glance and the angel subsided, after giving Derek a conspiratorial wink.

Derek did not quite approve of this jocular angel William. Derek felt more akin to the archangel. He also took his duties quite seriously. That was why he was so incensed at the accusation.

"If you know that the Dark Angels approached me, my lord, then you must also know that I turned my back on them and their evil lies."

"As you turned your back on Heaven," said Archangel Michael with asperity.

Derek faced his superior defiantly. "I am a true knight, my lord. I took vows of honor and loyalty in life and I remain true to them in death. It was God who broke faith with me."

"As I feared," said Archangel Michael. "You are not suitable. You are far too stubborn and rebellious."

"On the contrary," William argued. "He is quite wonderfully human. He'll be perfect for the job."

Derek had no idea what "job" they were talking about and he didn't plan to stay to find out. "If you will give me leave, my lords, I must return to my command." Derek bowed.

Archangel Michael fixed William with a stern look. "You are the one who will have to supervise him while he is on Earth. He will be your responsibility. Are you certain you trust him?"

The archangel lowered his voice. "Remember, William, you will be on trial yourself. We are giving you one more chance. If you bungle this assignment . . ." He shook his head gloomily.

"I'll be back painting sunsets," said William. He rolled his eyes. "Not that I mind the work, but it's the same thing day in and day out. Pinks and reds, purples and golds splashed across the sky . . ."

"Do not be whimsical, William," said Archangel Michael. "Sunsets are a natural phenomenon. Please keep to the subject at hand."

"Sorry, Archangel," said William meekly. "No sense of humor," he whispered in an aside to Derek.

"What did you say, William?" the archangel asked.

"I was wondering if you had made a decision regarding Sir Derek?"

Michael frowned in thought, then said, "You may explain the assignment to him. The decision will be his. He may not want to undertake it."

Derek bowed in silence, inwardly seething, outwardly composed.

"The situation with the Dark Angels is growing dire," said William gravely. "They have resorted to using mankind to aid them in the battle to overthrow God and take over Heaven. It is a sad fact that some mortals choose to join the Dark Ones. This has been true since time began, but we were able to prevent the Dark Angels from gaining direct access to mankind. They had to work through intermediaries—humans who had fallen victim to their lies—and thus their task was more difficult.

"Now, however, as you have heard, several of the most powerful Dark Angels were able to break out of Hell and enter Earth. They have direct access to humans and, we believe, they are plotting to plunge the world into chaos and bring all humanity to the brink of destruction. While we angels fight to save mankind, these powerful Dark Angels will take over Heaven and make slaves of the mortals on Earth. You have seen the lost souls of Hell, Sir Derek," Angel William added sorrowfully. "You know what torment they endure. Think of all mankind suffering like that."

"The Fallen get nothing more than what they deserve, my lord," said Derek harshly.

"Some mortals *are* truly evil," William agreed sadly. "And they deserve their punishment. But most mortals are merely weak and misguided. We never give up on anyone—as you yourself know, Sir Derek."

He made no response. He pretended not to understand what the angel meant. Instead, he asked bluntly what they meant to do.

"Do you propose sending me to Earth to battle these Dark Angels?" Derek rested his hand on the hilt of his sword. Perhaps this assignment wouldn't be as bad as he'd feared.

Archangel Michael's eyebrows shot up. He looked at William in alarm.

"No, no, not that," said Angel William hastily.

"We do not want a heavenly war breaking out on Earth. Mankind has problems enough, as it is. We want you to collect information and bring it back to us. We know which humans are being targeted and we think we know why. We just don't know what the Dark Angels plan. That is what you must find out."

"I am a warrior, not a spy," Derek said, glowering.

"Think of it as reconnaissance," said William soothingly.

"You could send any of the lesser angels on such a mission. Even a cherub such as Sampson," Derek said disdainfully. "These humans you mention have their own guardian angels, as well. They can provide you with information. I do not understand why you chose me?"

William and Michael exchanged glances.

"You had better tell him," said Michael.

"Because there *is* an element of danger," William admitted. "The angel guarding the human we want you to watch over has gone missing."

"Gone missing?" Derek repeated, shocked. "How is that possible?"

He knew, as did all of Heaven, that angels who accept the responsibility of guarding a human from birth to death are among the most loyal and dedicated of all angels.

"We have reason to believe that the guardian was slain, Derek. By the Dark Angels. Their powers are strong on Earth. You must not underestimate them."

"My own powers are formidable," said Derek proudly.

Angel William gave a deprecating cough. "I am sure they are, Derek, but . . . um . . . you will be prohibited from using them. Mankind must never, never suspect that a crisis of this magnitude has developed. There would be panic. Humans might lose their faith in us. This mission must be handled with the utmost subtlety. As a Knight Templar, you were a monk as well as a warrior. You must become more like a monk now—patient and circumspect, quiet and careful."

Derek had been a monk, but he hadn't been a very good one. Some vows had been easy for him to keep, such as vows of loyalty and courage. Vows of obedience were another matter.

"Why do you not simply assign another guardian angel to this human?" he asked.

"The archfiends would realize that we know about them," Michael replied. "We want to lull them into complacency. That's why you must maintain your distance, Derek."

Derek considered this a stupid plan; one that was placing the human at risk. He would have argued, but he caught the archangel's stern eyes, reminding him it was not his place to question the wisdom of his superiors. Doubtless, they knew what they were about. They were the generals, overseeing the entire field of battle. He was but a simple soldier.

"So if I go to Earth, I am to be human again?" Derek asked.

"Yes," said Angel William. "I hope that will not be a problem. We will do what we can to help you make the transition."

Derek was silent, thinking. He wasn't sure if going back to human flesh and frailties would be a problem or not. So many centuries had passed since he'd left all that behind. He could scarcely remember what it meant to be human.

He was still suspicious that this was yet another ploy of the angels to try to teach him a lesson. However, the Dark Angels had escaped Hell on his watch. He felt responsible.

"I will do what you ask of me, my lords."

"Excellent." Angel William was pleased. "The human female you've been assigned to watch—"

"Human female?" Derek interrupted. He frowned. "Why would the Dark Ones target a human female? Of what importance could a mere female be to the side of Darkness? You must be mistaken. The fiends would certainly seek out a male human."

Archangel Michael lifted his eyes to Heaven. William seemed a bit flustered. He pretended he hadn't heard the interruption and continued on.

"The female's name is Rachel Duncan. She is twenty-seven years old and she works in finance. We believe the Dark Angels have chosen her in order to try to disrupt the world financial situation."

"A woman involved in finance?" Derek asked incredulously. "How is this possible? Women are frail and fragile creatures. They lack the capacity to understand such complex matters."

"I told you so, William," muttered Archangel Michael.

"Yes, well . . ." William coughed again. "Times have changed since the fourteenth century, Derek."

"Obviously not for the better," Derek stated. "If women are being permitted to enter into business dealings, no wonder the world is in chaos."

"I need to speak to you, William," said the archangel. *"Alone."*

Derek bowed to his superiors and, turning on his heel, he left the chamber. The archangel shut the gate firmly behind him.

Waiting again in the antechamber, Derek pondered his new assignment. He was to be made human again. And he was to be tasked with watching over a woman.

He'd known very few women in his life. His mother had died giving birth to him and he had been raised by his father. He'd had his share of pleasure with women. Before he had taken his vows as a knight, many lovely ladies of the court had been pleased to welcome the handsome young man into their beds or coupled with him in the hay. He had thought himself in love at various times. There had been one woman in particular . . . But he had never married or been tempted to marry. War was his true mistress. Derek had joined the Knights Templar at the age of sixteen and he had died at the age of twenty-six. Fighting had left Derek little time for love-making. His love had been the battlefield, winning glory for himself and the knighthood.

As for women, he considered most of them lovely, flighty creatures, given to whims and tantrums, scarcely reasonable. Much like children, they were unable to fix their minds on any serious matter, and so it was men who had to do their thinking for them. Derek decided that he would simply confront this Rachel Duncan as one would confront a child, ask her questions, and demand that she give him answers.

This assignment was going to be quite simple, after all.

Inside the chamber, the archangel was shaking his head. "I am having second thoughts about this, William."

"Sir Derek will, of course, have to be immersed in the ways of the twenty-first century," said William.

"Obviously," returned Michael dryly. "Though I suspect there's only so much you're going to be able to do with him. You can take the boy out of the fourteenth century, but I'm not sure you can take the fourteen century out of the boy."

"He won't be on Earth long," William said. "And I will be there to keep an eye on him."

"Somehow that fails to comfort to me," said Archangel Michael.

"Perhaps this experience will finally open his heart to God," said William.

"Or perhaps we will lose him utterly," said Michael grimly. "Derek de Molay has always walked the border between dark and light. This may cause him to cross over."

"I have faith," said William, smiling.

"A fine angel you'd be without it," Michael retorted caustically.

"Then I may proceed? I have your blessing?"

"Yes," said the archangel, adding with a deep sigh, "I have the feeling you're going to need it."

"I'll just go tell him," said William, pleased. He walked out of Heaven and into the antechamber, leaving the gate open behind him.

Michael, with a long-suffering sigh, summoned Sampson to close it. When the cherub was gone and he was alone, Michael went over the plans. He was sending to Earth on an important mission a benign, simple-souled angel whose halo was more than a little tarnished to watch over a rebellious knight known for his arrogance who already had one foot in the fire.

Michael smiled broadly to himself. Matters were proceeding according to plan.

Two

Wait for it . . . Wait for it . . .

Rachel watched as the ball dropped into the machine. She squeezed the aluminum bat between her fingers as she remembered to control her breathing and keep her eye on the ball. Leaning back into her stance, she steeled her body. The ball shot out of the pitching machine as if it had been shot out of a cannon and Rachel was ready. She stepped into the swing and smacked the baseball dead center.

THWAK!

That would have been a line drive, baby! No one could have caught that ball, she told herself.

Funny thing was, Rachel didn't even like baseball. She never went to see the Sox play. She could not get fired up over the Cubs. Her job had been unusually stressful lately, and she needed to blow off some steam. Stress was a part of the job at the Chicago Mercantile Exchange—the Merc for short—where a broker could make millions of dollars in seconds. Or that same broker could lose millions in the same amount of time. Be wiped out, lose everything—house, car, future, even your life. Some saw suicide as the only way out of disgrace and ruin. And it could all happen in the time it takes to sneeze.

Brokers on the Merc handled the stress in different ways. Some went drinking after work, using the alcohol to sterilize their wounds. But the booze had the bad effect of pickling their brains. That's how they lost their edge. And booze left you feeling out of control.

Rachel couldn't stand that. She prided herself on being in control of every facet of her life. Well, most of her life. The career part of her life. Her love life was a different story.

THWAK! Another line drive, this one down the third base line.

The Merc was an impressive building located in the heart of Chicago, Rachel spent most of her time in the upper echelons of the pits. The pits were just that: sunken arena-type rooms where men—and now women—either placed trades for large financial corporations or were the independent traders, the maverick cowboys of the Exchange. Rachel was one of those who worked for a firm. She liked the relative security of her position. She made money for other people, receiving an excellent salary and hefty bonuses.

There were no high-brow meetings and expense account lunches at the Merc. The pits were barely contained chaos, and only those with strong wills and stronger stomachs survived.

Rachel had learned her lesson years ago. Being hung over at work cost you dearly. She'd lost her focus once, after a night drinking champagne cocktails (the European kind, made with brandy and bitters) and she'd made a mistake. Those champagne cocktails had cost her firm a half million dollars and almost cost her the job. Rachel promised herself she'd never be hung over at the Merc again. So instead of champagne cocktails, she now goes to the batting cages when things got rough—and today things had been rough. She'd just lost a big client and, once again, come near to losing her job.

Wait for it. Wait . . .

THWACK. A dribbling grounder to the pitcher. She'd be out at first.

The only reason Rachel hadn't been fired was because she was one of the best on the floor of the Merc. She traded what was called the Paper. She filled orders for her firm and their biggest clients and she filled those orders faster and more accurately than most of her male counterparts. And she was endlessly ridiculed for it. Her "handle"—the letters that were displayed on her trader's jacket—was RCHT, for Rachel T. Duncan. Of course all the boys on the floor called her Ratchet. She didn't mind the nickname or the teasing. It made her a member of the boys club that was the Merc. She'd earned her moniker.

Rachel loved the excitement in the pits, where the traders were crammed in shoulder to shoulder, belly to buttocks, pushing and shoving, waving their arms, and screaming to be heard. Her body would sway with the bodies of rest of the traders in waves of frenzy. She yelled out her orders so loud that often she would come home with no voice left. Every day when the opening buzzer rang, a surge of adrenaline pumped into Rachel's veins, and she was a warrior, going to do battle, fierce and aggressive on the floor.

Rachel was unstoppable and she was attractive and she knew it. She used her looks to her advantage, always arriving at the Merc looking as if she'd just stepped off the pages of *Vogue*. Some women faulted her for that, but Rachel paid no attention. She never understood how looking and smelling like an unmade bed was some sort of statement of feminine equality. Men who were tall used their height to gain attention. Men with broad shoulders and muscle-bound arms elbowed their way through the crowd in the pits. Why should Rachel not use the beauty God and her genes had given her to gain the same advantages? Besides, she had the brains to back it up and she knew it and so did the other traders.

If, as sometimes happened, a man mistook her for a fragile, weak-willed and weak-minded woman, and tried to push her out of her spot, she'd smash the high heel of her shoe into his instep. When she heard the interloper's yelp of pain, she'd bat her eyelashes and smile sweetly at him and say, "I'm so sorry. Did I hurt you? I thought you were trying to muscle in on my territory."

If he tried again, she'd kick him in the shins. Eventually, he'd get the idea. She'd go to battle again and again until she had all the space she needed.

Rachel looked down at her watch and realized she'd been in the batting cages for over two hours. Her hands were starting to blister and her arms were sore. She decided to head home.

She parked her car in the garage and walked to the lobby of her building that was located near Chicago's north side. Her condo had the coveted lake view, and she loved it. And it wasn't just the status. She liked looking out over the lake at night, seeing the lights of the buildings reflected in the water, like mirror images of the stars. She liked the luxury of living in a nice part of the city, and she loved all the amenities that came with a five hundred thousand dollar condo.

Rachel walked up the stairs of the building. The doorman, Alex, was there to open the door for her. He was a sweet man, been married for years.

"Hello, Miss Rachel. How'd we do on the market today?" Alex asked.

"Not good Alex. Not good at all."

"I'm sorry to hear that, but I can smell a big rally coming soon y'know. I have a sense about these things."

"I hope you're right. By the way, Alex, when is your new baby girl due? Soon I thought," Rachel asked, changing the subject. She didn't want to discuss or even think about work.

"The doctor says any day now. My wife says if it doesn't happen soon, she's going to pull the baby out herself."

"Hopefully it won't come to that," Rachel said, laughing and heading toward the elevator.

"You have a good evening now, Miss Rachel. G'night."

"Good night, Alex."

"Oh, by the way, Miss Rachel, I'm starting my vacation. There'll be a new guy here tomorrow."

Rachel paused. "I didn't know you were planning to take your vacation now."

"To tell you the truth, I didn't either," said Alex. "Mr. Fraym, the building manager, discovered that I had lots of paid vacation time built up and I should take it or I'd lose it. Works out fine, because I'll be home to help my wife with the baby."

"Sounds wonderful. Have fun." Rachel waved at him. "Tell Marie I'll be thinking of her."

She punched the elevator button for her floor, then leaned on her bat and yawned as she ascended. Did she have anything to eat in the fridge? She couldn't remember. She thought there might be some Lean Cuisine dinners. She hoped so. She didn't want to cook and she didn't want to go out again.

She unlocked the door to her apartment and turned on the light, dropped her car keys and purse on the dining room table, and headed toward the kitchen. She pushed Play on her answering machine to listen to her messages while she searched the refrigerator.

Beep.

"Ratchet Girl, where are you? We're all at Mario's. You haven't been out for a drink after work in ages. It's Thursday. Didn't anyone tell you that Thursday night is the new Friday night? It's all the rage. You should be here. Call me."

Rachel knew the voice. One of the guys from the office.

"Ugh, please. Never," Rachel muttered.

No Lean Cuisine meals left. She grabbed a plastic container of leftover taco dip from the fridge.

Second beep.

"Rachel, it's Tom, I wanted to compliment you on those hot shoes you were wearing today. Do you have any idea how distracting you are while I'm trying to think about Pork Bellies? I think I screwed up three orders today. Call my cell."

"Try getting a divorce first, jackass," Rachel told the machine. She went to the pantry, looking for corn chips.

Third beep.

"Um, hi, Rachel; it's, um, Matt. You left so quickly after the close today we didn't get a chance to um, chat. You seemed pissed. Is everything okay? Um, call me if you want to talk. Bye."

"How old are you, Matt? Jeez, what like, sixteen maybe? What on earth would we talk about? What you're planning to wear to the prom?"

Fourth beep.

"Rachel, it's Zanus. Just wondering how your day went. Give me a call when you have time."

Rachel smiled at the last message. She left it on the machine and erased all the others. She stood at the sink, eating stale chips and dip, washing them down with an open Diet Coke she'd left on the counter that morning. She tossed the plastic dishes into the sink. She wasn't much for cooking or cleaning.

Andreas Zanus, or Zanus, as he liked to be called. She'd been dating him for a few months now and things were going well. In fact he'd swept her off her feet from the beginning. He was the man every woman dreams about—handsome, attentive, and rich.

When he found out that she liked champagne, he'd flown her to France in his private jet for a long weekend to taste the best from the Champagne region. They'd traveled the beautiful countryside in a limo, drinking chilled champagne and eating strawberries dipped in chocolate.

Only last week, they had eaten at a Thai restaurant, and she'd raved about the food. He'd offered to take her to Bangkok for real Thai food. She had laughed at that and accused him of teasing her. He told her he wasn't kidding and, the next day, he'd handed her two first-class tickets for Bangkok. She couldn't afford to take the time off work, but it was the thought that counted.

Zanus was just the right age for her—old enough to have ditched all the immaturity younger men carried, yet not old enough to start collecting Social Security. He was tall with a good build. He had black hair, with enough gray frost to make it interesting. His eyes were dark and melting, his skin bronze. He dressed impeccably; the finest suits, the best tailors, the most expensive shoes. Even his blue jeans, when he wore blue jeans, came from Neiman Marcus. He was thoughtful, brought her little presents, nothing embarrassing or extravagant, but everything suited to her taste.

So far there were only two drawbacks to Andreas Zanus. The first was that she didn't love him. She knew she should be in love with him, because he was the sort of man any woman would fall in love with, but she wasn't there yet.

The second was that he was a client. He'd been assigned to her by her manager, Mr. Freeman. Zanus had actually requested her, in fact. He had told Mr. Freeman he'd been talking to some of her other clients and he liked what he'd heard about her. She'd already made a hefty bonus off her work for Zanus, and she'd been silently thanking Freeman for this for weeks. If Freeman knew she was dating her client, it wouldn't look good. But there were lots of inappropriate relationships going on at work. As long as hers didn't become gossip or do anything to interrupt her earnings, she would be fine.

That was the part that scared her and maybe that was why she hadn't let herself fall in love with him. If this affair went sour and she lost him as both a lover and a client, she might lose her job.

All Zanus had to do was make a complaint about her, maybe claim she was trading sex for business or some such thing. Her ethics would be questioned. She would be finished. Her reputation on the floor would be compromised and the other traders would make it unbearable for her to work.

There was no such thing as privacy at the Merc, where men outnumbered the women one hundred to two. The guys all knew Rachel was single, and they all firmly believed the sole reason she worked at the Merc was to meet and marry a wealthy trader. She couldn't blame them for thinking that way, since some of the women who worked there *were* looking for rich husbands.

Not Rachel. She had her own money, good friends, a great job, and her family. Rachel had grown up in Evanston, north of the city. Her family was well off, and had been for generations. Her parents were retired now and rarely home. They were currently cruising around the world on the Queen Elizabeth 2. Her mother sent postcards to Rachel from all of their exotic ports of call.

The last one had been Curacao. Mom had written that it was the place to be if you liked to drink different flavors of the liquor made from bitter oranges for which the island was famous, but other than that, there wasn't much to say for it. Though they'd gone to the Caribbean to bask in the sun, the sun in Curacao was too hot. The shopkeepers were too friendly, she didn't trust them. All of which meant her mother was having a great time. Mom loved to complain. And the person she complained about most and loved the most and understood the least was her daughter.

Rachel loved her parents, even if they didn't understand her fascination with trading or finance. Rachel had an MBA from the University of Chicago, and they had never understood her reasoning behind her chosen major, economics. Why did she want to work in someplace called the pit? Why did she have to work in a place where fat, smelly brokers stepped on you or pinched your butt to try to distract you or yelled obscenities at you? Why couldn't she be a real estate agent like Paul and Irma's daughter, Mitzy? No one ever stepped on Mitzy.

They also didn't understand why she wasn't married yet. Rachel was an only child, and her mother was desperate to see Rachel wed and pregnant. (Mitzy was married with two darling little girls and another on the way.) Of course the unspoken understanding was that Rachel would give up trading once she found a husband to take care of her and settle down. Rachel had nothing against getting married or children. She did have something against getting married and having babies this very minute and she certainly had a problem with giving up her career and letting a man take care of her—i.e., control her.

Rachel planned to do it all—have her career, have a husband, and have kids. There were no boundaries for women anymore. But she didn't want to rush into anything with anyone. She valued clarity and what was clear for her right now was work. Rachel concentrated on her work, concentrated on being the fastest, most accurate, most sought-after broker on the floor.

Some of the men in the pit made the scathing comment that Rachel Duncan had ice water running through her veins. They meant it as an insult, but Rachel considered that a compliment. Now all she had to do was get out from under her boss's thumb, find money enough to become an independent trader.

Mr. Freeman was a fair enough guy to work for, but as long as she was tethered to company rules and guidelines, Rachel didn't believe she could realize her true potential. Sometimes big trades, huge trades, came down the line, and Rachel didn't have enough authority to snatch them up when the timing was right. It was all very frustrating.

She finished off the dip and picked up the phone.

"Hi, there," she said when Zanus answered. "My day went fine. How was yours?"

They talked business. She hoped he would ask her out for this weekend, but, though he was very charming and paid her several compliments, he hung up without making a date.

Probably for the best, Rachel thought, trying to shrug off her disappointment. He is a client. She wondered if there was anything good on television. Glancing through the guide, she decided there wasn't. She stripped off her clothes, tossed them in the general direction of the laundry hamper, and slipped into a Cosabella nightgown. It had cost too damn much for a nightgown, but she loved the feel of silk against her skin.

Lying in bed, she closed her eyes and mentally prepared for her day tomorrow, reviewing in her head the orders she'd need to have filled. The numbers flew like birds through her mind as she drifted off to sleep.

She was still dreaming of numbers when her alarm went off. She had dreamed that the numbers were white birds flying away from her and she couldn't catch one of them, no matter how hard she tried. The dream made her feel uncomfortable and she was glad the alarm had ended it.

Rachel headed for the shower. Her normal routine consisted of tying her long blond hair back neatly into a bun, applying minimal makeup—concealer for the dark smudges beneath her eyes, some blush, a hint of eye shadow, lip gloss—and a quick leap through a spritzed cloud of Annick Goutal perfume. The perfume was not designed to attract men, but to help her survive the stink of the trading floor when the going got hot. Finally, she put on a man-tailored blouse, no-nonsense-looking suit coat, matching pants, and, today, Stuart Weitzman pumps. Rachel looked at herself in the mirror.

She was tall, blond, slim with a good figure. Her eyes were green-gray, large, and she had what her dad termed "The Look"—a cold, intense stare that could freeze a man in his tracks at twenty paces. Rachel used The Look to get her way sometimes, but she had to walk a fine line, and so she always wore pantsuits to work. No short skirts. She didn't mind if the men were distracted by *her*. She didn't want to be distracted by them!

It was all about the numbers, baby.

Rachel left her apartment and rode the elevator down to the lobby. A car usually picked her up for work. She owned her own car—a Volkswagen Passat—but she drove that around town. The parking fees at the Merc were insanely high so it was cheaper for her to hire a car service. Only the car wasn't there yet.

She looked at her watch. She was on time. Mildly irritated that the car was late, Rachel stood tapping her foot impatiently inside the entrance, keeping out of the wind that came roaring off Lake Michigan. She suddenly felt the hair on the back of her neck prickle, like she was standing beneath an air conditioner blowing cold air on her. Only there was no air conditioner. Someone was staring at her.

Rachel turned to say, "Good morning, Alex—"

She stopped midsentence. The man wearing the livery of the doorman was definitely not Alex. This man was handsome; really, really handsome—devastatingly handsome. He was maybe thirty with a body that went to the gym, yet didn't brag about it. He had blond hair and crystal blue eyes and a strong, take-it-on-the-chin jaw. And this handsome man was scowling at her like she'd done something to offend him.

"Oh, I'm sorry. You're obviously not Alex," said

Rachel, taken aback. "You must be new. I'm not quite awake yet, I guess . . . I'm Rachel Duncan. I'm in unit twenty-two-fifteen. I guess maybe Alex's wife had the baby . . ." She realized she was babbling like a schoolgirl and she made herself shut up.

The new guy didn't say anything. He stood there glaring at her in complete and utter silence. Was he mad that she'd mistaken him for someone else? If so, he *could* let it go, for heaven's sake! Rachel felt her neck prickle again, this time in hot embarrassment. She was suddenly annoyed that he wouldn't say a word to ease her obvious discomfort.

What a jerk!

Fortunately her car pulled up in front of the building. She turned and gave the doorman The Look. Then she shifted her gaze to the door and stood there, waiting. He didn't seem to get it at first. He just stood there like a bump on a log.

She looked back at him. "You're a doorman," she said coldly. "You're paid to open doors. Right?"

He grudgingly walked over to the glass door and held it open. She breezed past him without a glance. She hoped he froze to death in the backlash of the artic chill she sent his direction as she walked by.

The nerve of some people. She'd at least tried to apologize for calling him by the wrong name. But what was his right name? Damn, she hadn't thought to look at his name tag. And why was he giving her that awful look, like he resented her for something she'd done to him, and she'd never even seen him before. She was sure of that much at least. She would have remembered *him*.

Damn! Was he ever good-looking, she thought as she settled back into the black leather seat of the car. Six foot three, she guessed. Sandy blond hair that just kissed the collar of his uniform at the back. And icy blue eyes. Cold and hard on the surface, though. They weren't the eyes of a nice man. No, that look and those eyes weren't nice at all. But there was something underneath the ice, something smoldering. Fire and ice . . .

And, he had to be one of the best-looking men Rachel Duncan had ever seen in her life.

Derek's first day on the job did not start out well, and it went from bad to worse.

"We were able to get you a job as doorman at the building where Rachel Duncan lives," William explained the night before. "This way you can see who comes to visit her, who takes her out, that sort of thing. And you'll have time off in the evenings in case you need to run down some leads. She spends her days at work and she's safe there, though you wouldn't know it to look at the place. From what I hear, the pits of hell are less chaotic."

Derek had no idea what William was talking about and he really didn't care. He planned to be here only a short time. He missed his duties, missed his comrades. He had been in his human form for several days now, and though he was finally getting used to his body ("It's like riding a horse," William had told him. "You don't forget."), he was having difficulty adjusting to the human weaknesses and frailties. These included the fact that his body required sustenance on a regular basis. That his body felt pain and weariness. That a cold spring wind whipping off the lake froze his ears. That there were such things as alarm clocks that dictated one's comings and goings. He'd forgotten to set his alarm that morning.

"You're late, de Molay," Mr. Fraym had admonished as he thrust a uniform into Derek's arms. "I expect my employees to be on time! You'd better put that on as soon as you're finished filling out these tax forms. And don't complain to me if the collar itches and the pants don't fit. I don't care."

Fraym gave Derek a quick tour of the building, explained his duties, and then escorted him to the lobby.

"This desk is your post. You are not to leave it except to go to the bathroom. There are no cigarette breaks and no lunch breaks. You can eat your lunch here at the desk, but do it discreetly so the tenants don't see you. You are to keep the lobby neat. Water the plants, pick off any dead leaves. Open the door promptly for the tenants, and keep out solicitors and vagrants. You will call cabs for people and you will be pleasant. Guests should sign in, and all service workers should be accounted for. They aren't allowed in the front door, as a general rule, but sometimes there are exceptions. I'm paying you to be the eyes and ears of this building. Do you understand me?"

"Uh, yes, sir." Derek answered, not because he did understand, but because he wanted to get rid of this annoying man as soon as he could.

"Good, then. Put that uniform on and get to work."

As Derek went to dress, he realized suddenly that he was nothing but a filthy, simpering spy. Spies were necessary evils, Derek supposed. Monarchs employed them to keep track of what their enemies were doing and their enemies employed them to keep track of the monarchs. Generals used spies to find out what the enemy was plotting and thus gain a military advantage. But no honorable man would accept such a base and heinous task.

Derek had been a military commander for many centuries, and at the thought of what they'd done to him, how they had tricked him into accepting this post, Derek grew angrier by the moment. He had thought he was being sent on a mission of great importance. Instead, he—a man of noble birth—was going to be playing the role of servant and, if that wasn't bad enough, his task was to spy on a female! He was furious. He hoped those under his command never found out. He could imagine them rolling on the floor for eternity, guffawing over his silly uniform, and bowing and scraping and saying "Yes, Ma'am," and "Yes, Sir, thank you, Sir" in imitation of him.

Derek finished putting on the uniform and

took his post just as a woman came out of the elevator. She was blond, tall, slender, and lovely and she looked annoyed. Derek snorted. He'd rather fight dogs for table scraps than bow and fawn over some silly woman who couldn't open her own damn door. She said something to him, but Derek didn't hear her at first. He was too busy thinking of how he was going to tell William that he could take this assignment and shove it up his ass.

Then Derek heard the name Rachel Duncan. That sounded familiar and suddenly he realized that this was the female. This was the woman he'd been sent to spy on. The knowledge didn't make him any happier, except that now he had someone to blame—her. This was her fault. She had gone over to the enemy. The demons had selected her because she was obviously weak-willed. Well, she could quite literally "go to the devil" as far as he was concerned.

He took a good look at her, standing there in the entranceway, and he noted something different about her. Different from all the other humans he'd seen during his brief time on Earth. He asked himself what there was about her that set her apart. She was one of the loveliest women he had ever seen, but that wasn't it. He compared her mentally to the other humans with whom he'd interacted this very day—the annoying Mr. Fraym, for example. And then Derek knew.

Rachel Duncan was alone.

Not alone as in the fact that she was the only

person in the lobby. She was horribly, terribly alone. No loving angel hovered over her. No angel was there to guide her. Even Mr. Fraym had a guardian angel, an angel who elbowed him in his conscience if he was tempted to do something wrong; an angel who watched out for him, reminding him to look both ways when crossing the street or urging him to quit smoking.

Rachel Duncan no longer had a guardian angel, and Derek recalled William saying that her angel had gone missing, perhaps even been destroyed by the archfiends. She was alone and vulnerable and, what was worse, she did not know it. She did not understand her danger.

Derek had just come to this startling realization when Rachel said something to him about opening the door.

Confused by his thoughts and startled by her frank gaze, Derek belatedly remembered his duties. He opened the door for her and held it while she stalked past him. She looked angry, clear through. He supposed he couldn't blame her. He'd behaved rudely. He was going to apologize, but she was gone before he could say a word.

As she passed him, Derek smelled the scent of her perfume. The fragrance was heady, sweet, and it brought back vivid memories of palace gardens and exotic lands. What was it? Gardenia. Derek had not thought or smelled the scent of gardenias for many long years. The fragrance lingered in his nostrils and the image of her, alone and in danger, lingered in his mind.

"Hm, hm." A man cleared his throat.

Derek looked up to see a man standing in the lobby staring at Derek. The man held two large suitcases in his hands. Walking over, he dumped them down in front of Derek.

"Don't just stand there like an idiot. Carry these out to my car," he barked, annoyed.

Derek did as he was told. He didn't like it, but he was no longer thinking about asking to be sent back to Purgatory. He couldn't get the fragrance of gardenias out of his mind.

Rachel Duncan didn't need someone to spy on her. She was a woman, alone and vulnerable, frail and weak.

"She needs protecting," Derek told William over the phone that night, after he was off duty.

"That's not your job, Derek," William said, sighing. "Perhaps she does need protection. Your job is find out who from. And you're not going to gain her confidence by being rude to her!"

"I did not mean to be," Derek mumbled. "I was caught off guard."

"You have to apologize," William said sternly.

Derek was silent a moment, then he said, "You are right. I do."

"You agree?" William was amazed. He'd expected an argument.

"I did not behave as a gentleman toward a lady. I will ask her forgiveness."

"Not on bended knee," William said worriedly.

"I know," Derek replied with a smile. "I am not in the fourteenth century anymore."

And yet, as he hung up this miraculous device known as a telephone, he couldn't help but think that what Rachel Duncan needed was a true knight.

Three

Saturday morning, Rachel woke to the chatter of voices coming from her radio. She'd set the alarm for seven A.M. and never hit the snooze button. Hitting snooze was a slippery slope. It led Rachel to frantically racing around the condo with her hairbrush in one hand and her shoes in another, trying to gulp down coffee and simultaneously put on eye shadow, all in the forlorn hope of making it to work by the time the markets opened. She hated doing this; she felt disorganized all the rest of the day. Not to mention the time she'd shown up at the office wearing mismatched shoes or the time she'd accidentally put lipstick on her eyelids. That day she had made a vow—never to hit snooze again.

She didn't hit snooze, but she didn't get up either. She lay in bed, snuggling beneath the down quilt, and her one-thousand-thread-count Egyptian cotton sheets. They were so warm and her pillow was so soft that she stayed where she was. It was Saturday, after all.

She smelled coffee. The automatic coffeemaker had come on. The smell was tempting, but the coffee wasn't going anywhere. She lay in bed and thought, oddly, about the doorman with the ice blue eyes.

He had been on duty yesterday when she'd come back from work. He had opened the door for her with alacrity, springing up from his chair the moment he saw her emerge from the car. His gaze was serious and very intense. She had the strangest impression—that he knew her, or knew something about her. He seemed stern and angry, though this time she didn't think the feelings were directed at her. He appeared to want to say something, for he had cleared his throat twice and coughed once.

Rachel had swept past him haughtily, putting him in his place, letting him know she was still mad from the rude way he'd treated her that morning. In the end, he hadn't said a word to her. Rachel couldn't help feeling that she should have eased up on the guy. His first day on the job and all that. She found herself wondering what the doorman's voice was like.

Zanus, he had a wonderful voice—it sounded the way black velvet felt. Her thoughts went from the doorman to her client, who was maybe more to her than a client. She lay there, remembering how it had all started.

"I want you to take on a new client, Rachel," Mr. Freeman had announced. "Mr. Andreas Zanus. He's a venture capitalist with money out the wazoo, and I want you to treat him like he was made of gold and double-dipped in platinum. Nothing is too good or too expensive for this guy. Do you understand?"

"Yes, Mr. Freeman. I'll do my best to keep Mr. Zanus happy."

"I hope you mean that. I think you should know he asked for you by name."

"He did?" Rachel was taken aback.

"It seems he's been following your career. Talking to some of your other clients, that sort of thing. He's very impressed with you. I want you to get to know him, Rachel." Freeman winked at her. "You know. Be charming."

Rachel stared at him blankly. Was he really telling her to do what she thought he was telling her to do?

"I gave Zanus your direct number so he'll be calling you for a meeting. The firm is counting on you, Rachel."

She had not been looking forward to being charming to Mr. Zanus. She had been resentful, in fact. She had pictured him: flabby, bald, pretending to know all about commodities when, in fact, he knew nothing.

Boy, had she been wrong—about everything!

Zanus made it very easy to be charming; and she found herself trying not to be *too* charming around him. He had made it very plain that he thought they should be sleeping together, but Rachel was not prepared to cross that line. Not that she didn't want to, and she had to repeat her mantra every time she was tempted to succumb to his touch.

He is a client. He is a client. He is a client.

She could lose her reputation, her career. She was not willing to lose everything she'd worked so hard to achieve by sleeping with a client.

And so the trip to France, the dinner in Rome—separate bedrooms. Good-night kisses at the door. She wasn't a prude. She certainly wasn't saving herself for marriage. That horse had left the barn a long time ago. She was being careful.

But not only that. There was something missing.

"Spring has come to Chicagoland!" the radio was saying in its damnably cheerful voice. "Highs today in the mid-fifties with a forty percent chance of rain this afternoon."

"What am I doing lying here dreaming about men?" Rachel asked herself. "I should be thinking about money!"

She made her bed while she was still in it, a little trick she'd learned from *Cosmo,* which involved pulling the sheets and the comforter up to cover the pillows and then sliding out from underneath them. She wasn't much of a housekeeper and she wouldn't have concerned herself about making her bed, but she disliked crawling into cold sheets at night. Bad enough she had to crawl into bed alone.

Rachel used the quiet time on Saturday morning when no one was stirring and her phone wasn't ringing to go over her charts for the past week. It was important to keep your eye on the big picture, as well as the day-to-day ride on the market. She charted the prices for the week, and then studied the graph to see if a trend emerged. A trend could be anything—a head-and-shoulders curve, a slow downward sloping dive, a fast upward swoop. She could usually find some sort of sign that would tell her if the market was going to surge or pull back over the next quarter.

Rachel printed out her chart and posted it on a large cork bulletin board wall that decorated one of the walls in the condo. The cork board looked really tacky, didn't quite fit with her decor. She didn't mind. Someday, when she'd made her millions, she'd replace the cork board with a Picasso.

She was standing as far back from the chart as she could, squinting at the paper, trying to see where the curve was going, when her phone rang. The land line, not her cell. That startled her. No one she knew was up this early on a Saturday. Not even her mother.

That thought made her nervous. Maybe something had happened on the cruise. People were always disappearing off cruise ships. Perhaps

Dad had suffered a heart attack. She looked at caller ID and breathed a sigh that was part relief and part hesitation. It was Zanus. Even after three months of dating, he still made her a little nervous, like any minute he was going to tell her their wonderful time together had all been a mistake. It was just one of those things. Oh, and by the way, he was going to yank his millions out and sue her firm. But maybe all that would change if she would sleep with him. She picked up the phone.

"Hello?"

"Rachel?" said his voice, very deep and resonant. "It's Zanus. Sorry to disturb you so early, but I have something important to talk to you about."

"Okay," Rachel said, her heart sinking. Good conversations never started that way. Breakup conversations started that way.

"We've been together a few months now, and you have been wonderful—both on the job and off. I want to take you out for a special dinner this evening. I am sorry I didn't call sooner, but I thought I might have to fly to Cairo this weekend. As it turns out, the meeting was postponed. I know that you probably have already made plans—"

Sweet of him to lie like that. He knew perfectly well she wasn't seeing anyone else.

"—but I thought I would take the chance. Are you free tonight?"

Rachel was startled. Zanus hadn't seemed the type to get sentimental over anything, much less her. Then she realized what this must be about. They had been spending a lot of time together and they had not yet had The Talk.

"Uh, let me look at my calendar," Rachel said.

She shut her eyes and slumped down in the chair. The Talk—where you decide if you are exclusive, and feelings are discussed and general nervousness and discomfort ensued.

Rachel hated The Talk. She had been hoping that with Zanus, these subjects would never came up. Why should they? Theirs was a business relationship. Or it had been up until now. She really did like him, but she didn't want to blow whatever they have by revealing too much too soon. Damn, she hated this. But he was her client and, beyond that, he was special to her. She couldn't very well back out. Besides, she felt a flutter of excitement. Maybe The Talk with him wouldn't be so a bad, after all.

"I can cancel my other . . . thing." She was a little flustered. "Dinner would be wonderful."

"Excellent. I'll make reservations at Charlie Trotters. Are you familiar with that restaurant?"

"Uh, why, yes," Rachel said. She couldn't believe it. She had been wanting to eat at Charlie Trotters forever. It was only the very hottest restaurant in the city. Charlie himself was a culinary legend. "But you won't get a table. You have to make reservations months in advance."

"Leave that to me, my dear," he said with a chuckle. "I'll pick you up at eight. Late seating starts at nine."

Trying to sound casual, she continued, "Charlie's not in his raw food phase anymore, is he?"

She hoped that didn't sound too snide.

Zanus only laughed. "No, Charlie's not in the raw phase anymore, thank goodness. I didn't care for it either, to be honest. But the man didn't gain his reputation by being ordinary, did he? I'll pick you up tonight at eight."

"Yes, eight is fine."

"Perhaps, later, I can come to your place for a drink," he said.

"Uh, yes. Sure. Maybe. I'll see you at eight." Rachel hung up and collapsed on her couch and thought things over.

In her excitement over Charlie's, she'd forgotten about The Talk. She had been worried that this might be the Let's Just Be Friends Talk, but what if it was the Tonight I Get to Try Out Your 1000-Thread-Count-Sheets Talk. What would she say to that?

Sure Zanus's voice was wonderful—his fingernails manicured, his Thomas Pink shirts pressed with the perfect amount of starch, his cologne specially made for him in France. But wasn't this just ego disguising itself as a man? She had been dating him for three months and Zanus hadn't even bothered to ask her if she wanted to go to Trotters or if she preferred someplace else. Thinking back, he'd never asked her where she wanted to go. He took her places he picked out.

Two months ago, he'd called her the night before to tell her that they were spending the weekend champagne tasting in France. Then there had been the weekend in Rome for the opera and a fourteen course dinner with his business partners. He'd at least given her a couple of days notice on that one. Now he was taking her to one of the best, most expensive restaurants in the entire United States. And he'd never asked if she *wanted* to go there.

Trotters had a set menu and if you didn't like what he was serving that night, you didn't eat. Of course, she would have chosen Trotters above anywhere else in the city, but Zanus didn't know that. Or did he? Did her know her that well?

She wouldn't have said no to any of the places he took her, and she didn't. But, like tonight, he never actually asked her if she wanted to go somewhere. He called, showed up, and they left. The one thing she was able to control in their relationship was the sex.

Good lord, girl, you're being silly! she scolded herself.

Those weekends had been a dream come true for her. Why should he ask her if she wanted to go, when, of course, she did? A girl would have to be six sandwiches shy of a picnic to turn down a romantic weekend in Europe with the man of her dreams. Was he a male chauvinist pig for knowing that? And if he wanted to have sex with her, he was just being a normal, healthy, American male.

Zanus was a dream, and Rachel wanted to smack herself in the head for trying, once again, to mentally sabotage this relationship. Zanus was amazing, and she had the feeling that she did not need to dread The Talk, after all.

What if tonight I say yes? Rachel asked herself, feeling the flutter in her stomach generate electricity that surged through her body.

Any man would think they were past due for a romantic liaison, but thus far she'd limited love-making between the two of them to some hot and heavy kissing in the back of the limousine.

He is client, she told herself. *So what? If we care for each other . . .*

But did she? That was the question.

Rachel looked around the apartment. Her decorating scheme consisted of Diet Coke cans on the counter, *Wall Street Journal*s on the floor, and underclothes draped over the backs of chairs. Then she looked at herself in the mirror. She never bothered to shower on Saturday or put on makeup. She was wearing track pants that she'd picked up on sale at Wal-Mart and a tank top that didn't match.

Rachel thought bitterly that Sarah Jessica Parker would never be caught dead wearing Wal-Mart track pants, not even on Saturday mornings. And if Sarah Jessica was going to Charlie Trotters with Big, she would look absolutely fabulous.

Rachel went to her closet, pulled out her one good evening dress, and groaned. There was that red wine stain over her right breast. She'd meant to send it to the cleaners after she'd last worn it in Rome. Besides, he'd seen her in this dress at least twice now.

Rachel panicked. *What am I going to do?*

She let herself go during the week because a manicure was too easily ruined in the pit, they would last two days at best. She wanted something new to wear; something that would knock his socks off. She needed a blowout, because her hair had not been properly trimmed and styled in ages, and her habit of plucking at her split ends when she was nervous didn't help matters. Her cuticles were ragged, her fingernails blah. She looked down at her toenails and winced.

Rachel took a deep breath and hit the shower. While flinging soap suds around, she made plans. She was within walking distance of Michigan Avenue. She hadn't really been listening, but she thought the man had promised that the weather was going to be fine today. Chicago in the springtime was fun. The tulips would be blooming on Michigan Avenue. Everyone was in a good mood, thrilled they'd survived another brutal Chicago winter, and glad to be out of the house.

She'd make a day of it.

Where to shop? When in doubt, a girl should wear Chanel. She'd start there. She began to put on what she usually shopped in—her gym pants—then realized that the salespeople wouldn't be likely to take her seriously if she looked like she'd just come from the gym. She put on slacks and a yuppie-looking sweater that had been a Christmas present from her mother. On her way out the door, Rachel grabbed her jacket and keys, and it was while going down in the elevator that she thought again about the doorman.

Rachel gave an inward sigh. She didn't want another unpleasant run-in with him.

What if he's there in the lobby? She mulled this over. *If he gives me that look again, I'll just walk past him as if he were invisible. Better to pretend he doesn't exist. A rude doorman is not going to spoil my day.*

Still, she thought, as the elevator descended, it would be nice to see if his eyes were really as blue as she remembered them.

The elevator stopped on the lobby floor. Rachel stepped out hesitantly, looking around for the doorman with the blue eyes.

He wasn't there. The night man was still on duty.

Telling herself she was relieved, Rachel made a beeline for the door and out onto the sidewalk. She was halfway to Michigan avenue before she realized that it was only 8:30 A.M.

The stores didn't open until 10 o'clock.

Rachel looked at her reflection in the window of Nordstrom's: Her nails were polished—French manicure. Her hair was cut and now swept over her shoulders in the latest style that happened to look extremely good on her. She carried myriad bags in which were three pairs of new shoes, one classic yet steamy Chanel suit—black. She had even splurged to have her makeup done by a professional at the salon.

She needed a day like today—date with Andreas Zanus notwithstanding, Rachel had let herself go, not caring about her appearance. She'd been so worried about making money, she'd forgotten how to spend it. She made a vow to treat herself to a day like today at least twice a year. She'd forgotten how good it felt to be a woman!

Bags in hand, she started walking back toward her condominium and it was then thunder rumbled and a drop of rain hit her square on the nose. Dismayed, Rachel looked up. The sky was turning an ugly gray color. Was it supposed to rain today? She hadn't paid any attention to the weather report. The wind picked up. And just as Rachel was remembering that her umbrella was on the floor of the hall closet, the heavens opened and the rain came down in sheets.

She looked around wildly for a taxi, but, of course, everyone else in downtown Chicago had the same idea. Those taxis that were out on Saturday morning were immediately snatched up.

She ducked under an awning to take cover, but it was too late. She was already soaked, her hair and makeup ruined. Well, those were things that could be fixed. She was determined that nothing was going to ruin this day. Rachel pulled her trench coat up close around her, and set out in the rain for home. Actually, once she'd consigned herself to being wet, walking in the rain was kind of fun. She sloshed gaily through puddles, shook back her wet hair from her face, and grinned at people huddled under their umbrellas, who stared at her as though she were a lunatic.

"I'm a lunatic with three pairs of new shoes!" she told a complete stranger. "So what? They make me happy! And," she added to herself with a little sigh, "it's been a long time since I was happy."

Did Zanus make her happy? Yes, of course, he did. What girl wouldn't be happy flying off to a heavenly weekend in France? Never mind that he never asked her where she wanted to go, what she wanted to do. Never mind that they talked about work. Never mind, never mind, never mind. Today was her day. A happy day. And tonight would be a happy night.

Rachel walked up to the door of her building, her keys in one hand and all of her parcels in the other. She'd forgotten all about the doorman, until he opened the door for her.

Yes, his eyes were as blue as she'd remembered. Bluer, in fact.

"Oh," she gasped, startled, then she added lamely, "Thank you, uh, Derek." She looked at his name tag.

He took hold of some of her bags and carried them inside. "I can take these parcels to your apartment for you," Derek offered, and his voice was deep, yet had a gruff quality about it, as though he was also embarrassed.

Parcels. Who said "parcels" these days? But he was still regarding her with that same intense look, only this time he wasn't angry. He seemed to be concerned, deeply concerned.

Why? Because she gotten wet in a rainstorm? What was up with this guy?

"No, no. I can manage my . . . parcels," Rachel said hastily.

Too hastily. Like she didn't trust him to ride up in the elevator alone with her. Which she didn't. He made her feel uncomfortable, the way he looked at her. But she didn't want him to know that. Now she was the one who was being rude.

She flushed and then, because he was still staring at her intently with those amazingly clear blue eyes of his, she mustered all the haughtiness she could manage—which wasn't much, considering that she soaking wet—and swept past him.

Well, she didn't exactly sweep. She squelched.

Rachel was suddenly conscious that her hair was a straggly mess. Her eye liner was running down her face, undoubtedly making her look like a raccoon, and her wet shoes were making loud squishing sounds as she walked across the marble floor, leaving puddles in her wake. Hard to be haughty when you squish when you walk.

"I'm sorry about the mess I'm making," she said, flustered.

"Please do not worry about it," Derek said, following after her with her bags.

She was making her soggy way toward the elevator, when he circled around to stand in front of her.

"Could we talk, milady?" Derek asked. He spoke very formally, almost sternly.

Rachel stared. "What did you call me?"

"Could we talk?" he repeated, flushing.

She was about to say no, she had nothing to talk

about with doormen, but then he said, "I'd like to apologize for the rude manner in which I behaved yesterday."

Rachel sighed. Why did he have to be so good-looking? And those eyes. To use an old cliché, he had the eyes of an angel. "Well . . . okay." What the heck? She did want to know why he had acted so strangely when she mistook him for the other doorman yesterday morning.

He brought up a chair. "Please, sit down. You look exhausted. Miss Duncan, right?" He spoke her name awkwardly. He did everything awkwardly, as though he wasn't used to being around women. Not shy, exactly, a man's kind of man.

Yet, with those looks, he must have to beat off the women with a stick. Maybe that was the problem. Too many women hounding him. Or maybe a bad relationship . . .

Stop it! Rachel scolded herself. *He's my doorman!*

Rachel was glad for the offer of a chair. Her feet were killing her, and, once she sat down, maybe she could discreetly dump the water out of her shoes.

"Thanks, Derek." She gave up on haughty, went for bright and perky. "Shopping is really wearing on a girl. I have a date tonight, you see. He's taking me to Charlie Trotters."

Rachel knew she was babbling, but she couldn't help herself. And why had she said that about a date? Was she in high school? How obvious could she get? Was she really trying to make this guy jealous?

Shut up, Rachel! she told herself, blushing hotly. *Just shut up!*

Derek cleared his throat. He looked embarrassed, and she breathed a little sigh. Maybe he hadn't noticed she was acting like she had the starring role in *Legally Blonde*.

He stood in front of her, tall and straight and stiff, as though he was a Marine standing in line for inspection. When he spoke, it sounded as though he had his speech memorized.

"My name is Derek de Molay, and you may have guessed that I am not from around here." He cleared his throat again. "I am new to city life and I have not quite learned how to handle myself in certain situations. Plus, I have never been a doorman. I am still not sure what I'm supposed to be doing or not doing."

"Derek," said Rachel, "this really isn't necessary—"

His voice and his look grew stern again. "And it seems to me that this city is a dangerous place for a woman alone. I am surprised that such a beautiful woman as yourself would choose to live here . . . by yourself. . . ."

He paused, then added ruefully, "I am probably making this worse. Now you'll think I am a chauvinistic swine."

He certainly had an unusual way of phrasing things. Rachel would have ordinarily thought he was a chauvinistic pig and lashed out at him, but she was tired and she had to get ready for her swanky dinner date. And he had called her beautiful. Even though she looked like a drowned cat, he'd called her beautiful. No matter that she really shouldn't care what this Derek thought of her, it was nice to be complimented.

She looked into the blue eyes and knew that he wasn't a rude, boorish chauvinist pig. She didn't know quite what he was, but he wasn't that. He was what he said he was—a guy who was used to wide open spaces, who was maybe a bit naive. Maybe he was from someplace like Montana, where men wore cowboy boots and held open the door and tipped their hats to a lady, or so she'd heard. Or maybe he was just taking his job too seriously. Okay, she could understand that. She'd give him another chance.

Rachel stood up. "Apology accepted, Derek. But I assure you I can take care of myself. I've taken two courses on women's self-defense and passed with flying colors. Not to mention the fact that every day I engage in some sort of physical contest with the other traders in the pit. And I've lived in this neighborhood for six years without incident. I feel quite safe."

Rachel thought that this was at an end, when she realized that he was following her toward the elevator. He still had her bags. She couldn't very well tell him not to go up with her now, not after his apology.

They came to the elevator. He punched the button for her and they stood there waiting. She looked at him. He looked at her. An awkward silence fell between them, and Rachel was immediately irritated. Why should she feel awkward around the doorman? Why should she feel anything?

"Well, I better get upstairs before I catch pneumonia." Rachel glanced at the bags. "If you could bring those up—"

"I will be glad to." Derek followed her into the elevator.

Odd, but she could hear the unspoken "milady" at the end of his sentence.

Two floors of uncomfortable silence, then Derek said suddenly, "So who is this man you are seeing tonight?"

Rachel was mildly annoyed, but perhaps this was his idea of small talk. "He's . . . uh . . . someone I've been seeing awhile . . ."

"What is his name? How well do you know him?" Derek pressed.

Rachel was now extremely annoyed. "I don't think that's any of your business."

He frowned at her, the blue eyes were intense, his expression stern. "You do not understand. You are . . . *alone*!"

"Yes, I am alone," Rachel retorted, her annoyance heating to anger. The nerve of this guy! "And I intend to keep it that way."

Derek said nothing more. He shifted his gaze away from her, stared moodily at the numbers flashing past in the elevator's screen. Finally they reached her floor. The doors couldn't open fast enough for Rachel.

"I'll take the bags," she said in frozen tones. "Thank you."

Derek handed her the bags in silence. He hit the button and the doors closed on him.

"Note to self," said Rachel, putting her key in the lock. "Avoid nosey, creepy doorman!"

Four

Rachel frantically rushed around her condo, throwing out newspapers, stuffing dirty clothes in drawers, and cleaning and dusting every surface. Then she set about undoing all the damage to her hair and face from the storm that afternoon. She was nervous about tonight, about what might happen after dinner.

She was standing in front of the mirror, reapplying the eye shadow—trying to remember just how the stylist had put on the three different colors—when the reality of what this date might mean hit her. No man was a saint. Eventually Zanus would be expecting her to sleep with him. In fact, she didn't know any other man who would have dated her for three days, let alone three months, without wanting to hop into the sack. He wasn't gay. His passionate kisses in the back of the limo revealed that he wanted her.

Rachel didn't know for sure why tonight was to be the special night, except the way he'd asked her out and the fact that he was taking her to a restaurant where the bill for the two of them would probably top her mortgage payment seemed to indicate that he was ready for something to happen between them.

Rachel thought all this over as she laid out her new dress on the bed, placed the new strappy black-and-gold heels from Neiman Marcus on the floor underneath it, and added her hottest pair of Saturday-night panties and matching bra—all black lace. Black being the ultimate power color.

Always be prepared, she told herself.

She spritzed on new perfume—Passion by Annick Goutal—and added new earrings and a matching necklace from Tiffany & Co. Not diamonds, but a very modern-looking, brushed gold piece that stood out in gleaming contrast to her black dress.

"Perfect," she said, admiring herself in the mirror.

When Rachel's phone rang, she nearly jumped out of her new heels.

Stop it, she told herself. *This is just another date, like any other date you've had with him. You don't know what's going to happen tonight.*

"Rachel? It's Zanus. I'm downstairs."

"Oh, is it that time already?" she said, as if she hadn't been looking at the clock every fifteen seconds. "I'll be right down. Just give me one moment."

She drew in a deep breath, picked up her purse, her keys, and left.

Forgetting her coat.

Derek watched as the limousine pulled up in front of the building. The car's windows were tinted and he could not see inside. The driver left the engine running, and Derek stepped outside to see if the limousine's occupant wanted him to open the door, but no one came out.

Derek stood outside the entrance and waited to see if he could catch a glimpse of the car's occupant, while still keeping an eye on the lobby. Moments later, the elevator doors opened.

Rachel stepped out and glided through the lobby toward him. Her hair stirred with the motion of her movement. The heels of her shoes made a tapping sound on the marble floor. Her beauty and the danger she was in pierced his heart, and he was suddenly swept back in time to another scene, to another marble hall—this one in a castle.

Lady Isouda. He had been fourteen. She was twenty-two and married to his liege lord. Derek saw her in his mind's eyes, dressed in black, like Rachel, except that Isouda's gown had been adorned with pearls. Wise in the ways of the world, Isouda had known that Derek had been infatuated her, though no words were exchanged between them except those that were proper for a noble lady and a young courtier. Once she had permitted him to dance with her and he had been in ecstasy. And, once, she had given him a ribbon from her hair.

He had allowed himself to imagine that she was desperately in love with him and that only her husband stood in the way of their happiness. Later, when he was older and more experienced, he had realized that she was only being kind to a lovelorn youth.

Lady Isouda had been a strong woman herself, Derek recalled suddenly. Once their castle had been attacked while her noble husband was away in a distant land. The lady had undertaken to lead the castle's defense herself; and though, of course, she had not taken up arms, she had conceived the strategy that had driven off the attackers. He remembered her the day of the assault—her beauty in her black dress and her peril; how he had pledged his young fourteen years of life to her.

Strange. Derek had not thought of Lady Isouda in centuries. And yet, once upon a time, he had believed that she was God's gift to him—but that had been before God had disappointed him, let him down. Was it possible that God was trying to make amends? Was Rachel God's gift to him?

No, Derek reminded himself sternly. God didn't give gifts to mortal men. God taught lessons, severe lessons. The God Derek knew was a God of wrath, not of love.

Still, he couldn't help but think that Rachel was undeniably beautiful, elegant, and graceful. Tonight, certainly, dressed in her finest, she was stunning, but he had been struck by her beauty this afternoon—the laughter in her eyes and the rainwater glittering like diamonds in her hair, not seeming to mind that her makeup was smeared over her face.

And she was in danger, in peril not only of her life, but her immortal soul. She was strong, but she was also proud and stubborn.

And Derek had offended her yet again. Not only offended her, he'd made her mad. Derek shook his head. When it came to women he was, like William had said to him, like a bull in a china shop.

He held open the door for Rachel. She cast him a glacial glance.

"I am sorry," he said. "It is just that I love the taste of shoe leather."

She looked at him, puzzled.

"That is why I keep putting my foot in my mouth," he said.

She thawed out, even gave him a smile.

The driver of the limo stepped out to open the door for the car's occupant. Rachel halted beneath the building's awning to await her companion. A cold wind had sprung up after the rain, blowing in off Lake Michigan, and she shivered and clasped her arms around her.

Derek wondered why she hadn't worn a coat. The bitter thought came to him that she had been too excited over her date.

The man stepped out of the car. He was tall,

with black hair and eyes dark as the pits of hell. He was somewhere in his early forties, and even Derek, who knew nothing about clothes and cared less, could see that he was impeccably and expensively dressed.

Derek glanced at Rachel. Her eyes shone. Her smile for this man was radiant. She was enchanted with him. He could see that plainly enough.

And Derek knew why.

This was no man. This was an archfiend in disguise. Derek didn't need a sign from God to know that this man was dangerous, not just to Rachel, but to anyone who crossed his path.

"Hello," Rachel said a little breathlessly, kissing him. "You look magnificent. Really, you've outdone yourself this evening."

Zanus stood back to admire her. "And you are as beautiful as a dream."

"Thank you." Rachel laughed. "Compliments of Chanel."

He regarded her with concern. "You're shivering."

"I didn't bring my coat," Rachel said. "It was so warm today. I didn't think—"

"Please, take mine." Zanus removed his overcoat and settled it over Rachel's shoulders. She protested, but he smiled and shook his head.

"We must get you in the car before you freeze."

He put his arm around her, strong and protective and commanding. Derek saw Rachel stiffen a little and he hoped she would put this guy in his place, as she'd put him in his place in the elevator. But Zanus smiled at her and she seemed to melt. Meek and demure, she permitted him to usher her down the stairs.

Derek, watching, had to remind himself that he was an observer. He couldn't follow his own inclination, which was to punch the fiend in the throat and leave him sprawled on the sidewalk.

Zanus gestured to the driver that they were returning to the car and now Zanus was reaching for the handle of the car door. Derek, running down the stairs, beat him to it. A leap and a bound and he was there to open the door for Rachel. As she passed by him, clutching Zanus's coat around her, Derek tried to send her a mental warning.

I am here for you, he told her silently, his eyes gazing into hers. *You do not know what this man is. He is more dangerous than you can ever imagine. If you want to tell this fiend to go back to Hell's flames where he belongs, I will stand by you and protect you.*

Derek felt so strongly that he was sure he must be reaching her, and for a heart-stopping moment, he thought she was going to follow his urging.

Rachel halted to stare at him, mesmerized.

"Please, Rachel, get in," Zanus said from behind her. "Before you catch cold."

Rachel blinked and, with a final, confused glance at Derek, she smiled at Zanus and slid into the limo's black leather interior. She was not looking at Zanus, however. She was staring at Derek and there was a wondering expression on her face.

Derek stepped back and Zanus walked past him. The man's hell-pit eyes fixed on Derek—eyes so empty that, despite himself, Derek felt a shiver at the base of his spine.

"You're drooling, boy," Zanus said in a smooth voice, just low enough that Rachel could not hear. Pulling a bill out of his wallet, he handed it to Derek. "Don't wait up."

Derek didn't take the bill. His right hand was clenched and he was having to use every bit of his mental discipline to keep from planting that fist on Zanus's square-cut jaw.

Zanus smiled as though he knew what Derek was thinking. He stuffed the bill into Derek's pocket, then stepped into the car, shut the door, and the limo drove off.

"He does not know who I am!" Derek realized and he smiled grimly. "The archfiend takes me for nothing more than a love-sick doorman. Well, my friend, we'll see about that!"

His fist relaxed. He discovered he was literally shaking with rage. He watched the limo until the red taillights were out of sight.

Derek had never felt so frustrated. He had the power to halt that limo with a thought. He had the power to rip open the metal frame with his bare hands and yank Zanus out and with a call to the cherubim gatekeepers, he could send him back to the nether regions where he belonged. He had the power to reveal to Rachel the fiend's true nature.

But he didn't. Instead, he stood, flat-footed on

the sidewalk, with Zanus's one hundred dollar tip in his pocket. He couldn't to do anything except watch the archfiend drive off with the first woman to have ever touched his heart. Not the infatuation of a boy. The love of a man.

But he wasn't really a man, he reminded himself. He was an angel, a holy warrior, sent to Earth on a vitally important mission. He couldn't risk giving away his identity. He was human now, and forbidden to use his powers. He had to obey orders.

Much as he hated to admit it, those orders made sense to him now. He had seen firsthand how dangerous the Dark Angels were to mortals. He had to learn as much as he could about what the fiends were plotting.

Orders or no orders, he planned to keep watch over Rachel. He intended to stay at his post until he knew she was home safe and sound.

When the night man came on duty, Derek handed him the hundred dollar bill and sent him home.

Five

Rachel was sitting at a beautifully appointed table at Charlie Trotters. She'd drunk some wine, undoubtedly a little too much, but it was exquisite; like drinking kisses snatched in a vineyard in southern France. They had finished dinner and were waiting for dessert and coffee and brandy.

Zanus excused himself for a moment. As soon as he left, waiters swooped down to pick up and refold his napkin. They also refilled her wineglass.

Rachel sipped the wine, enjoying the beauty of her surroundings and the memory of a fantastic meal. She had been worried over nothing. They had not had The Talk. Their conversation had been interesting, as always; Zanus was a fascinating man, well read, knowledgeable. He did not monopolize the conversation, but encouraged her to talk and he listened to her attentively. This had been the perfect date. He was the perfect man.

Why, then, did she have the feeling that something was missing?

"He's charming, thoughtful, romantic, handsome," Rachel muttered into her wineglass. "Everyone who meets Zanus thinks he's perfect. Well, not everyone."

Rachel's thoughts went back to the unsettling interlude with Derek the doorman. She was standing at the limo door, arranging her skirt, when their eyes met. She had the strangest feeling he was trying to tell her something, send her a warning. She would have written it off as mere jealousy and been flattered and even amused except that there had been a moment when those blue, blue eyes looked into hers that she felt a shiver go all through her. A moment when she'd wanted to forget the limo and grab hold of him and cry, "What is it with you? Tell me what you know!"

But why should he know anything? And why should she care if he did? It was all very confusing. Rachel drank more wine and wondered what was keeping Zanus. Perhaps he had to make a phone call. Cell phones were verboten in Charlie Trotters. And what about the end of the evening? She wanted to sleep with him. She really did. She was thinking of this when Zanus returned to their table.

Reaching into his pocket, he said, "I asked our waiter to hold off on that crème brûlée for a minute so that I could give you this."

He drew a long velvet box out of his pocket and placed it onto the table in front of her.

Rachel was speechless as she looked at the box, then up at Zanus.

"You didn't—"

"Please open it before you tell me I didn't have to get it for you." He smiled at her.

Rachel opened the box. Inside was a diamond bracelet with two strands of diamonds arrayed on either side of one perfect strand of emeralds. Rachel gasped and then caught her breath. She placed her hand over her mouth and gazed at the bracelet in awe. She looked at Zanus.

"It's wonderful. I've never seen anything like it." She touched the bracelet in disbelief.

"That's because they don't make anything like this anymore. This is a vintage piece. It has history." He reached for the box and took out the bracelet.

"Let me help you put this on."

"Thank you. This is such a wonderful gift, I didn't expect this. You've been so wonderful to me . . ."

"I like being wonderful to you," he said. "Diamonds and emeralds become you."

Rachel admired the jewelry. In that moment, she felt completely and perfectly happy and she scolded herself. He was perfect. Which meant there must be something wrong with her. Must she always overanalyze every word and gesture? Why couldn't she let herself be happy in a relationship? She could almost hear her mother's voice, asking her that very question.

"This evening has been perfect," she said, smiling into his eyes.

"So perfect that I do not want it to *end,*" he said and he took hold her hand.

Was it her imagination or had his voice lingered on that last word?

He confirmed it by his next words. They were tender, caressing, but there was a meaning behind them she couldn't ignore.

"A man cannot wait forever, Rachel," he said softly. "I know you have reservations because I am your client." He hesitated, then said with a smile, half kidding and half not kidding, "Perhaps, it might be better if I wasn't—"

"No," Rachel said hurriedly. "Please. I know. I've been overly cautious. It's just that . . ." She looked into his eyes and saw desire. And she felt the same. Of course she felt desire. He was wonderful, after all. Oh, what the hell! Life was short. Gather ye rosebuds while ye may.

She smiled at him. He smiled back. All was settled.

For the rest of the evening, she was consumed by a fever of nervous anticipation. Rachel was acutely conscious of each one of his touches—when his fingers pressed the small of her back to guide her through a doorway, when his knee brushed against hers or his hand rested over her hand. Every touch seemed to be a deliberate and calculated move on his part. Each was perfect. He never held her hand too long, so as not to become sweaty. He never pressed her too hard, and his knee never kissed hers long enough to be forward.

Of course he is experienced with women, Rachel thought. What did I expect? A fumbling pubescent boy? No, dear heart, you wanted a man, and now you've got one. A *real* man. Stop sabotaging this for yourself.

"You are awfully quiet, my dear. Is something bothering you?" Zanus asked during the ride home.

"No," Rachel smiled at him and squeezed his hand. "Nothing's bothering me."

He leaned over to kiss her passionately. He reached both hands up to hold her face. His eyes were so dark that Rachel couldn't tell where the black of his pupils ended and the iris began. His eyes were drawing her near and she relaxed, letting herself fall into them.

The limousine pulled up in front of Rachel's building.

Rachel drew back from the kiss and asked nervously, "Would you like to come up for a drink? A brandy, maybe?"

"Yes, a brandy would be nice," Zanus said with a knowing smile.

Rachel had to rearrange her clothes in order to step out of the car. Zanus helped her out. He looked to the driver, then back at Rachel.

"Should I send the car home?"

It was a loaded question and they both knew it. She thought of the dinner and the bracelet.

"Yes," she answered softly.

As they entered the lobby, she was very thankful Derek wasn't there. And then they stepped into the elevator and she forgot Derek. For she suddenly remembered the state of her apartment. She'd cleaned this afternoon but wasn't sure if her cursory job would be up to snuff for him—some men were fastidious, Zanus seemed to be that way—but if Rachel had an army of servants like he did, her place would be immaculate too. *Maybe if I keep the lights turned down, he won't notice that I didn't dust.*

"Um, my place may be a little messy," she said, flushing.

Zanus stopped her. He took her head in his hand and gently kissed her lips. Then he whispered in her ear, "I am coming up to see you, not your apartment. Messy or clean, I'm not reporting you to the Martha Stewart militia."

She laughed and he kissed her again.

As she unlocked the door and turned the light on, Rachel quickly peeked around for any obvious dirt she had overlooked that afternoon. Seeing nothing, she moved to the kitchen to find the brandy and Zanus walked into her living room.

Rachel brought out the brandy and sat on the couch. Zanus sat down beside her. Relaxing, he put his arm around her. He took a sip from his glass, then set it down. Rachel took a gulp from hers. This should feel so right, but it was feeling all wrong. Did she really want to do this? She could call it off now, fake a stomach ailment or something. This was their first time together and Rachel worried about the implications to their business relationship. What if things between them changed? This was why you didn't sleep with a client! But already, it had gone too far for her to stop without seriously offending him.

"Come here." Zanus took hold of her hand and pulled her to him and kissed her.

"We will do this properly." Zanus stood up and took off his shirt off to reveal strong and well-muscled arms and chest. He lifted Rachel up from the couch and carried her to the bedroom.

After it was over, Rachel waited tensely for Zanus to hold her, so they could fall asleep in each other's arms. Fortunately, he merely gave her a kiss on the cheek and rolled over to his side of the bed.

Rachel scooted away, not wanting to touch him. She was exhausted, but she couldn't sleep. She kept wondering: Why did he have sex with me? The act had been so mechanical on his part. No feeling, no passion, no love. Just an act. What had she just done? Why did she suddenly feel cheap?

A man gives you a diamond bracelet and you hop into bed with him. What did you expect?

Rachel told herself to shut up. Why should she feel guilty for making love with Zanus? He'd always been kind and respectful of her. He had let her set the boundaries of their relationship. Maybe that was the problem. He'd said that their evening was going to be special and Rachel had assumed they would talk about where this relationship was headed. Only they hadn't discussed their relationship. They had talked about everything *but* their relationship and their feelings for each other.

She had been dreading the conversation, true, but she still thought the timing for it was right. She hoped that if they talked things through she'd have a better understanding of his thoughts on the future, and whether she was a part of that future or not.

Yet, he had given her that beautiful bracelet. Maybe he wasn't the type to talk about his feelings. Maybe he was using his bracelet to say what he couldn't. He wouldn't be the first man she'd met that couldn't discuss his feelings and instead showed them with gifts.

Still, something wasn't right about him. He never asked her what she wanted, where she wanted to go, or what would made her happy. He did what he wanted and assumed that she would be ready to follow him anywhere. Even though she was the one who had invited him up to her apartment, she knew quite well that the dinner and bracelet were a ploy to make her feel obligated to sleep with him. He had even tried to blackmail her, she realized suddenly, with a cold feeling in the pit of her stomach. That business about the night ending.

What he'd really meant was that if she didn't say yes their relationship would be ending! She'd seen it so clearly, yet she'd lied to herself.

He was manipulating her. Zanus had orchestrated this whole evening to get her into bed.

But why? She supposed he'd enjoyed the sex, as any man would, but he could have spent less money and achieved the same result by buying this month's issue of *Hustler.*

So what now? Where do we go from here?

Rachel watched the clock crawl through the hours and listened to him breathing softly beside her. He didn't even snore.

God, he was perfect!

Six

Derek stood on the sidewalk across the street, watching Rachel's window. He'd been at his post for hours, waiting for her to return from her date. He'd hoped that she'd come back alone. He hoped she would discover Zanus's true nature and tell him to leave her alone. He'd hoped for that. He had almost even prayed for it, but then he remembered that God didn't answer prayers. At least, not his prayers.

Derek watched the limo arrive, and he ducked back into the shadows so they wouldn't see him. He noted Rachel's disheveled appearance as she stepped out of the car, and he heard Zanus send the car away for the evening, a note of triumph in his voice.

Derek watched the lights come on in Rachel's apartment. He waited for her to come to her senses. Waited for Zanus to walk back out.

"I will be glad to call you a cab," Derek muttered.

But Zanus didn't return. The lights in her windows went dark. Derek stood there in the chill night air, aching inside. He was furious at her, so angry his rage hurt him; and he was worried about her, so worried he was almost sick with it.

First his rage talked. She must be blind or stupid not to see through Zanus's disguise, that arrogant, pompous attitude, that extravagant show of wealth? Fine, let her succumb to his charms. She deserves whatever's coming to her.

And then he thought of the danger she was in. No guardian angel there to protect her. What woman wouldn't fall for Zanus? He was handsome, suave, charming. Even Derek had to admit that. What did the archfiend want with her? What was he after? William suspected it had something to do with her work in the financial markets, but they needed proof. Which was where Derek came in. Except what could he do? He was just the doorman.

Rage spoke up again. Stupid, stupid woman. She'd placed herself in jeopardy. The forces conspiring against her were the very forces she'd invited into her bed. Derek had taken the master key to her condo with him, just on the off chance it might be needed. He longed to unlock the door of her apartment, burst in, kill the archfiend on the spot. That would be going against orders, however. Archangel Michael would be furious. The heavenly forces would lose their chance to find out what evil the fiends were plotting.

Derek was powerless to stop Zanus. He had to control himself, wait until the fiend made his move. Then, hopefully, he could step in and save Rachel—from herself. Until that happened he had to stand here in the cold, clutching Rachel's key so tightly in his hand that the sharp edges of the metal bit into his flesh. Blood dripped from his palm and soaked into the lining of his coat pocket.

He stood sentinel duty all night in the chill darkness, watching Rachel's window, guarding her, as best he could.

The next morning, Rachel woke to the smell of bacon. She rolled over, looking for Zanus, remembering her night with him. She felt embarrassed and uncomfortable about facing him. She wished he'd just slipped away into the dawn. She was tempted to try pretending to be sleeping, hoping maybe he'd grow tired and leave.

But, no, he was cooking for her. Might as well get it over with.

She rose from the bed, reached to the back of her door for her robe, and slipped into the bathroom to clean herself up. Looking in the mirror, she wiped the sleep and leftover mascara out of her eyes, then brushed her teeth. Rachel walked into the living room to find Zanus in his underwear making French toast and bacon.

"Good morning, angel," he said to her.

Rachel stood staring. "Where did all this food come from? I didn't have any bacon, eggs, or bread for that matter. And what time is it?"

Zanus handed her a cup of coffee. "Here, sit down and drink this. You're not quite awake yet, are you?" He moved back to the stove to finish cooking. "To answer your first question, I noticed the sad state of affairs inside your refrigerator. Do you really live on taco dip and Diet Coke? I went out to the convenience store and bought some rations. In answer to your second question, it's eight A.M. I am an early riser and saw no reason to wake you. No rest for the wicked, and all of that."

Rachel drank her coffee, thinking this was probably the single most confusing morning of her life. They were sitting at the kitchen table, drinking their coffee, when Zanus broached the subject of her work.

"So have you made a decision yet?"

"Decision about what?" she asked, though she knew perfectly well what he meant.

"You know about what—those trades I want you to place. We talked about it some last night. The timing is right. The market is hot and you know it. Remember how we discussed your future? Your talents are being wasted at your firm.

Freeman doesn't see it. You're brilliant in the Merc. Imagine what you could do if you were allowed to be in there totally unfettered, without the firm's leash around your neck."

Rachel had heard all of this before. She and Zanus had held this very same conversation last night. Suddenly she realized that this was, for them, The Talk. No discussion of where their personal relationship was headed. Discussion of where their financial relationship was headed.

At least, she thought, he's not giving me a kiss on the cheek and saying he'll be sure to call. At least he's thinking about the future. She felt better about last night.

"Freeman is taking advantage of you," Zanus said persuasively. "He's paying you a pittance and making a fortune off your brains. You should quit, go out on your own."

"As I've explained, my dear, the only way I could do that would be to have my own seat on the exchange, and I don't have that kind of money. The last seat sold for millions."

"What if there was a way to raise that kind of capital? Would you do it?" Zanus stopped flipping bacon and turned around to look at Rachel.

"In a minute!" she said, laughing. "But I'm not good at robbing banks. Those orange prison jumpsuits make me look washed out."

She smiled at him over her coffee mug.

Zanus wasn't smiling. He was serious. He

turned off the stove. "There is a way, Rachel. At least a way to get started, I have a friend who has a Globex computer. You could trade with him electronically."

"You've really been thinking about this, haven't you?"

Zanus spoke with such conviction, Rachel was starting to become a believer herself. She had dreamed of owning her own seat after her first year on the floor, as she watched most of the other brokers either burn out or bottom out or both. She had always succeeded. She had always come out ahead. She was nowhere near burnout. She was good. Damn good.

To be out from under Freeman's narrow-minded, risk-avoiding, conservative approach to the market was extremely attractive to her. If she had her own seat, she could make trades that were in her best interests. She could trade without having to consider her clients or the firm. She would assume all of the risk and reap all of the reward. It was every successful trader's dream.

But seats were limited and extremely hard to come by. They were usually passed down through families, from father to son or, in rare cases, from husband to wife. That was because an independent trader could trade against value of the seat, use it as leverage. She could make enough to retire at the age of thirty or maybe become a venture capitalist. Rachel could be her own boss.

All she had to do was say yes to Zanus. *Let him*

seduce me once more, she told herself ruefully, but with a feeling of excitement.

She knew what kind of trades he was proposing. They weren't exactly illegal, just unethical. She'd never done anything like it, but she knew plenty of brokers who had, and gotten away with it. The risk was minimal, in fact.

Zanus sat down beside her, ran his hand over her arm.

"I have been thinking about this a lot, Rachel. This is an opportunity you can't afford to miss."

Rachel felt dizzy for a moment. She must still be exhausted from too much wine and not enough sleep last night. She was inclined to agree with Zanus. If she were caught making these trades, she could be reprimanded. Sometimes the managers would overlook such things, though, if they thought you were worth the trouble of keeping. In other words, if you made money. Firms would sometimes even pay the fines levied on brokers. How much trouble could she really get into for this? She had a perfectly clean record.

Zanus looked at her intently. "Rachel, what have you got to lose? And, after all, you did sleep with me last night. I'm your client. I could tell your boss."

Rachel looked at him in alarm.

"Relax," Zanus said, smiling. "I'm teasing. Think about the money."

He was right. Freeman had been making money off of her sweat for years. She was entitled to this.

"Okay, I'll think about it," she said, feeling a flutter of excitement. "Send the details to my PDA this week."

He came around the table and kissed her.

"Let's celebrate. Thursday night we'll go out."

"Thursday is my book club night." Rachel reminded him.

He should know that by now, she thought. He knew this was important to her or, at least, he should know. He'd asked her out on Thursdays before and a couple of times he'd even tried to make her change her plans to suit him. She hoped he wasn't going to do that now.

To her surprise, he said, "I know Thursday is book club night. I think we should all go out to celebrate. I've been wanting to meet your friends."

Rachel laughed nervously. "Honey, I don't think that's such a good idea. It's kind of a Girls Only, No Boys Allowed thing. No one brings along a date."

Zanus gave Rachel a hurt look. His voice cooled noticeably. "Is there some reason you don't want your friends to meet me?"

"No, of course not!" Rachel said. "It's just that we don't talk about things that you like to discuss. We gossip and giggle and act like idiots when we're together. I'm just afraid you'll be bored."

"Is that why you don't want them to meet me? Because you think I am boring?" He was teasing, but she could see he was starting to grow angry.

"I didn't say you were boring. I said I thought

we would bore you— Oh, never mind. Look, I'm sorry. I would love for my friends to meet you. They've heard all about you. We'll do dinner on Thursday. Okay?"

Rachel was a bit puzzled by his insistence on going to her weekly dinner with the girls. But this one wasn't worth an argument. Not in the least.

Zanus smiled with satisfaction. "Ah, I finally get to know what goes on when you sneak away on Thursday nights and don't call until morning! Thanks for being a good sport about it. What book are you reading this week? I want to be prepared."

She was tempted to tell him, *Little Women*, just to see if he would really read it. She refrained. He couldn't take a joke very well.

"Don't worry," she said. "We stopped reading books a long time ago."

Seven

The bell rang and trading finally halted for the day. Some of the men threw their cards into the air and cursed the world for their bad fortune. Others maneuvered to close out their trades or settle a dispute. Rachel ran to the bathroom, as usual. There were no breaks while the market was open. No time to eat, no bathroom stops. You didn't dare leave the pits while trading was going, especially if it was going in your favor, and for Rachel, it had been a very good day. Pleased with herself, she was about to head back to her office to review her day and prepare for the next, when her cell phone rang.

"Hi, Rachel," said the crisp, professional voice. "It's Lyla. Mr. Freeman would like to see you in his office after market close."

"Okay, Lyla. Please tell him I'll be there. Thanks."

Rachel snapped shut the phone. She felt sick to her stomach. She knew it. One of her clients had insisted that she make some trades for him that had turned out to be bad, bad, bad. She had advised against them, but, as usual, this arrogant jerk knew best and now he was probably throwing all the blame for his losses on her.

Now Freeman was going to fire her. It wasn't like she was a rare commodity. There was a line a mile long of others panting hot and heavy to take her place on the Merc. Sharp young men and women fresh out of business school. Big corporations like the one she worked for didn't care about turnover, burnout, drug addiction, attrition, or any of the problems faced by other industries. All her company cared about was the bottom line.

Well, maybe this is my chance, she thought, as she walked slowly down Wacker Drive to her office building. Maybe this is where I say, "You can't fire me, I quit." It was an odd twist of fate that she'd considered just last night to make those trades with Zanus's friend.

When she stepped into the elevator, she ignored those who greeted her. She didn't even say hello to her coworkers as she passed them. She was wondering suddenly what it would be like not coming here everyday. What it would be like to be all on her own . . .

Freeman summoned her into his office with a wave of his hand. He was on the phone, in the middle of a conversation with someone. She sat down in the big chair opposite his desk, feeling like when she was in grade school waiting for the principal to call her mother because she'd smacked Danny Feeney for spitting water at her.

The conversation was taking a long time. Freeman gave her a shrug and rolled his eyes, indicating he was helpless to break it off.

Mr. Freeman was an attractive man. Tall, thin, he always wore nice suits and had a tan from the golf course in the summer, the tanning bed in the winter. Unfortunately, his personality didn't match his good looks. He was a trader from the old school. He had a sub-par education. His entire motivation for trading was simply to grow rich enough to retire early and upgrade to a trophy wife. The only problem was the more money he made the more he spent.

He and the current Mrs. Freeman (who knew quite well she would get half of everything in the inevitable divorce and probably had her half already staked out) owned a lavish estate in Lake Forest. They bought expensive cars, took pricey vacations. He wasn't doing bad for a man in his mid-forties with a full head of hair, but he hadn't saved a dime of his money.

As a person who planned for every eventuality, Rachel couldn't understand it. He could never see beyond his next new car, the next vacation home in Florida. And he couldn't figure out why he was always halfway to being broke. That's the reason he'd left the pit to become a manager. He had to keep up with his bills. As a manager, his paycheck was not subject to market volatility or his own mediocre skills as a trader.

Freeman hung up the phone and closed the door to his office. "Rachel I've just gotten off the phone with your client. He's—"

Rachel cut him off. "In my defense, Mr. Freeman, no one could have gotten him a better price on that order. He was being totally unreasonable and he refused to pull the trigger when I told him—"

To her astonishment, Freeman nodded.

"I know, Rachel. You're right, of course." He grinned at her. "Luckily, I'm not talking about *that* client. I'm talking about Mr. Zanus. He's quite impressed with you."

Rachel could feel a serious red flush creeping up the back of her neck. She'd hoped to keep the fact that she was dating Zanus under wraps at the office. If Freeman found out, she didn't want to know what would happen.

"I'm glad he considers my work satisfactory," she said cautiously.

Freeman's grin expanded. "Satisfactory! Rachel, he says you are the best he's seen, and if you didn't already work for me, he'd steal you away to work for him. That's a pretty nice compliment, and as you know, when I receive that type of positive feedback from a client, I like to reward my employees."

Oh no, Rachel groaned inwardly. Freeman's idea of rewarding people always meant public humiliation. What was it going to be this time?

Would she have to give a speech at the next board meeting? Or, worse, a motivational talk for her peers before the market opened. She could see the traders now, snickering at her when they thought Freeman wasn't looking.

"That's really *not* necessary," she said earnestly. "I'm just doing my job—"

Freeman smiled at her. "Relax, Rachel. You're not going to have to make a speech or anything. Zanus has asked if you could spend some more time with him outside of the office. He's shown a great interest in the inner workings of the market and the floor. I want you to pay him every attention. Teach him more about what we do and how we do things here. Do you understand?"

"Yes, absolutely." Rachel could have kissed him in her relief. "I'll do my best to keep Mr. Zanus happy."

Rachel smiled to herself. Zanus had been very clever. Now she could be seen outside of work with him and, if Freeman heard about it, he would think this was all his idea. Of course, this would just be for a short time, until she'd made enough money to quit the firm. But, for now, no questions would be asked.

And with that Freeman stood up, shook hands with her, and sent her on her way.

Rachel felt a warm rush of gratitude toward Zanus who had been clever enough and sensitive enough to try to smooth her way. She'd been completely mistaken about him, she decided. So he wanted to sleep with her and he'd gone to great and expensive lengths to obtain his objective. Wasn't that a compliment?

Walking out of the office, Rachel saw Lyla, Freeman's secretary, give her the eye. Rumors would fly that she was sleeping with Freeman to keep her job, but that was nothing new. If she'd really slept with half of the men she was rumored to have, she'd be a very tired woman.

As she settled into the car for the ride home through rush-hour traffic, she let herself dream about the day when she would have her own seat. When she wouldn't have to worry about the stupidity of clients or Freeman's inanities. She even let herself think about what life might be like married to Zanus. Her mother would be ecstatic and insist on planning everything. She couldn't trust Rachel to handle it, after all.

Fine with me, Rachel thought, leaning back into the leather seat and allowing herself to dream . . .

The car rolled to a stop in front of her condo. The door opened and there was Derek, holding the door for her.

He looked her straight in the eyes and it was so intense, so penetrating, that it took her breath away. For a moment she couldn't speak or think.

Why did he do this to her? Why did he make her feel nervous and jumpy and flustered? Why did his hand, strong and firm, taking hold of her hand to assist her from the car, cause her pulse rate to go sky high? She was going to marry Zanus in Hawaii. She should not be thinking about how great it felt for the doorman to touch her hand.

"Derek, I will be going out tonight," Rachel said, rewarding him with a smile. "Please have a taxi come by for me at eight P.M."

She started to walk off.

"Are you seeing that man in the limo again?" Derek demanded harshly.

Rachel turned around to face him. "What possible business is it of yours?"

"Where are you going tonight?" he asked, as if he hadn't heard her.

Rachel stared at him for a moment, taking back every good thought she'd had about him. Now she was a little afraid. Was he becoming obsessed with her? She turned and continued walking, refusing to dignify such a question from a doorman—even a handsome doorman—with an answer.

"I need to know so that I can tell the cab company, Miss Duncan," Derek said coolly, following her into the lobby.

"Oh, right," said Rachel, flushing. Now she felt stupid. Paranoid and stupid. "I am going to a restaurant called Fuse. It's in the Hotel 71."

He wrote down the name on a notepad. Rachel continued walking toward the elevator, mentally kicking herself. *Why do I let him get to me? Why do my brains seem to turn to bean dip whenever he's around?*

She was nearing the elevator when she heard his footfalls coming up behind her.

"Rachel, I have to talk to you," he said urgently. He took hold of her hands. "It is important—"

The elevator door opened. There stood the Ericksons—a wealthy couple, blue bloods, prominent socialites—staring at the two of them holding hands.

"Dear me," said Mrs. Erickson. "I hope we aren't interrupting."

"You are, actually," Derek said, glowering at them.

The two stared at Rachel, mildly shocked.

Rachel snatched her hand from Derek's grasp.

"Mr. and Mrs. Erickson," she said politely, cursing beneath her breath. Mrs. Erickson was the biggest gossip in the building. By tomorrow afternoon, everyone would know Rachel was having a fling with the doorman.

"Lovely evening, isn't it?"

They murmured that it was and walked on. She entered the elevator and for a moment she thought Derek was going to charge in after her, but apparently he recalled his duties. He stalked off to open the door for the Ericksons, who were giving each other knowing smiles.

She punched the button and sighed in relief when the doors closed. And she put out of her mind the warm, firm feel of his hands holding hers . . .

Derek was not around when she went downstairs to meet her taxi—thank goodness! The night man was on duty and Rachel didn't know him very well, which was probably a good thing. Rachel had called the manager to put in a complaint about Derek's behavior. But, as usual, Fraym's machine had answered. She had left a terse message and hung up.

Her taxi was right on time, however. Derek had managed to do something right.

"Hotel 71," she said, and sank back in the seat to watch Chicago flash by.

She loved this city at night. Loved the wonderful architecture, loved the lights that were around her and above her and even below her, reflected in the river that was the city's lifeblood. It was April. Spring was in the air, though there was still snow in the shady corners. She felt rejuvenated and refreshed. Not only the lights and the city, but she was meeting her girlfriends for dinner. These were not friends from work. They were her solace from work.

This was also the first time Zanus would meet her girlfriends. Rachel wasn't sure she liked the idea, but the girls were thrilled. They had wanted to meet this fabulous man they'd heard about. Rachel had admittedly done considerable bragging about him but now she wished she hadn't. What if they didn't like him? What if he didn't like them?

Rachel had met Lana and Kim and Beth through a book club she'd joined. The book club hadn't quite worked out, however. They all loved to talk about books. The problem was, they had such different tastes they could never agree on what book to read next. More and more Rachel and Lana, Kim and Beth, found themselves going off on their own, forgetting to discuss the book in favor of talking about each other. They decided to form their own book and social club. They did still talk about books. They would tell each other what they were reading and share their opinions. That way if a book appealed to one friend and not to the others, they weren't forced to read something they didn't want to.

They all liked each other, and they led such different lives that each found the lives of the others fascinating. Their conversations always steered a path toward personal discussions instead of the book they were supposed to be discussing. The current book they were supposed to be talking about was one Rachel had recommended. *Leg the Spread: A Woman's Adventures Inside the Trillion-Dollar Boy's Club of Commodities Trading* by the author Cari Lynn. The book was about life in the pits from a female perspective. Rachel had urged them all to read it, saying it would help them understand her better.

Lana had rolled her eyes and said she doubted anything would help her understand Rachel, but she'd give it a try.

Lana was a television executive. Brash and beautiful, she never took crap from anyone and was always championing some cause. She was very much take-charge and gave the impression that she could handle any situation she encountered. Lana was single and she really liked men. In fact, Lana went through men like most women blow through tissues.

Rachel admired Lana's boldness. Nothing embarrassed Lana, and she could care less what anyone thought of her. Rachel thought it would be very liberating to walk in Lana's shoes for a day or two.

Lana's older sister, Beth, was the only married one in the group. She was practical, whip smart, and preppy. She always looked perfectly put together and appeared to be totally in control of herself. She was honest to a fault—the fault being that some things should remain unsaid. Beth and her husband owned a very successful small business together. Beth was typically the reserved one in the group, but on rare occasions she would completely cut loose with the girls and they'd all roll into bed in the early-morning hours. When Beth took it into her head to pull an all-nighter, there was no stopping her.

And last there was Kim, a chemist who worked for a large pharmaceutical company. Kim was also smart, practical, stubborn and pretty with long brunette hair that she would never dream of cutting. Kim was polite, quiet, and seemed delicate. She was often taken for a pushover. But those people who made this mistake were soon proven wrong. Kim had a supervisory role at her company and she never accepted less than perfection from herself and her charges.

Rachel entered the lobby of the Hotel 71, decorated in ultramodern, with plants growing out of a coffee table and jet black elevators. She went to the restaurant bar—one of the new hot spots in town, all steel and chrome and funky lights and young professionals. The place was crowded, no table available, and so she sat at the bar. Zanus said he would meet her there; he had some business to take care of at the office, but he would take her home.

Rachel thought again how strange it was that he'd insisted on meeting her friends. Most men she'd dated could have cared less about her girlfriends. He'd seemed angry over her reluctance to bring him. She should be pleased; this was a sign he was thinking about her, interested in what interested her. She couldn't help but find it a bit odd, though.

She wondered if she was worried about jinxing her relationship with him. Introducing the friends was a big step. The next step was meeting the parents. Her stomach gave a little flutter at the thought. Fortunately hers were on QE 2 heading for the South Pacific.

"Dirty martini," she told the bartender. "Straight up, and salty. And throw in a extra olive, will you?"

Rachel sipped it and started to relax and unwind, but she couldn't get Derek completely out of her mind. *Rachel, I have to talk to you. It's important.* Why? What about? She couldn't help but be curious. She told herself he was just creepy, but, the truth was, he wasn't. He seemed to be genuinely, sincerely concerned about something and it had to do with her.

A hand on her shoulder made her jump.

"Hello, darling." Zanus greeted her with a discreet kiss on the cheek. "Sorry to startle you, but you were so absorbed in your thoughts you didn't see me."

"Sorry about that," she said, flushing. She was thankful that no one had yet invented videothoughts, otherwise he would have seen a full-size picture of Derek.

"Have you been waiting long?" he asked politely.

"No, I haven't. I just ordered a drink."

Zanus ordered a single malt scotch (the most expensive on the bar list) and sat on the stool next to Rachel.

"So where are the ladies?"

"Oh, they're probably running a bit late. Would you like to go to our table now?" Rachel asked.

She and Zanus were seated and soon her girlfriends trickled in. Kim was the last to arrive, exasperated about some sort of terrible chemical mix-up at work. Rachel made the introductions and they all listened to Kim's story about the joys of having to be decontaminated.

Zanus was charming, of course. Rachel felt foolish for having reservations about introducing him to her friends. He made them all feel at ease, encouraged them to talk, answered their none-too-subtle questions with grace and charm, telling them nothing while giving the impression he was telling everything. Rachel watched him, fascinated.

Dinner was moving along smoothly. The entrees

were served, and Lana was regaling them with a story about one of her conquests, when Rachel noticed that Zanus wasn't listening. He was staring over her shoulder toward the bar. She turned to look but couldn't see what was so interesting.

She took advantage of an intense conversation between Lana and Beth to lean over to Zanus and said softly, "So who do you keep staring at up at the bar?" she asked. "Is it that redhead with the legs up to her chin? I have to warn you—I'm the jealous type."

He seemed taken aback by her question, as though unaware he'd been so obvious. Then he shook his head. "If you must know, I am the one who should be jealous. That new doorman of yours is standing at the bar. And he won't stop staring at you."

"What?" Rachel said, aghast. "You must be mistaken."

She turned again and then she saw him.

Derek was sitting at the bar, watching her.

"Why would he be here?" Rachel said, perplexed.

"That's exactly what I want to know," Zanus said grimly.

Rachel's friends had stopped their conversation to stare at the bar. Derek didn't even have the grace to appear embarrassed at being caught or to look away. He kept staring straight at her.

"Rachel, who's the new admirer?" Lana asked and winked at Zanus. "You better take care. He's awfully handsome."

Lana believed in keeping boyfriends on their toes, playing one off the other. Rachel could have cheerfully strangled her.

"It's nobody," she said weakly. "It's just the doorman at my building."

"Rachel, is that really your doorman?" Beth gasped. "Wow! He's hot."

Zanus was glaring at her accusingly, as though this was somehow her fault. She felt the blood rush to her face.

"I don't know why he's here. He's a little strange. I think he might be foreign or something." She was hoping they'd drop it, but she should have known better.

"Really?" asked Kim, interested. "I think he looks Swedish. Those blue eyes. I have relatives in Sweden. Perhaps I should go introduce myself—"

"No!" Rachel grabbed her. "Don't you dare! Look, could we just not talk about it? If we ignore him, maybe he'll go away. My, isn't the veal wonderful?" she said loudly.

Zanus threw down his napkin. "Rachel, I'm going to get to the bottom of this."

"No, please don't," Rachel begged. She felt hot all over. "Just leave him alone. I've already spoken to the manager about him. Let's finish our dinner."

Zanus remained seated. Her friends, seeing her discomfort, rallied around her. Lana took charge of the conversation, asking Zanus about his thoughts on Rome, saying she was going to be visiting there soon and could he recommend a hotel? He told her about a beautiful hotel at the top of the

Spanish Steps and the two were soon lost in their discussion. Rachel noticed that although he appeared to be giving his complete attention to the conversation, Zanus kept a close eye on Derek.

Derek, to Rachel's chagrin, was keeping a close eye on her. She had never in her life been so embarrassed. When Beth gave her a glance to let her know that she could take this opportunity to go compose herself, Rachel was quick to take advantage. She excused herself to go to the restroom.

She was standing at the sink, pressing a cold towel over her flushed cheeks, to the detriment of her makeup, when the door opened. She was looking in the mirror and she stared in shock to see Derek striding into the ladies' room.

Eight

Derek came straight up to Rachel. "I need to talk to you."

"What the hell is your problem?" Rachel demanded. "You can't come in here!"

"I need to know the name of the man you are with," Derek said urgently. "What do you know about him?"

He was standing in the middle of the bathroom in his doorman's uniform. His intense blue eyes were fixed on her and he didn't look crazy, but maybe he was the kind that after the killing spree, the neighbors all said he was such a nice, quiet guy. They never would have suspected.

A woman standing at the sink was washing her hands for an extra long time.

"Please, Derek," Rachel said quietly. "Just leave me alone. I don't want to get you fired, but there are laws in this city against stalking—"

"I am not stalking *you*," he said impatiently. "It's him. That man. What is his name?"

Rachel was so angry and embarrassed she didn't even realize what he was saying. She just wanted him to go away. "I don't have to tell you anything, Derek. You're my doorman, for God's sake. Get out of here now."

"Damn it, woman, I do not have time for your snobbery," Derek stated angrily. He was commanding, powerful, and she suddenly had the strangest image of him in a different kind of uniform. Military. It was all over him, from his upright stance to the direct and bold way he confronted her. "I need to know that man's name."

Now all the women in the restroom were not only staring, they'd halted their own conversations so they could hear better. The one woman was still washing her hands.

Rachel did a slow burn. "I don't know who you think you are, Derek de Molay, but you need to leave now. Immediately." She turned her back on him.

Derek didn't leave. On the contrary, he actually crowded in next to her, elbowing aside a woman trying to get to the towel dispenser.

"Listen to me, Rachel Duncan," he said in a low voice. He stood close to her, talking earnestly to her as if he and she were the only two people in Chicago. "I am not asking questions out of idle curiosity. I have been sent here to gather information and I do not have time to waste. Something in your life is very wrong!"

He was so compelling, so serious that she couldn't help but feel a shiver of fear go through her. Not fear of him. Fear of something unseen, unknown. She stared at him, unable to speak.

He made an impatient gesture. "Do you think I enjoy being a . . . a doorman?" He almost couldn't get the word out. His fist clenched. "Bowing and scraping to people all day long. It is demeaning for one of my birth. But I do it because . . . Well, never mind that."

He put his hand on her shoulder. "You have to listen to me, Rachel—"

His hand on her shoulder sent thrills of electricity all through her. She knew she should be offended. She was used to men trying to overpower and intimidate with their masculinity and she knew how to deal with that sort of crap—a high heel into the ankle can work wonders. Yet, here she stood, tingling at his touch. There was something compelling about this man that had her fascinated, kept her mesmerized. He was so earnest, so intent, so caring. She was suddenly tempted to melt against his chest, feel him put his arms around her.

The thought shocked her, jolted her back to reality. Good grief, had she lost her mind? She was a modern-day business woman being interrogated in the ladies' room by an obsessed doorman. She was being made to look foolish and she could *not* allow this to go on.

Quietly, Rachel said to Derek, "Take your hand off me."

He hesitated a moment, then he did as she asked. She stepped around him and swung open the door to return to the restaurant, only to run smack into Zanus.

"Darling, I was getting worried and I came to check on you." He paused, staring over her head at Derek. Zanus's voice hardened. "What is going on here?"

"Nothing, dear," she said hurriedly, trying to crowd him out of the door. "It was just a misunderstanding. He's not from around here and wandered into the wrong restroom. Let's go finish our dessert."

Rachel started to walk back toward the restaurant, hoping Zanus would follow. Her plan didn't work.

"I want to have a word with you," Zanus was saying to Derek.

She looked back to see him standing in the open ladies' room door, barring Derek, keeping him—and all the women—penned up in the restroom.

"Should I call nine-one-one?" a woman asked worriedly.

"Hell, no," said the woman at the sink. "This is just getting interesting."

Rachel hastened back, put her hand on Zanus's arm.

"Please, don't make a scene—"

"I don't believe he wandered in here by mistake." Zanus shrugged her off. His face had hardened. His voice was so cold that it made Rachel shiver. "I think this man has an unhealthy interest in you, my dear."

"And what is *your* interest in her?" Derek asked coolly.

"Zanus, please!" Rachel pleaded. "Come sit down!"

Zanus did not seem to hear her. He was staring at Derek, as though trying to place him. Suddenly, Zanus's eyes widened. Then he said softly, "I'll be damned."

"I think that boat has already sailed," Derek said dryly. He raised his hands. "Look, I do not want any trouble—"

Zanus clenched his fist and punched Derek, hard, in the midriff. Rachel gasped in horror and shock. Derek, grimacing in pain, bent double, trying to catch his breath. A woman in the restroom screamed.

Zanus, shaking a bruised hand, took hold of Rachel's arm and tried to steer her away. "Come back to the table—"

Rachel was frightened by the look on Zanus's face. If he'd been flushed with rage, she might have understood, but he was icy-calm, tight-lipped, his dark eyes glinting.

"I think we should leave," Rachel suggested in a low voice.

He glanced, frowning at her, and she realized suddenly that she was being blamed.

"You haven't finished your dessert," he said coldly.

"I don't want any dessert. People are staring. Let's just pay the bill and get out of here—" She tried to pull away.

Zanus's grip on her arm tightened, and Rachel gave a little gasp.

"Let go," she said. "You're hurting me—"

Derek's hand, coming from behind, grabbed hold of Zanus's shoulder, breaking his grip on Rachel. Derek spun Zanus around and slammed his fist into Zanus's jaw, sending him crashing back into a table. The people sitting there jumped to their feet, the men exclaiming, the women screaming. The table and Zanus went down. Glasses shattered, drinks spilled. Now the place was in an uproar. Someone called out that he was dialing 911 on his cell.

"Stop this, both of you!" Rachel cried, her embarrassment and confusion giving way to anger.

Neither man heard her. Zanus was struggling to his feet. Derek stood over him, fists clenched.

Rachel couldn't see for her rage. The room was a blur. She had a dismayed impression of thudding feet, voices shouting, "Security! Let us through!"

The woman who had been at the sink was beside her, wanting to know if she was all right. And her friends appeared around her.

"Rachel!" Kim gasped. "What happened?"

Beth was behind her and Lana was there, on the other side of her. They all talked at once.

"We were just coming to find you—"

"We saw that guy talking to you—"

Security finally arrived on the scene. Two big bruisers in suits had hold of Derek and were dragging him back. Another big guy was helping Zanus solicitously to his feet.

"Mr. Zanus! Are you injured? What seems to be the trouble?"

"Sorry about this, Ralph," said Zanus, coolly straightening his tie and brushing broken glass off his suit pants.

Of course, Rachel thought, they would know him here. It seems everyone in Chicago knows him.

"This man was stalking this woman. Rachel, come here," Zanus ordered her peremptorily. "Explain what happened."

Rachel shrank back among her friends and tried to disappear.

"I have to get out of here," she said through clenched teeth. "If my boss finds out I was in the middle of a bar fight, I'll be finished. My coat. I left my coat with the coat check . . ."

"C'mon!" said Lana. "Ladies, circle the wagons!"

They formed a circle with Rachel in the center and started walking hurriedly toward the coat check room, which was near the lobby.

Rachel was trembling with anger by this time. She didn't know who she was most furious at—Derek or Zanus or both. Right now, all men on the planet could evaporate in a puff of smoke and she'd be happy. Arriving at the counter, supported by her friends, Rachel pointed. "That's my coat. If you could hand it to me?"

The young man behind the counter had been leaning out of his stall, trying to see.

"What's going on in there?" he asked, turning to get her coat off the hanger.

"Men being idiots," Rachel said coldly. She reached for her coat.

The young man held onto it. "Claim check, please."

Rachel started to open her purse, then she remembered that she'd given the claim check to Zanus! He was always considerate about little things like that, retrieving her coat, paying the tip, helping her on with it. She wasn't about to go back and meekly ask him for it. Not after the way he was acting.

"Damnation!" she swore. "That's my coat! I should know it!" She should indeed. Brand new, Dolce and Gabbana, the latest style. She seized her coat, tried to yank it free.

"It's the liability, lady," he explained, keeping hold of it.

"Rachel, come here!" Zanus called.

"Wow, he sure is mad," said Kim softly.

The security guys had Derek by the arms. They were marching him toward the lobby, where the manager was on the phone. Probably with the police.

"That's her coat," Lana was saying to the young man, who by now had Dolce and Gabbana in a death grip.

Rachel shoved open the half-door separating her from the coat room. The young man retreated before her. She took hold of her coat and stomped down hard on his foot, digging in her heel as hard as she could. He gave a yelp of pain and grabbed for his foot.

She took her coat, flung it over her shoulders, and struggling to put her arm in the sleeve, she walked toward the lobby.

"Rachel!" Zanus shouted, furious.

"We'll run interference," Beth offered.

"Get out of here before the police come," Lana told her. "I'll make sure your name stays out of this." She pulled her press badge out of her purse. "I never leave home without it."

"Call us as soon as you're home. Let us know you're safe," Kim said.

Rachel nodded and kept walking.

Derek regretted hitting Zanus. The archfiend had realized he faced one of heaven's own holy warriors and had purposefully provoked him. Derek had reacted out of instinct and frustration—the instinct of a trained warrior and the frustration of trying to reason with an illogical and irrational female.

"Blast the woman! Is she daft? Why doesn't she just answer my questions?" Derek muttered to himself, as the security guards were hauling him toward the lobby.

His eyes fixed on Rachel, who appeared to be locked in some sort of struggle with the coat check boy. She was pale, her eyes blazed. She cast a glance at Derek as the security guards marched him past, and the look she gave him might as well have been a spear driven into his chest. He almost winced.

Once again, he'd bungled it. He'd embarrassed and humiliated her. He'd played right into Zanus's hands. Though, if Rachel had just done as he'd asked, she would have spared him a lot of grief.

"Keep moving, bub!" said one of the guards, and gave Derek a shove.

He could have escaped. Big as they were, the guards were obviously not trained warriors. But it would mean another fight and Derek was in enough trouble already. He hoped to be able to talk his way out of this.

He glanced over his shoulder, saw Zanus shouting for Rachel, who was ignoring him.

Derek swore, cursing himself. He'd been a fool! He'd meant well, but in trying to extricate Rachel from danger, he may have put her in dire peril. Zanus knew he'd been discovered. And neither Derek nor William still had any idea what was going on.

He had to extricate himself from this situation and report to William—immediately.

"See here, gentlemen," said Derek, swallowing his pride—a bitter lump that came near choking him. "I am sorry about what happened back there. It was all a mistake. I will apologize to that—I will apologize to the fellow."

"You can give the desk sergeant your apology after he's done booking you," the guard grunted.

"The hotel manager's on the phone with the cops right now," added the other guard. "Mr. Zanus is looking to press charges. Assault and battery, disturbing the peace."

"Stalking," said the other guard grimly.

Derek's immersion in modern life provided him vivid images of policemen clapping handcuffs on him and hauling him away in a squad car. Standing before a camera holding a placard with a number. Fingerprints. Body searches. A cell with a bed and a toilet . . . Rachel alone and unprotected.

Hotel guests drew back away from Derek and stared at him as the guards marched him past the bank of elevators into the small lobby. The manager was just hanging up the phone.

"Cops will be here," the manager said. "I'm not sure when. Busy night on the streets apparently. Take him into the back room—"

Derek wasn't about to be taken into a back room or anywhere else for that matter. He hadn't wanted to do this, but it looked like he would have to fight his way out. He was tensing his muscles, ready to do battle, when loud shouts coming from the front entrance caused the guards to slow their pace and turn to see what was going on.

Derek turned, too. He recognized the person doing the shouting—a middle-aged man with grizzled hair, a six-day growth of beard, wearing a moth-eaten sweater, baggy trousers, a ragged shirt and dirty tennis shoes.

"William!" Derek exclaimed in astonishment.

The archangel's speech was slurred, his eyes bloodshot, and he swayed on his feet as he poked the bellman in the chest with his finger.

"You obviously have no idea who I am!" he was shouting. "I am Ashley Barrington Mace the Second, and I am a guest at this hotel! I demand that you stand aside, my good man, and let me pass!"

The bellman was manfully barring the entryway, keeping his head turned to avoid the reek of cheap wine that was so strong Derek could smell it from across the lobby. "I am sorry, sir, but I can't allow you to come inside in your condition. If you wait while we check your information."

William lurched into the bellman, grabbing hold of the collar of the uniform to keep from falling, and exhaling gusts of wine-soaked breath.

"Enough of this nonsense. Take me to my room, my good man!" he said imperiously.

The bellman tried to fend him off. "Security!" he yelled.

"Must be a full moon tonight," one of the guards grumbled. "All the loonies are out. You keep hold of Stalker Pete here. I'll go—"

"Bah!" said William, shoving himself off the bellman. "I'll go myself."

The archangel in his guise as a vagrant dodged nimbly around the bellman and made a dash for the lobby. Running at breakneck speed, William almost did break his neck. He tripped on the upturned corner of the carpet and went flying.

The projectile vagrant plummeted headfirst into the belly of the guard holding Derek. The guard went over backward with a grunt and a loud, "Ooof!"

Both Derek and William leaped on top of him, pinned him to floor.

"Oh, my God!"

Derek looked up to see Rachel standing there, staring outside at red flashing lights—cop cars just arriving.

William struck Derek on the side of the head.

"Run, you fool! Run!" William hissed.

"Archangel William!' Derek gasped. "I have to tell you—"

"Not now!" William glared at him. The guard was floundering beneath them, and it was taking them both to keep him pinned. "Run! And take Rachel with you!"

"But—"

"You've caused the poor girl enough trouble for one night. Get her out of here before the cops come. I'll keep the guards distracted long enough for you two to get away."

Derek decided this was sound advice. He scrambled to his feet and made a dash toward Rachel.

One minute Rachel was frozen by the sight of flashing red lights through the lobby windows, and the next Derek was suddenly beside her, gently but firmly propelling her toward the door.

"Just keep walking," he said to her calmly, "like nothing's happened."

Rachel started to pull away from him, but the policemen were climbing out of the car and walking toward the entrance. She was the cause of a bar fight and she'd just stolen a coat! She'd be taken downtown for questioning and her name would appear in the paper. What if her boss found out?

"Slowly," said Derek. "Don't run."

Rachel began to walk toward the door. Derek had his arm around her protectively.

Behind her came the sounds of scuffling, then the vagrant gave a pathetic yelp. "My neck! I've broken a vertebrae!" He began to moan. "I'm going to sue this hotel!"

"It's a shame, the way they treat homeless people!" said an indignant young woman dressed all in black with a bolt through her nose.

"I hope he does sue," said someone else.

"I'm a lawyer, sir," a man said, kneeling down beside William. "I saw the whole unfortunate incident. Don't move. Let me give you my card."

"This brute won't let me up!" William howled. "He's holding me hostage. This is battery! I need an ambulance, stat."

The policemen barged into the lobby. They cast a glance at Derek and Rachel.

"Keep moving," Derek said softly into her ear. Aloud he said to the policeman, "I think a man has been badly hurt in there. You might want to send for an ambulance."

The policemen nodded and hurried past. The first sight that met their eyes was William moaning in pain, stretched out on the lobby floor. People were yelling in confusion. The guard tried to make a lunge for Derek, but the policemen halted him.

"Not so fast . . ."

Derek and Rachel walked out the hotel entrance. They didn't stop, but kept walking. Rachel glanced through the window, saw Zanus talking urgently to the policemen. The guard was angrily jabbing his finger at the front door. The police looked uncertain and then Lana was there, in their face, waving her press badge and jabbering.

"I think they're going to come after us," Rachel said, panicking. "Get a cab!"

"No time!" said Derek grimly. "We'll have to run for it."

They could hear more sirens in the distance. Pulling the lapels of his uniform coat up around his neck, Derek tucked his chin down and started to run down the sidewalk. Rachel dashed after him. People stared at them and scrambled to get out of their way.

"They probably think we're Bonnie and Clyde and we just robbed the place." Rachel suddenly felt a mad compulsion to giggle wildly. It was all so ludicrous.

She kept running, but she was falling behind. And then she slipped, turned her ankle, and cried out in pain.

Derek looked over his shoulder, came hurrying back to her.

"Do you want to get caught? Come on!" Derek ordered.

"If you haven't noticed, I'm trying to run in three-inch heels!" she snapped.

"Take off the stupid shoes. Here, hand them to me." He reached out to her.

"Are you insane? These are Jimmy Choo's. They cost me four hundred dollars, and I don't take them off for anyone."

She started to try to run, but she could barely walk. Derek slid his arm around her waist, supported her as she limped along at his side.

"Are they still after us?" she asked fearfully.

He looked back over his shoulder. "No sign of them. We should still keep going, though, if you can make it."

"Not a cab in sight," Rachel muttered.

They kept going. Limping along, hanging onto Derek, Rachel couldn't believe what she'd just done. She'd run from the police and from Zanus, who was only trying to protect her, and gone off with the guy who was stalking her. Did this make any kind of sense?

She'd have some explaining to do tomorrow to Zanus, but she decided she wouldn't worry about that right now. She was too wired and keyed-up to think straight. All Rachel knew was that pressing against Derek's muscular body made her feel safe and warm, his arm around her was comforting.

"Did you really pay four hundred dollars for a pair of shoes?" he asked suddenly. "You can barely walk in them."

"Yes, but the heels make a damn good weapon," said Rachel briskly. "How do you think I rescued my coat?"

She looked up into his eyes, blue eyes that were no longer ice blue, but as blue and inviting as the Caribbean ocean on a summer day. He smiled at her and she couldn't help it. She smiled back.

"I am sorry about what happened," Derek said. "It was all my fault. It's just . . . I seem to lose my head when I am around you." He eyed her. "You are a very exasperating woman."

Rachel didn't know whether she'd been complimented or insulted. She was puzzling it out when her cell phone rang. She knew by the ring tone who it was.

"Are you going to answer it?" Derek asked.

"No," she replied.

The phone finally shut up, only to ring again two minutes later.

"Stop a minute," she said.

Derek halted. She reached into her purse, picked up her phone, and shut it off.

"Zanus?" he guessed grimly.

"I don't want to talk about it," she said. "Hey, there's a coffee shop. I have an idea. You can buy me a cup of coffee and while I'm drinking it, you can call me a cab. It's the least you can do after nearly getting me arrested."

Derek was in a quandary. He was finally alone with her. He wanted to explain everything, tell her the truth or as much of it as a mortal would be likely to understand. He wanted to explain to her why she was in danger, but that was going to be difficult. He could only imagine what she would say if he told her that Zanus was a demon from the fiery depths of hell. She was already half convinced he was crazy. This would finish him off.

The truth would not only risk Rachel's life, it would risk the entire angelic mission here on Earth. But he still needed answers.

Inside the shop was warmth and the fragrant smell of coffee. They sat down and a girl came to take their orders. She sprinted off to work her magic with the espresso machine. Sitting across from Rachel, Derek could clearly see that she was exhausted. Their coffee arrived and they both enjoyed it for a moment in companionable silence. Then Derek said, "About Zanus—"

"Lovely spring we're having, isn't it?" Rachel said.

Derek smiled. He could take a hint. "When I was young, I used to love this time of year. Springtime where I lived was beautiful. I would spend hours alone fishing in a little creek near our manor—home," he amended hastily.

Rachel nodded. "Yeah, I used to fish with my dad in Lake Geneva. I baited my own hook and everything." She sighed deeply and leaned her head on her hand as she stirred her coffee. She looked suddenly weary, lost, and forlorn.

"Believe me when I say again that I am sorry for the trouble I have caused you," Derek said.

Rachel stared down at the coffee mug. Then she looked up at him and smiled. "And I'm sorry about that crack I made about doormen. You're right. I was being a snob. But you shouldn't have provoked Zanus. And Zanus shouldn't have gone after you like that. So you're forgiven. I have a question though—what do you have against him?"

"I just do not like the fellow," Derek said evasively.

"But you don't even know him," Rachel pointed out.

"I know people like him. And they are bad, the lot of them." That at least was the truth.

"But you don't know me," Rachel said, exasperated. "What I do is none of your business. Zanus thinks you're stalking me and I'm beginning to believe he's right."

"Then why are you here with me?" Derek asked with a half-smile.

"I don't know," Rachel said, sighing and running her fingers through her hair. "I honestly don't know."

Derek kept silent, waited for her to continue. She didn't look at him. She looked back at her coffee.

"Why did you tell me there was something wrong in my life?" she asked hesitantly. "How could you know anything about my life?"

She paused, then said, half joking and half serious, "You're not CIA, are you? Homeland Security? You don't think I'm funneling money to terrorists, do you? Because I'm not. Or is it Zanus? Do you think he's a terrorist? I can assure you, he's not."

He's more dangerous. He doesn't just want your life. He wants your soul! Derek was desperate to tell her, but he couldn't. He was floundering here, not really sure what to tell her. He began to realize that William had been right. Dealing with humans was not easy. He opened his mouth, but before he could reply, she went on.

"You're not CIA," she said. "No offense, but a CIA agent wouldn't be this inept. What are you?" She looked at him, looked at him intensely with her beautiful eyes, and his heart thudded in his chest so loudly he was afraid she might hear it.

"I'm your doorman," he said, trying to be funny.

She didn't smile. A little frown line appeared in between her eyebrows.

"It's just . . . I've had the strangest feeling that something is wrong. And I don't know why. My job is going great and so is my love life, despite what you think. Still, I'm left with this feeling that I'm all alone with no one to turn to. I felt like this as a kid once. My mom and I got separated at the shopping mall and I was in this big scary place surrounded by strangers."

Rachel shrugged. Then she smiled at Derek and made a joke of her own.

"Maybe my guardian angel has deserted me," she said with a laugh.

Derek choked and spewed coffee down the front of his uniform.

"Are you all right?" Rachel picked up a napkin and dabbed at the stain.

"Went down the wrong way," he said, when he could talk.

She stared at him. "I don't know why I'm telling you all this. Maybe it's for the same reason we spill our guts to people we sit next to on airplanes. You're *not* stalking me, are you?"

"No, I am not stalking you," Derek replied. "I know we just met and the fact that I am trying to protect you seems strange to you, but . . . well . . . you remind me of someone I used to know. Someone who was very dear to me."

"Recent breakup, huh?" Rachel said, sympathetically.

"No," said Derek. "It was a long time ago. A very long time ago."

"It couldn't have been that long. You're not that old. What are you? Twenty-five?"

"I'm older than I look. Wiser, too," he added ruefully, "although I guess I would have a hard time proving that!"

Derek looked outside. "Our taxi's here. How is your ankle? Can you walk?"

Rachel slid off the stool and gingerly put her weight on her foot. "It'll be sore for a day or two, but I'll be fine. I'll just have to wear sensible shoes to work. Bleh." She made a face. "Thanks for the coffee. And for listening to me. But, please, from now on, no more following me into restaurant bathrooms. And no more snide comments about Zanus. My private life is my own. Off limits, even to my doorman. Agreed?"

"Agreed," said Derek. He rose to his feet, offered her his arm for support. "I may not be a guardian angel," he said awkwardly, "but I would like to be your friend."

"I can always use another friend," said Rachel.

They made the taxi ride back to the condo in silence. Rachel sat as far from him as possible. She seemed lost in thought and he didn't disturb her. As they were pulling up in front of the condo, Rachel opened for her purse.

"I'll pay," she began and then she gasped. "Oh, dear God. It's Zanus!"

The unmistakable black limo was parked in front of the building. The lights were off.

"Get down!" Rachel cried. Reaching over to Derek, she seized hold of his collar and dragged him down into the seat. "Don't let him see you. I'm in enough trouble as it is."

Derek wanted to ask who was stalking whom, but he kept quiet and he kept his head down. Rachel threw some money at the cab driver.

"Don't get out," she ordered Derek. "Wait here until he leaves." She slammed the door shut and walked hurriedly over to the limo. Zanus got out. He looked grim and stern.

"The dude's going to wonder why I'm stickin' around," the driver observed.

"Yes," said Derek. He hated leaving Rachel, but it would be worse for her if Zanus saw him. "Drive off—slowly."

The cab driver grinned. Apparently this was the highlight of his evening. He eased the cab out into the street. Derek risked lifting his head to take a peep out the window. Rachel and Zanus were deep in conversation. He looked taken aback. Rachel glowered at him in anger. She appeared to be giving him a tongue-lashing.

The cab crept down the block. Derek peered out the back window. He saw Rachel turn and walk into the building—alone. Zanus stood a moment on the sidewalk, staring after her, then he got into the limo and it pulled away.

Derek leaned back and relaxed.

The cab rounded the block, pulled up again in front of the building.

"What do I owe you?" Derek asked, fishing in his pocket.

"Nothin'. The lady took care of it. Say, that dude's not a crime boss or something, is he? 'Cause he looked like trouble. You better watch your step, mister."

"Yeah, thanks." Derek opened the door and got out of the cab. He was walking toward the stairs that led up to the entrance when he saw a shadow detach itself from the shrubs and move toward him.

"We need to talk," said Zanus.

"No, we do not," said Derek and he kept walking. He glanced up at Rachel's window. The light was on. Zanus looked up there, as well.

"She might be watching, so I'll make this short and sweet. I know who you are," Zanus said.

Derek looked around with a smile. "Then you also know that I'm good at chopping up demons such as yourself and tossing you back into the slime pit where you belong."

"You can't win," said Zanus. "You're at a disadvantage. You're an angel." He sneered. "You're too good for this world."

"If you do know me," said Derek mildly, "you know I am not all that good. I never made it into Heaven."

He walked up the stairs, leaving Zanus standing there. Derek didn't look back. He didn't need to. He could feel Zanus's eyes on him. Derek had spoken very boldly, but his heart was heavy. Zanus was right. The archfiend could use his hellacious powers and Derek was prohibited from using his power for good, and that left him at a dangerous disadvantage. He didn't buy that argument Archangel Michael touted—about not wanting to reveal themselves. How could good win over evil when good had its hands tied? He'd talk to William about it.

Derek sighed deeply. He had a feeling William wasn't going to be at all pleased with him . . .

Derek heard Zanus's footfalls moving rapidly down the sidewalk. He heard the limo door open and shut. Derek waited outside the door until he saw the limo's red taillights disappear into the night. He looked up at Rachel's window, saw her light had gone out. She was safe. For tonight at least.

What was he going to do about tomorrow?

Nine

The next morning Derek parked himself behind the front lobby desk. He leaned back in his chair, and rubbed his eyes. He couldn't wrap his mind around what had happened last night. Rachel's guardian angel was missing in action, and Derek had no idea why or for how long Zanus had wormed his way in her life. All he understood was that Rachel was in grave danger and how in the name of all that was holy could he help her?

She had gone to work as usual that morning. She had given him a smile that was friendly, if a little wary. She had been afraid he would be too familiar, perhaps. He had been careful to be especially polite and formal. He couldn't help but ask her, as he held the door, if everything was all right.

"Fine," she told him, as she stood at the door,

waiting for her car. "At first Zanus was angry, but then he cooled down and apologized. It's a good thing he didn't see us together last night, though." Rachel grimaced. "He would have been furious. As it was, he admitted I was right, that he'd been out of line, and he should have let me handle things. Oh, and Lana left me a message. She and Zanus managed to keep my name out of the press. So—all's well that ends well."

All isn't well! He did see us together last night, Derek thought, but he couldn't tell her, because that would lead to questions from her that he wouldn't be able to answer.

Her car arrived. She got in and they drove off.

So what did he do about her?

He might simply tell her the truth, but then he imagined how the conversation would go.

"You see, Rachel, every person on Earth is assigned a guardian angel. Sometimes an angel will volunteer for the job. This might be one of your ancestors or a friend or loved one who has passed on. If there are none available, another angel is assigned the task. The rule is, everyone is protected. The guardian angels aren't allowed to intervene in your life. They can't leap in front of the bus that's about to smash into your car. They provide spiritual protection. They battle the demons here, as we battle them in Limbo. Your angel fights for your soul, Rachel, and if that angel is gone, your soul is in jeopardy. You sense that your angel is missing. You're right. And it was your boyfriend who killed your angel."

Derek shook his head and smiled ruefully. *Yeah, right. It's here she stares at me like I've lost my mind and then runs screaming for the exit.*

He'd learned enough about mortals to know that in this age of technology and science, a lot of people would scoff at the idea of guardian angels. If we can't see it or feel it, we don't believe it, they would say. But at the same time, these same people did believe in electrons and neutrons and protons. They couldn't see them, but because science said they existed, people believed in them. All very strange. He might be wrong about Rachel, but he had the feeling that she would be one of the scoffers.

To make matters worse, Derek knew things were starting to get personal between them. She was no longer a mission. She was a lovely face; fragrant hair; dark, fiery eyes. Even when she wasn't around, he heard her voice and breathed the scent of her perfume. She was delicate and beautiful and, at the same time, courageous and fearless. At one point, he'd thought she might actually punch out that poor guy who had hold of her coat. She hadn't been afraid when they were running from the police. She had seemed to find it almost exhilirating. She liked adventure. She liked taking risks. She had a look in her eye he'd seen in men in battle. Nothing scared her.

Telling her that her guardian angel was missing and that Zanus was somehow behind it would not scare her—even if she believed him, which she probably wouldn't. Somehow he had to make her understand. She needed to be less courageous. She needed to be afraid. Fear was the key to self-preservation.

Derek woke with a start. He hadn't gotten much sleep; he'd been up most of the night thinking about Rachel and Zanus and wondering what to do. He must have fallen asleep in his chair. He wondered groggily what had awakened him and then he heard it again. Someone was rapping loudly on the glass lobby door.

Derek looked out and sighed. It was Angel William, still in his shabby coat and disreputable hat. Derek knew he was in for it. He had no choice, however. Derek unlocked the door and held it open.

William stormed inside. He was out of breath, gasping for air.

"Police in this city . . . stubborn . . . quite stubborn . . ." He had to stop to pant.

Derek brought him a chair and William sank into it.

"William," Derek began, "we've got a problem—"

William snatched off his shabby hat and started hitting Derek with it.

"You bet we have a problem! Somewhere out there, a village is missing its idiot!" William shouted, bashing Derek with the hat. "What in the Sam Hill is wrong with you? Do you realize what could have happened last night? You could have been arrested! If it hadn't been for my intervention, you would be in prison and I would have been forced to leave you there. We angels simply can't organize prison breaks. I shudder to think what Archangel Michael will say about this. I'll have to report it, of course—"

Derek raised his arms to defend himself against the blows. "I am sorry, William, but if you will just let me explain—"

"Explain? Explain what? That you're a Neanderthal? We expected such behavior from cavemen. Their brains had not yet fully developed—which must be your problem, you dunderhead! You simply cannot walk up to a strange woman in the ladies' powder room and demand to know the name of the guy she's dating," William said vehemently, emphasizing each word with a blow of the hat.

He finally stopped, worn out. Sitting back, he used the maltreated hat to fan himself. "That kind of behavior will get you locked up, and deservedly so. Not to mention the fact that I had to run six blocks while being chased by a very angry policeman who, though somewhat tubby, was in excellent physical condition."

"I am sorry," said Derek as contritely as he could, "but there is something wrong—"

"You bet there is." William snorted. "You're the wrong man for this job, that's what's wrong."

"No, William, listen to me. This Zanus—Rachel's boyfriend—is an archfiend."

William sucked in a breath. He looked as if he were ready to fire off another diatribe, and then

Derek's words hit home. William gaped at him, so shocked that for a moment he couldn't speak. Then he frowned deeply.

"Are you certain about this?"

Derek nodded firmly. "He as much as admitted it to me last night."

"Why would he admit it to *you*?" William asked, skeptical. He looked at Derek, and then groaned. "Oh, no. Tell me you didn't! Tell me he doesn't know who you are!"

"What if he does?" Derek returned impatiently. "Maybe it will make him think twice before he does anything. We have to think about Rachel. She's utterly alone, unprotected, and *he's* right there waiting to make his move."

"This is bad," said William shaking his head. "Very bad. I was afraid that something like this might happen."

"Then why didn't you insist that Michael give Rachel another guardian angel!" Derek flared in sudden rage. "How could you both leave her down here with that demon—"

"Now, calm down, son," said William. He regarded Derek in concern. His expression grew grave. "You're not getting attached to this mortal, are you? Because if you are, you will have to be sent back at once—"

"No, of course not," said Derek. "I'm not attached to her in any way. She is just a job to me."

Angels weren't supposed to lie, but Derek deemed it necessary. If William suspected for one moment that Derek was becoming emotionally involved, he'd send him back to Purgatory before this assignment was finished. And it wasn't altogether Rachel. There was now something personal between him and Zanus. Derek didn't trust anyone to handle this mission except himself.

"It is not easy, dealing with these mortals," Derek complained bitterly. "They're too complicated. They have all these urges and emotions that get in the way, clutter things up."

"Emotions like falling in love," said William, fixing a stern gaze on Derek.

"That is it exactly," said Derek, deliberately choosing to misunderstand the archangel. "Rachel thinks she is in love with this Zanus—"

"I wasn't talking about Rachel," Williams said. "I'm talking about you!"

"I am not in love with her," Derek said angrily.

William eyed him a moment, then said, "Good. Have you considered the consequences of what would happen if *she* fell in love with you?"

"I do not think there's much chance of that," Derek muttered.

"You're probably right," William said.

"You do not need to agree so fast," Derek said, casting the angel a reproachful glance.

"Derek," said William severely, "you want to gain her trust, not her affection. You are only on Earth for a short while. When this assignment ends, you will return to your duties. You will disappear from her life and she won't understand how or why. You could hurt her terribly."

"I think I can safely assure you, William, that there is no danger of Rachel Duncan falling in love with me—" Derek began.

He was interrupted by a banging on the door. It was two of the tenants. By the angry expression on their faces, they had been standing there for some time. Derek, glad to be able to avoid William's piercing gaze, hurried off to let them inside.

"What do they want?" William demanded irritably.

"They want to come into the building," said Derek, over his shoulder. "They live here. This is my job—"

"Oh, right." William began to twirl his hat around in his hands. He was shaking his head in consternation and muttering to himself.

The couple, both dressed in tennis attire, swept through the door in an icy blast of chill displeasure. Derek made his apologies, but the man brushed those aside.

"Do you realize how long we've been standing there?" the man asked Derek angrily.

"Not to mention the fact that you weren't there to help us out of our limo," said the woman.

"All because you were too busy conversing with a . . . a vagrant!" The man cast William a scathing glance.

"This person should not be here." The woman took a handkerchief from her purse and held it to her nose. "This building is *not* a homeless shelter!"

"Well, maybe it should be, lady!" William cried, bounding to his feet.

Derek tried to intervene, but William shoved him aside. The archangel was incensed.

"I'll have you know that the way you people treat the homeless in this city is a disgrace." William shook his finger at the couple. "An absolute disgrace! Particularly for you, Jimmy Raye Cyrus."

The man's mouth sagged open. He had been red with rage, but now all the color drained out of his face. He was as pale as the underside of a dead fish. He swallowed.

"You must have me mistaken for someone else. That's not my name—"

"Oh, yes, it is. That's what they called you back home. None of this high-falutin James Raymond Cyrus the Third malarkey. You were born plain old Jimmy Raye and your own grandfather was a homeless vagrant, though they were called hobos in the days of the big Depression. Your grandfather rode the rails when he was young, working odd jobs here and there until he scraped together enough money to start the little garage business. Then came your daddy and he took over and by his hard work he turned that little garage into a chain of fancy auto parts stores that can be found in every major city from here to California. Not that you would know, would you, Jimmy Raye? You haven't paid any attention to the business that's been in your family for years! You're too busy playing tennis."

"I'm very sorry for this, Mr. Cyrus," Derek said, as he grabbed hold of the furious archangel and tried to drag him out the door.

Mr. Cyrus didn't say anything. He was staring at William, a dazed expression on his face. His wife was making up for his silence. She was sputtering with rage.

William broke free of Derek and charged back to the attack.

"And let me tell you this, Jimmy Raye," William went on. "If it hadn't been for your daddy fixing things up with the draft board during Vietnam, *you* might be one of those homeless vets sleeping out under the el."

"James! Why are you standing there listening to all this?" his wife demanded. "The man is obviously crazy."

"Yes," said her husband weakly. "He's . . . quite insane."

"Come along, James," said his wife. She gripped his arm and started him heading toward the elevator. He went with her, but he continued to look back at William, at one point even stumbling over the trash can.

His wife glared back at Derek. "This is all your fault. I'll be speaking to Mr. Fraym about this."

"I am very sorry," Derek said for the sixteenth time. "It won't happen again, I assure you."

He finally succeeded in wrestling the archangel out the door.

"Well done," said Derek. "Now I will lose my job."

"I'm sorry, but that pompous south-end of a northbound horse had it coming," William fumed.

"It's not so easy, dealing with mortals, is it?" Derek asked dryly.

The archangel gave him a sheepish grin.

"No, I guess it isn't." William cast his eyes heavenward. "Now I'm the one who'll be in trouble with Archangel Michael. You don't think Jimmy Raye will get you fired, do you? We need you here."

"Fortunately Mr. Cyrus is always half soused. You could smell the whiskey on him. Must do wonders for his tennis game," said Derek. "He probably won't remember much."

"More's the pity," William growled. "Now, what are we going to do about Rachel? I didn't fully understand her precarious position until now. Did you talk to her last night? What did she tell you?"

"She's been completely taken in by that Zanus." Derek started to pace around the sidewalk. He told William all about their conversation. He also told William about Zanus's threats.

"This is bad," said William. "Very bad."

"Bah, I've dealt with the likes of him before."

"You don't understand," said William gravely. "It's worse than you imagine. I came to tell you that I received information from Archangel Michael only this morning that the demons are planning something big."

"Something big? What is it?"

"Unfortunately we don't know," said William.

"But isn't this what you archangels do for a living—keep an eye on things, on the guardians and their charges?" Derek was grim. "I'm beginning to think all of you are in over your heads."

He expected William to indignantly refute this, and was unpleasantly surprised when he didn't. William only shook his head and looked even more serious.

"Archangel Michael believes we're dealing with a powerful archfiend—one of the upper echelon. This Zanus may be the one. You must be extremely careful around him, Derek. You haven't dealt with the likes of him before. He's one of the generals. You are no match for an archfiend."

Derek snorted and waved his hand in disdain.

"I mean it," said William. "And there's another problem. The archfiend knew who you were. How?"

"I don't know. I guess he must have seen through my disguise. I saw through his quickly enough."

"Because you were looking for a demon."

"Yes, so what do you mean? What are you hinting at, William?"

"The archfiend saw through your disguise because he was looking for you," William answered slowly. "He was looking for a holy warrior. He knew we were onto him."

"But how did he—" Derek paused, shocked. "That would mean . . ."

"He was tipped off," said William grimly. He looked suddenly terribly old and frail. "There's a traitor somewhere."

"Are you saying an angel told him? That's unthinkable!" said Derek.

"We know some archfiends slipped past the holy warriors. We thought they had all gone straight to Earth, but perhaps not. Perhaps they have infiltrated our ranks—"

"I don't believe it." Derek was adamant.

"I'm afraid you're going to have to, son. Which means you must be ever more vigilant in protecting this woman *and* yourself. Removing her guardian angel was only their first step. We can't anticipate what they're going to do next. This is a new situation for us. The demons are using new tactics and, unfortunately, they have us at a disadvantage. They can use their powers and we can't use ours."

"That doesn't make sense. I was going to talk to you about that very thing," Derek said. "Why should it matter if we reveal ourselves to mortals?"

"Because then they would become dependent on us, Derek," said William. "Like spoiled children. Like that Jimmy Raye Cyrus. His parents gave him everything he wanted. They leveled out all life's bumps and filled up the potholes so that he had a nice, smooth ride. And now look at him! He has nothing to do all day but go looking for life at the bottom of a whiskey bottle.

"If mortals knew that angels were here to take care of them, they'd never do anything for themselves. 'The poor aren't my responsibility. Let the angels help them.' That sort of thing."

Derek wasn't convinced. He had been a warrior and a strategist his whole life, and there had been times when he'd had to lead his men into battle without intelligence about the enemy's position or strength. Derek also knew that such battles often ended badly. It was obvious to Derek that the archangels were not prepared for this type of battle. It was also obvious that he was going to be on his own. He couldn't count on Heaven for help apparently.

But then, he never really had been able to count on Heaven. He'd always relied on himself. And that was what he intended to do now.

"If Zanus attacks me, I'll have to fight him," said Derek.

"He won't attack you—at least not physically. If he'd been going to, he could have done so last night. He's in much the same predicament we are. He knows we know about him, but he doesn't know how much we know. He has to find out."

"What do you mean, not physically attack?"

"He's an archfiend. They're much more subtle than that."

"Zanus was not subtle last night," said Derek, rubbing his midriff that was still sore from the punch Zanus had given him.

"He wanted a reaction from you and he got it, didn't he?" William shook his head. "You played right into his hands. If it hadn't been for me rushing in to save your bacon—"

"Yes, sir. I understand," Derek said, flushing. "I admit what I did last night was stupid. But I'll be on my guard from now on."

"I hope so," said William. He didn't sound overly

confident. "You'll need to gain Rachel's trust, convince her that you are not the threat. I hope you didn't scare her last night."

Derek snorted. "She wasn't frightened. I thought for a minute in that restroom she was going to punch me *and* Zanus. She wanted to dice us into little pieces and feed us to the cat. Besides, we talked afterward. We went out for coffee and I apologized, and she is fine with me now."

He shrugged and added bitterly, "She told me to stay out of her life, but otherwise than that, we are fine."

William wasn't listening.

"Cat . . ." he murmured. "Now there's an idea."

"What are you mumbling about?" Derek asked, exasperated.

"Uh? Oh, nothing," said William. "Now listen here, son. You are not to ask her personal questions and you cannot confront her. You are to *observe her comings and goings,*" he said, laying emphasis on each word. "And especially note who she's with. We must know more about this Zanus person and gauge how much influence he has over her."

"I can tell you that," said Derek angrily. "She's in danger. We should do something."

"We are doing something, Derek," William said sternly. "We are doing what we have been told to do. When you command a regiment, you do not tell every soldier the battle plan. You tell them what they need to know to do their jobs and then you expect them to obey your orders. If they don't, if they go off on their own, they could not only get themselves and their comrades killed, they could put the entire campaign in jeopardy. We don't know Heaven's battle plan, Derek. We only know our small part of it. If we go against orders, we could be putting everything at risk—including Rachel."

Derek stared at him in grim silence. He hated to admit William was right.

William softened his tone. "I understand. You are a man of action, rushing in where angels fear to tread. But you better tread carefully here, Derek."

He eyed Derek, then said, "I think I'm going to ask Michael to assign you a partner."

"Absolutely not!" Derek said heatedly.

"You have no say over this, I'm afraid, son. It's too important. You can't watch over Rachel twenty-four hours a day. I'll put in a request for someone to help you guard Rachel. Someone who can be with her when you can't and, at the same time, feed you information."

"I do not need anyone, I tell you!" Derek had never worked with a partner before and he didn't plan to start now. He'd learned not to trust others as a rule, and that rule had served him well. Above all, he didn't like the thought of anyone else trying to get close to Rachel.

"Your partner will report to you daily. I know you don't like it, but time is of the essence here, Derek. You said it yourself. Now that Zanus knows we're onto him, he'll have to act more quickly. Rachel will be in even greater danger."

William regarded Derek intently, trying to read his thoughts.

Derek met his gaze defiantly. He hoped William did read his thoughts. His thoughts ran along the lines that this whole mission was going straight down the toilet. His superiors had no idea who or what he was up against. They had bad intelligence, and now he was being assigned a partner who could very well be an infiltrator.

"Your partner will be in contact with you soon. Try to get some rest, son," William added solicitously, patting Derek on the shoulder. "I'll be in a cardboard box under the Fullerton Street bridge if you need me."

William wandered off down the street.

Derek worried about Rachel. She was at work. Standing in the place they called the pit. He imagined ugly dark figures hunching over her, huddled around her, wings extended to cover her with dark shadows, their sharp talons outstretched, trying to seize hold of her. He saw their eyes glowing red with demon fire and it was all he could do to keep from racing out to the Merc to check on her, assure himself that she was safe.

He restrained himself because that was the very thing he'd promised her he *wouldn't* do.

Ten

Rachel struggled through her day in the pits. Fortunately this Friday was a quiet day on the market, not much going on. Zanus knew better than to call her while she was working, but sometimes he'd send her a text message or leave her voice mail telling her where he had made reservations for dinner or that he had tickets to the latest hottest play. She didn't hear from him today.

Her phone rang almost the moment the market closed. She answered it with a fast-beating heart.

"Hi," she said, trying to sound casual.

"Hello, Rachel." He seemed cool. "I know we usually go out to dinner and a show on Friday evening, but I'm going to have beg off tonight. Something has come up and I need to deal with it."

"Of course. I understand," Rachel said. "I'm really tired after all the excitement last night. I don't think I could have stayed out late anyway." She paused a moment, then she asked, "You're not still mad, are you? About what I said. I was upset—"

"No, of course I'm not mad," he answered and his voice warmed. "As I told you, something's come up. I'll call you tomorrow."

He hung up. Rachel snapped her phone shut with a sinking feeling in her heart. She told herself that Zanus was a man of business, a man with financial concerns the world over. Of course, situations were bound to "come up." It was just odd that they happened to come up the night after the two of them had their first quarrel.

She had been extremely angry to find him parked outside her condo last night, waiting for her like a parent waiting for a teenage daughter out after her curfew. She had also been a little worried that he would see Derek and so she had launched into her speech, telling him in no uncertain terms that the problem with Derek the doorman was her problem, not his. She was perfectly capable of dealing with him without a big, strong man rushing in to protect her. She'd had matters under control. He'd been the one to start the brawl. He had delivered the first punch and so on and so forth. She had been vastly relieved to see Derek's cab drive off. Smart thinking on his part!

Zanus had listened to her, and then he'd had the grace to apologize. She was perfectly right. He had been out of bounds. He had even said how much he had enjoyed meeting her friends and that he looked forward to getting together with them again. Then he had given her a kiss and gone away.

And then he hadn't called all day, and when he did call, it was to cancel their date.

She wondered if she should call him, then told herself not to be stupid. She would sound clingy and needy. If he was going to end their relationship over something like this, better she should know now. She would spend a quiet evening at home. Maybe order in Chinese and watch one of the old Doris Day movies her mother had given her for Christmas. Her mother was always hopeful that someday Rachel would come to her senses and turn into Doris Day.

She hadn't slept at all last night and so she decided she'd go straight home, skip her daily trip to the office after market close if they didn't need her. They didn't. Not surprising. Mr. Freeman almost always played golf on Friday afternoon if the weather was nice, and today the sun was shining with hardly a cloud in the sky. Rachel cancelled the car and caught a cab.

On the way, she decided not to order Chinese but to treat herself. She had been so nervous in company with Zanus and her friends that she hadn't eaten much dinner last night. She told the cab driver to take her to the Drake, a beautiful old hotel on the lakefront.

The bar was packed with young professionals.

She had a dirty martini and then ordered a salad and a bowl of their famous Bookbinder Soup with sherry, along with a glass of white wine. Since the evening was nice, she decided to walk home. Perhaps the exercise would make her feel better.

Night had fallen by the time she was near home. Coming in sight of her building, Rachel slowed her pace. She wondered if Derek was still on duty. She hoped he wasn't. He'd been very polite and considerate this morning, but she was all confused about him and decided that the less she saw of him, the better. He had really been quite sweet last night, all things considered. He was certainly handsome and strong. Every time she thought about him putting his arm around her to help her after she'd turned her ankle, her stomach did acrobatics. And she'd found herself thinking about that a lot today, more than was good for someone who was in a serious relationship with another man—a man who was every woman's dream.

There was something mysterious about Derek that intrigued her. He hadn't really answered any of her questions, not straight answers, at least. He had said he hated being a doorman. If so, why was he? He was good-looking, well spoken, seemed well educated. And he had that unmistakable military air about him. She found it hard to believe that he couldn't have found another job if he wanted one.

And he definitely had something against Zanus. There had been a moment last night when she was certain the two of them knew each other.

Both he and Zanus had denied it, and she had no reason to doubt either one of them, but still, it was odd. And just as Rachel was telling herself she would be glad if Derek was off duty, she found herself perversely hoping to see him.

She was reaching into her purse for her keys, when a guy came dashing out of nowhere and bumped into her, hard, almost knocking her down. She felt a yank and looked down at her hands in the light of the street lamp and realized that she was holding her purse's strap. The purse itself was gone.

"Hey!" she cried, shocked to see a man running down the street with her purse in his hand. "That man stole my purse!"

People going past glanced over their shoulders, gave her a look of sympathy, and kept on going. Purse snatching was a common thing in Chicago and the thief was almost always never caught.

Rachel felt sick. Not only had she lost all her credit cards and her money, but her purse was new and quite expensive. The man was still in sight. She was looking for a policeman, when suddenly, Derek came bolting out the door of her building. Blond hair flying, he ran after the purse snatcher so fast that his doorman's cap whipped off his head and landed on the sidewalk.

Rachel stared, amazed. She'd never seen anyone run like that. His speed was uncanny. Rachel watched in awe as he quickly closed the gap between himself and the thief. She couldn't see what happened next. They had vanished into the shadows created by a burnt out streetlamp. Rachel waited in an agony of fear for Derek. She wished she'd kept quiet. What if the guy had a gun?

And then Derek appeared, her purse in one hand and the thief in the other. Rachel breathed a sigh of relief. Derek dragged the thief back toward the building. Calmly, he handed the purse to Rachel, then dropped the thug onto the ground at her feet. She was reminded, suddenly, of a cat doing the same with a mouse.

"Here is your purse. Are you hurt?" Derek asked anxiously.

Rachel didn't answer. She was staring, aghast, at the thief. Her anxiety for Derek evaporated at the sight.

"What did you do to him?" she demanded, her voice quivering.

Derek appeared puzzled at her reaction. He had been smiling as though he'd done something chivalrous, expecting her to knight him or something.

"I twisted his arm some to make him drop the purse."

"Twisted his arm! More like twisted his neck! I think you killed him!"

Derek looked down and his words dried up.

The thief, who was no more than a kid, maybe fourteen or so, lay on the sidewalk. Blood spewed from his broken nose that was splattered all over his face. He had a smashed lip and his face was swelling. His eyes were closed. He was unconscious.

"I did not do this to him, Rachel!" Derek said in

a dazed voice. "I swear! I barely laid a hand on him!"

By this time, a crowd had gathered. The very people who had ignored the purse snatching hurried over to see the blood. Rachel heard someone say he thought the poor kid was dead.

"You beat him!" Rachel cried, glaring at Derek. Her fists clenched. She could have beaten Derek up herself. "You brute! He's a kid, barely half your size, and he was probably hungry, and you beat him half to death for lifting my purse! What is wrong with you?"

People crowded around, some to make comments, others offering to try to help. And, of course, someone had called 911. It seemed to Rachel that half the population of Chicago was clustered around her, including that homeless man, the one who had charged into the Hotel 71 claiming to be Ashley Barrington Something. Rachel didn't exactly remember him, but she could never forget that hat. Suddenly everything—her worry over Zanus, the purse snatching, her fear for Derek, and her bitter disappointment in him all came crashing down on top of her.

Police sirens sounded. Red lights flashed. An ambulance was pulling up.

Rachel pushed her way through the crowd and ran into the apartment building. She ran to Mr. Fraym's apartment and met him just as he was coming out.

"What's going on?" he demanded. "Why are the police here?"

"Mr. Fraym, you'd better come outside. Right now!" she said. "It's the doorman."

Mr. Fraym looked grim. "What's Derek done now?"

"He's outside in front of the building standing over some poor kid he beat nearly to death for lifting my purse."

Fraym gasped. "He beat up someone in front of the building? Did anyone see this besides you?"

"There's a big crowd—"

Fraym's lips compressed and he headed for the door, Rachel hurrying along at his side.

Rachel was furious. All her warm and fuzzy thoughts about Derek vanished. He had seemed charming and kind last night, but at the bottom, he was a brute.

"This is the last straw," said Fraym. "I've had more complaints about him in a week than any other doorman collected in a year."

But, as he neared the door, Fraym slowed his pace. "What is going on—"

Bright white light flared into the lobby, coming from outside. The light hit Rachel square in the face, half blinding her. She shielded her eyes and saw a man with a large camera balanced on his shoulder standing on the stairs. Next to him was a woman holding a microphone. They were interviewing the homeless man with the disreputable hat.

"I saw it all, yes, ma'am." He peered through the glass door and pointed. "There she is!" he shouted. "That's her! She's the victim!"

The woman doing the interviewing said, "Quick, Mac, get a shot of her."

Mr. Fraym opened the door, only to have the female reporter shove past him and make a dart at Rachel. The reporter waved the microphone at her.

"Ma'am, were you hurt in the purse snatching? Did you know the thief? How much money and valuables did you have in your purse at the time?"

A large white van with Channel 7 News painted on it in huge letters was parked across the street. Rachel looked over the reporter's shoulder to see the paramedics escorting the thief to an ambulance. He was still bloody, but at least he was conscious and able to walk. Two policemen flanked him.

"What do you think of the hero who saved your purse?" the female reporter persisted. "What would you like to say to him?"

"I . . . don't know . . ." Rachel was bewildered, blinking at the dazzling white light. "Thank you . . . I guess . . ."

The female reporter gave her a disgusted look and spoke into the microphone, "Obviously this poor woman is in shock . . ."

Derek was being interviewed by another reporter. Rachel recognized him. He was a Chicago celebrity.

"You are truly one of a kind, Mr. de Molay," the reporter said, enthusiastically shaking Derek's hand and smiling for the camera. "Chicago needs more good citizens like you."

The reporter turned away from Derek, who looked extremely embarrassed.

"For those just tuning in this evening, our crew happened to be near the scene filming an in-depth piece on the homeless with our infrared camera when we caught this crime *as it was happening*. And we also got footage of local doorman, Derek de Molay catching and subduing this woman's attacker and returning her purse to her. We'll be airing that tape on the ten o'clock news. From Chicago's North Side, I'm Ron Hickford reporting."

The light of the camera turned off. The night seemed suddenly, incredibly dark.

"Okay, that's it for now, people," Ron was saying to his crew. "Let's get home and edit this baby. We have just enough time to make the ten o'clock report. Good work, Mr. de Molay."

He shook hands again with Derek, who was also being congratulated by people in the crowd and the police officers. To Rachel's chagrin, Mr. Fraym was right there in line. He shook Derek's hand and posed for a picture with him being taken by a reporter for the *Chicago Tribune*.

Dear God! Was every newsman in Chicago here tonight? She had led such a quiet, normal, peaceful life up until now . . . What was going on?

"Ma'am, would you like to make a comment now?" The female reporter was back in her face.

"Uh, no, no comment," Rachel said. She was turning, planning to escape back into the building, when a policeman came up to her.

"Ma'am, if you could step out to the squad car. We'll need a statement . . ."

Rachel gave them their statement. She didn't have much to tell, really. It had all happened so fast. Once the cop was finished with her, Rachel walked slowly up the stairs toward the front entrance. She caught a glimpse of Fraym with his arm around Derek, promising him a raise. Rachel shook her head. She started to open the door, but there was Derek opening it for her. Doing his job.

"Rachel," he said earnestly, "I want you to know, I did not beat that young man. Really. He must have hit his head when he fell—"

"Forget it," she said. She found it hard to look at him. She remembered the fear she had felt for him, how real, how terrible it had been for a moment. "You're a hero now. On the news and everything. Oh, thanks for retrieving my purse. They've taken it for evidence, otherwise I'd give you a reward—"

Derek gave her a hurt look. "I don't want your money," he said coldly. "I thought we were friends."

Rachel shook her head. She couldn't speak for the lump of tears in her throat. Derek's expression softened. His hand closed over hers.

"You're safe, Rachel. That's all that matters," he said.

His hand was strong and warm, his nearness comforting. She was tempted, once again, as she had been tempted last night, to lay her head on his shoulder and cry out her worries and frustration. Then it occurred to her that the hand holding hers was probably still drenched with the blood of his victim. She wasn't sure if she was more disappointed in Derek or herself for toying with the idea that she might have feelings for him. He had betrayed her. Zanus had betrayed her.

Rachel tore away from his grasp and walked through the door without a backward glance.

The crowds finally went off about their business. Mr. Fraym returned to his apartment, eager to call his mother and tell her he was going to have his picture in the paper. The light went out in Rachel's apartment. Derek stood on the door stoop talking with William.

"That was a close one," said William, mopping his forehead with what was left of his hat. "You nearly got yourself fired—again. Good thing I was around to keep an eye on you. We're not out of the woods yet, though. You've managed to lose credibility with Rachel—again."

"I did not hurt that young man," Derek said heatedly. "I swear to you, William, on my honor I would never do such a thing! No true knight would ever strike anyone who was defenseless, no matter what he had done."

"I believe you," said William, and he looked grave.

"Then what happened? The thief didn't beat himself up—"

"Oh, yes, he did—in a way."

"Don't talk nonsense—" Derek began, then he stopped to stare, appalled, at William. "Zanus!"

"I'm afraid so. That was no helpless teenager, Derek. That was a demon. He was sent to snatch Rachel's purse and afterward he used his demonic powers to make it appear that he'd been beaten to a bloody pulp. Of course, you played right into their hands. Zanus knew how you would react when you saw that Rachel was being threatened, and you did just as he hoped you would. You rushed to the rescue."

"But why would he do it?" Derek asked. "Why make me look like a hero in Rachel's eyes?"

"Do you look like a hero to her? Or do you look like a low-life schmuck who beats up starving kids?"

Derek remembered Rachel's horrified expression and he swore softly.

"I warned you to be on your guard. I told you Zanus wouldn't attack you physically," William continued relentlessly. "He doesn't have to. You're doing a fine job of destroying yourself on your own. Fortunately I was on hand. At least, I've saved your job. I'm not certain about Rachel. You may have irreparably harmed our cause there."

Derek shook his head dismally. "I should have seen this coming."

"Of course, you should have." William sighed. "I think I must take you off this case now."

"I will not go," said Derek firmly. "I can't go, William."

"Why not?"

Derek smiled bleakly. "Mr. Fraym just gave me a raise."

William answered his smile with one of his own, but the smile didn't last long. Growing serious, the archangel laid his hand on Derek's arm.

"Be careful, son. You've tangled with Zanus twice now. And you've beaten him twice. He won't be so subtle about getting rid of you next time. I'll leave you on, at least until your partner arrives on the scene."

Derek scowled at the mention of this partner. He would have liked to register another protest, but he was on shaky ground already. He figured it was better to keep his mouth shut.

"I can take care of myself," he said. *"And* Rachel. Don't worry."

"I do worry. Speaking of Rachel, she's really upset with you right now."

"Yes, I know. I bungled this. Again." Derek sighed. "I tried to explain, but she would not even look at me. I can't say that I blame her. After all, the evidence is against me. How do I explain it?"

"You may not have to . . ." said William thoughtfully.

"Can you fix things?" Derek asked.

"Not me," said William. "Zanus. He may be able to use his powers here, but there's one thing he can't do—he can't let ER docs start cutting open his demons . . ."

* * *

Rachel had just crawled thankfully into bed when her home phone rang. She peered at the caller ID and sat up and switched on the light.

"Yes, Officer, this is Rachel Duncan." She paused, listening in astonishment. "He did what? How can someone disappear out of an ambulance? You think he jumped! So I take it he wasn't badly hurt, after all. Just some scratches. You're right, it certainly did look much worse. Probably no chance of finding him now. When will I get my purse back? Yes, thank you for calling, Officer. I was concerned . . ."

Rachel hung up the phone and lay back on her pillow and sighed deeply. She owed Derek an apology. A big apology. And this was one she would be glad to pay.

As she drifted off to sleep, Rachel reflected that her life had certainly become a lot more interesting since Derek de Molay had arrived to open doors for her.

Eleven

Saturday morning, Rachel woke early with a mission. She would apologize to Derek. But she didn't get up immediately. After the events of the last two nights, her head and her heart both felt muddled. She looked outside her window. The sun was shining brightly. It was going to be a beautiful day. She decided to forget the charts and go for a run in the park. Running would give her time to think and clear out the cobwebs.

She brushed her teeth, pulled her hair back, and tied it with a scrunchie. She paused to stare at herself in the mirror.

Rachel felt silly for being so out of sorts. Zanus was really a great guy, even if he was jealous of Derek. Jealousy was good for a man. It was flattering to watch him go totally alpha male with Derek.

But what about Derek?

He was a complete mystery to her. His preoccupation about protecting her, his vague warnings about Zanus had her concerned, but she didn't know precisely what to be concerned about. Either Derek was right and Zanus did pose some kind of threat or Derek was a complete loon and she should run screaming for the hills. But if he was a loon, he was a convincing loon. She had to give him that.

And that strange business about the purse snatcher. The policeman had claimed he'd simply vanished. The theory was that he'd jumped out of the ambulance when it had stopped for a traffic light. But wouldn't someone have noticed? Or maybe these things happened in Chicago all the time. The policeman hadn't sounded overly concerned. At least, Derek was telling her the truth. The kid must not have been that badly hurt if he could perform such an amazing feat of acrobatics!

She was almost out the door when her home phone rang. She hoped it was Zanus. She looked at the caller ID, sighed deeply, and answered.

"Yes, Mr. Freeman. That was me you saw on the news last night. Yes, sir, I had to give a statement to the police. Yes, I had to tell them where I worked. I didn't say anything to the reporters. The name of the firm will not be involved. No, there's not going to be a trial. The police called me late last night. The guy escaped. No, sir, there's no need to worry. I don't think they're likely to catch him. Yes, sir. I've had my fifteen minutes of fame. I think I can promise you there won't be anymore televised appearances."

She hung up the phone and stood there glaring at it. Sheesh! She would be so glad to get out from under that idiot man's control. Blaming her—as if she'd gone out of her way to get her purse snatched so she could be on the nightly news. The deal with Zanus was sounding better and better all the time.

Rachel was still thinking about Zanus as she headed toward the elevator. She really needed someone to talk to so she could sort out her feelings. Perhaps she should talk to her mother. No, that wouldn't work. Her mother would like Zanus the moment she heard about how much money he was worth and the trip to France for champagne. Her mother would, of course, expect Rachel to quit her job and stay home to raise the children. She'd never understand Rachel wanting her own seat on the exchange. Besides, Mom was somewhere in the South Pacific by now.

Her girlfriends? For one thing, she could never call them at this hour of the morning! Rachel imagined Lana, complete with eye mask, groping about for the telephone and swearing a blue streak. Lana never woke up before two P.M. on Saturday if she could help it. Beth would have either been up all night with the baby and just got her to sleep or she'd be up early with the baby who had finally slept all night. As for Kim, she was going to be out of town this weekend, off visiting her parents who lived in Wisconsin.

Rachel wasn't really sure she could talk to them anyway. They had all called to make sure she'd made it home after their adventure at the restaurant. They liked Zanus, but they were far more interested in what was going on with Derek. In the end, Lana held out for Zanus, who had behaved like a perfect gentleman about keeping Rachel's name out of the paper. Beth thought Derek was being wonderfully mysterious and was so chivalric and good-looking! Kim took the practical viewpoint.

"It's as easy to marry a rich man as a poor one," was her advice.

Of course, Rachel wasn't planning on marrying either one of them at the moment.

I'll go running and figure this out for myself, she thought.

The weather was nice, with a warm breeze coming off the lake. The sun was already hot on the back of her neck. Rachel was wearing her exercise clothes—black stretch Capri pants, tank top, jacket, and running shoes.

She was kind of hoping Derek would be around, so she could make her apology and let him know the interesting news about the vanishing purse snatcher. He wasn't there, however, and she realized he must have Saturdays off.

Still, he lived in the building, didn't he? Maybe he would come outside for a brisk walk or maybe he worked out at the gym. She hung about outside of her building, stretching her calf muscles. Derek didn't show. She wondered with a grin if he was on the early morning talk shows, discussing his heroic rescue of her purse via satellite with Wolf Blitzer.

Stretched out and ready to run, Rachel set out at a slow jog around the block, then headed toward the park. She was about ten minutes into her run, when Rachel saw a familiar figure walking ahead of her. It was Derek, and trailing behind him on a leash was a dog. A sheltie, she thought, though she'd never seen one quite that rotund.

As she came closer, she saw that the sheltie was old and arthritic. The little legs moved stiffly, though, by the grin on the dog's face, it was enjoying the walk.

Derek and the sheltie were moving so slowly, and Derek looked so ludicrous—a big strong man with a little pudgy dog. Rachel had to stifle a laugh. Derek must have been walking that dog for an hour to make it this far. She could not pass up an opportunity to rib him for this, and, besides, she could make her apology.

Rachel stopped to catch her breath and smile at Derek, who looked astonished to see her.

"My hero!" Rachel joked. She leaned down to pat the sheltie, whom she now recognized as belonging to one of the older ladies in the building. "Is this your new partner in fighting crime?"

Derek looked relieved. He must have thought she'd still be mad at him.

"Yes, this is JoJo the Wonder Dog. Faster than a speeding bullet."

"I'm glad to see he's getting some exercise," Rachel stated. "The vet keeps telling Mrs. Pomfrey to quit feeding him foie gras and smoked salmon and biscuits dipped in sherry, but, by the looks of him, she hasn't done that."

Derek grinned. He brought out a plastic sack filled with chopped liverwurst. "This is his treat for walking this far. Of course, once he gets it, he sits down and refuses to budge. I generally have to carry him back."

He sat down on a bench and opened the plastic sack. "Watch this. He does the Liverwurst Dance."

Derek held out a piece of meat. JoJo began to yap and spin around in a circle with more speed and agility than Rachel would have thought possible. He was rewarded with the treat and Derek ruffled the little dog's fluffy ears.

Seeing Derek like this, walking patiently with this fat little dog, made Rachel realize that he couldn't have beaten that kid to a pulp last night. She had intended to apologize for her behavior yesterday, but she felt suddenly uncomfortable. She couldn't find a way to get the words out.

An awkward pause fell between them. Derek looked at the dog and Rachel looked furtively at Derek. Then, of course, they both spoke at once.

"Listen, Rachel, about last night—"

"About last night, Derek—"

They both stopped to laugh self-consciously.

"I feel terrible about that kid," Derek began.

"No, please don't say any more," Rachel said, flushing. "I overreacted. Besides the police called me last night. The kid wasn't hurt badly after all. Seems he was well enough to jump out of the ambulance and run away."

"Really," said Derek. He had a thoughtful look on his face.

"I'm sorry. You caught the thief and saved my Gucci handbag and kept me from having my credit cards stolen and identity theft and I don't know what else. And I behaved like a . . . a—"

"Distraught woman who has just had her purse stolen?" Derek suggested.

"You're being kind. I'm sorry."

"So am I."

He held out his hand. Rachel laughed and put her hand in his and they shook on it. He held on to her hand a little longer than necessary. Rachel felt a tingle in her blood and she drew her hand away only when she realized she didn't want to let go.

"Well," said Rachel, "I guess I better finish my run . . ."

In truth, she wasn't in any hurry to leave. Little JoJo had polished off the liverwurst, and, true to form, he plopped himself down in the grass and refused to stand back up. Derek tugged halfheartedly on the leash, but he wasn't really paying attention to the dog. He looked as though he were making up his mind to something.

He said suddenly and awkwardly, "Are you busy this afternoon?"

Rachel stared at him, startled. "Why do you ask?"

"I have this afternoon off," Derek continued, red-faced and flustered, "and I was wondering if you would like to have lunch with me?"

Rachel thought about the rest of her day. Zanus had not called her. She didn't have any plans, and the thought of spending another weekend working on her charts suddenly did not appeal to her.

"It's going to take me awhile to get my partner here back to Mrs. Pomfrey, so you could finish your run. We could meet here at noon."

He was being thoughtful and considerate. If they met here, no one in the building would see her going out with the doorman. Probably just as well for him, too. Mr. Fraym would not appreciate Derek fraternizing with the tenants.

Zanus would be furious if he found out, but then why hadn't he called her anyway? That irked her. She could have been killed last night. It was all over the news. Even if he was still angry with her, she deserved a call. He should be checking to see if she was all right.

"Lunch would be great," she said.

Derek looked pleased, so pleased that Rachel felt a little flutter in her pulse.

To cover her own flustered feelings, she pointed to the hot dog cart at the corner of the park. "Maybe if you put sausages in your pocket, JoJo would get up and move?"

"Now, there is an idea." Derek laughed. "I will meet you here at noon."

Rachel continued her run. She was looking forward to having lunch with Derek. She told herself it was because she was glad the awkwardness between them had ended. She didn't want to have to spend all her time trying to avoid the doorman.

"Makes leaving the building difficult for a girl," Rachel said to herself with a laugh.

She wondered where he'd take her for lunch on a doorman's salary. Probably that very hot dog cart. Rachel didn't mind. She loved hot dogs, as a matter of fact. Sometimes nothing tasted better.

Back home, Rachel showered, fixed her hair and her makeup, and picked out something suitable to wear. She would not dress up. He'd think she expected him to take her somewhere fancy. Jeans, a fitted long-sleeved T-shirt, and her flip-flop sandals. She loved her flip-flops. They screamed summer, but Rachel simply couldn't wait for summer to wear them. Today was warm enough and, besides, maybe Derek wouldn't find her choice of footwear silly this time. She just had to remember not to mention what she'd paid for them.

Rachel walked to the park, carrying her jacket, just in case. Derek was waiting for her. He was holding a well-stuffed, heavy backpack.

"Hello," Rachel greeted him. "What's in the bag? You haven't dog-napped JoJo, have you?"

"No," Derek said, laughing. "The sausages worked, by the way. We made it home in record time. Under two hours. The liverwurst gave me an idea. I thought we might have a picnic."

"A picnic sounds wonderful," said Rachel. She couldn't remember the last time she'd been on a picnic.

They set out, walking side by side, companionable but not too close. Making it clear they were friends, not lovers. The park was crowded. The weather was lovely, and people were out enjoying it. Footballs were being tossed back and forth. Some enterprising young people had put up a volleyball net. Others were flying kites or throwing Frisbees. Children and dogs were running around everywhere.

Derek picked a secluded spot beneath a tree whose green buds were just starting to show. He put down a small blanket that Rachel wondered secretly if he'd stolen from JoJo for her to sit on. He sat on the grass, heedless of grass stains on his blue jeans.

He opened the backpack and pulled out small packages wrapped in wax paper and tinfoil. There was brie cheese, Greek olives, crackers, bread, and ham. Rachel's eyes widened at the sight of so much food. He'd bought enough for an army. To finish it off, he brought out chilled white wine in a box and two plastic cups.

Rachel found it all charming and endearing. She couldn't help but think how Zanus would have done a picnic for her. For one thing, he probably would have never invited her to a picnic in the first place—he might ruin his pants. Second, if he did, there would have been a table with fine linen and champagne in a bucket and caviar and prime rib and a waiter to pour, and it would have all been very correct and not nearly so much fun.

She tried to picture Zanus drinking wine out of a box from a plastic cup. The thought made her giggle.

"So, Derek, how do you usually spend your free time?" she asked.

"I read books. I come to the park. On Sundays, I go to museums or the library."

Rachel had noticed a book in his backpack.

"Do you mind if I'm nosey?" she asked, reaching for it.

He shook his head, and she pulled it out.

She had expected to find him reading someone like Tom Clancy. Instead, the book was a weighty tome on the Knights Templar.

"Wow, this looks intense," Rachel said. "Are you studying for a degree?" That would explain why he was a doorman.

"No," said Derek, smiling. "I just do this for myself. I enjoy history, especially medieval history."

"Why that particular time period?"

Derek hesitated, flushing slightly, as though he found the question difficult to answer. "It's . . . um . . . well, I guess you could say . . . it's the paintings of that time period. I look at them and imagine what it would have been like to have lived back then."

Rachel was astonished and then felt ashamed of herself. She *was* a snob, as he'd accused her of being the other night. It had never occurred to her that a doorman could be studying medieval history and spending Sundays at the Chicago Art Institute or Field Museum.

"I don't know much about history," she confessed.

"The paintings depict a different lifestyle and a different way of thinking. Men were honorable back then. If a man gave his word, he would be willing to die rather than go back on it." He looked intently at Rachel as he spoke. "If a man loved a woman, he would do anything in his power to keep harm from coming to her."

Rachel gave a self-conscious laugh, tried to look as if she were unconscious of his meaning. This was hard, for her heart was beating fast.

"Men are different now," Derek added, his brow darkening.

He glanced at her, and she knew he was talking about Zanus.

She was mildly annoyed. "I don't believe all men of this era are dishonorable. Some know what it means to be a gentleman and *not* follow women into the ladies' room," she said archly.

Derek glanced at her, troubled. Seeing her grin, he realized she was teasing, and he winced and pressed his hand over his heart.

"You have struck to the quick, my lady," he said. "I am bested in the field. You win the tourney." He solemnly handed her a grape.

She just as solemnly took it and popped it in her mouth. She was seized with a sudden crazy desire to kiss him. Shocked at herself, she looked back at the book.

"Is the writer any good?" she asked hastily. "Does he know his stuff?"

Derek shrugged. "Fairly accurate. Of course, he was not there. He couldn't know what it was like. He doesn't understand . . ." He fell silent, lost in thought.

"You talk as if *you* were there!" she said teasingly.

Derek glanced at her, then he smiled. "I think I would have liked living back then. Life was a lot simpler. More brutal and rough, but simpler. Take courtly love, for example."

"What kind of love?"

"Courtly love. Men of that time period courted women. There was none of this pay for a couple of dinners and let's go jump into bed. Knights wrote poetry to their ladies. They worshipped them from afar. They sang songs to them and went on quests to prove their love. And sometimes all they received in return was a little smile, a sweet glance, a favor at a joust."

"Not even a kiss?" Rachel asked.

"Not even that. Many times the women were married to someone else. A true knight would never besmirch the honor of the woman he loved. He suffered for his love in silence, sometimes never even telling her. If, by chance, she loved him in return, she could not dare tell him. No such thing as quickie divorces in those days. The two loved from afar. Courtly romances were rarely consummated."

"That must have been hard on the women. They couldn't go off on quests for the man they loved. What about marriage?"

"Marriage and love were mutually exclusive at the time. Marriages were generally arranged by the families for either business or political reasons. Sometimes the bride and groom met for the first time on their wedding day. If the couple was lucky, they learned to love each other. If not, they suffered in silence. If a man fell in love with a married woman, he had no control over it. He was prey to love's passion."

"But discreet about it, yes?"

"Oh yes," Derek said. "That was the most enjoyable part—the secrecy. The danger, even." He gave an ironic smile. "In some cases, romance would have probably ended in a minute if the two ever really got together. She would find out that he was a dolt who paid someone to write the poetry he gave her and he would find out she smelled of garlic."

Rachel laughed. "So it was noble to be sneaking around?"

"A man was discreet because he should not boast of a conquest, thereby cheapening it. He is ennobled by love and so is she. Their love for each other makes them better people." He looked away from her, gazing far off into the distance.

"Is that what it was like for you?" Rachel asked quietly.

Derek jumped and spilled his wine. He looked at her, startled. "What do you mean by that?" he demanded.

She was surprised by his strong reaction. "Nothing," she said. "Only you told me that I reminded you of someone. I thought maybe—"

"Oh, yeah, right." He smiled, seemed unaccountably relieved. "Yes, you could say that, I suppose. I was young. She was much older. And she was married."

He pulled up some new blades of grass and began tossing them away, one by one.

"I'm sorry," said Rachel, seeing him deeply affected. "Did . . ." she hesitated, feeling awkward.

"Yes," he said, encouraging.

"Did your love for her . . . ennoble you?"

He smiled, soft and gentle. "I like to think it did. I think anytime you love someone, that love should make you feel as though you want to do great deeds, be brave and heroic. You want to strive for perfection, for the sake of the one you love, not your own. That way, if anything happened, and you lost the person you loved, you would feel pain, but you would also feel pride and gratitude, for you would know that because of the loved one, you are better, wiser, stronger."

He looked at her as he spoke.

Rachel drew in a shivering breath and realized that she'd stopped breathing while he talked, so as not to miss a word. She'd never heard a man express his feelings like this. She was speechless. She had the feeling he was talking about himself and about her. Especially the part about losing the person you loved.

"More wine?" he said, and he reached for her plastic cup.

"Yes, sure, thanks." She handed over the cup.

The box of wine was down by her feet. He started to pour the wine, but at that instant, he snatched off her flip-flops, jumped to his feet, and dashed off with them.

"Hey!" she cried. "Shoe thief! Stop!"

He let her catch him. She seized the flip-flops out of his hand and smacked him on the wrist with one of them.

"There's never a cop around when I need one," she said, laughing. Pointing to her flip-flops, she asked, "Say, do you like my shoes?"

"Is that what they are?" Derek asked. "There's nothing to them. You might as well be walking barefoot."

"They show off my feet. I may not have much else to brag about, but I do have pretty feet," said Rachel, looking down at her manicured toes with satisfaction.

"One thing you cannot brag about," he said. "You run like a girl." He dashed off again.

Laughing, she chased after him. He was a swift runner, obviously in top physical condition. She was going to ask if he had been in the military, but decided that if she kept asking personal questions, he'd get the wrong idea. Or maybe the right one. She didn't know. She was so confused.

They spent the rest of the afternoon goofing off, having fun. They threw grapes at each other, trying to catch them in their mouths. Derek dove wildly to catch the ones she cheatingly overthrew, ending up with grass stains down his shirt. She could have never done that with Zanus, she thought. He had a horror of looking ridiculous.

They laughed—a lot. She liked hearing Derek laugh. He laughed loudly and deeply, putting his whole body into it. Rachel couldn't imagine Zanus doing that either. In fact, she couldn't remember ever hearing Zanus laugh at all. He sometimes gave a chuckle at some of her wittier remarks, but she always got the feeling he was just being polite. He had no sense of humor. And he'd probably never heard of the Knights Templar.

You're not being fair, she scolded herself. *Zanus knows lots of things Derek doesn't, things you're interested in.*

That was true. She had tried, when they first sat down, to explain to Derek what her job entailed, how commodities like pork bellies and wheat and money, like the dollar and the Euro, were bought and sold based on what people thought they might do in the future. He'd listened politely, but after a while, she saw his eyes glazing over. He regarded her in perplexity (especially when it came to pork bellies). She had the feeling she might well have been talking a foreign language and quickly changed the subject.

That didn't stop her from enjoying herself. When, quite suddenly, gray clouds moved into the sky and it started to rain, Rachel found herself disappointed that their fun afternoon was at an end.

"Quick!" Rachel gasped. "Your food!"

"Never mind that," said Derek, regarding her with concern. "You're getting soaked!"

"I don't melt," she said, laughing. "Remember the other afternoon? I'm the idiot who likes walking in the rain."

"I remember," he said softly.

She looked up at him. He moved closer to her, his lips parting, his eyes half-closed. She felt a thrill go through her and she hesitated a split second, then turned swiftly away.

"We have to save this food," she said, not looking at him. "This will make lunch for you for a week."

They scrambled around, grabbing the leftovers, putting lids on plastic containers and stowing them in the backpack. She sneaked a peek at him, to see if he looked disappointed that she hadn't let him kiss her. She hoped he understood. They were friends—finally. She didn't want to ruin that. He glanced up, saw her looking at him, and he smiled, reassuring.

And then he threw a grape at her.

Twelve

The rain stopped as quickly as it started, though the skies continued to look threatening. Derek and Rachel headed for home at a fast pace, hoping to beat the next downpour. They were just leaving the park when Derek saw William, standing beneath a tree where he'd taken shelter during the storm. Sighting them, William started waving a battered hat and flapping his arms.

Derek walked faster, pretended he didn't see him.

"Derek," said Rachel. "I think that man is trying to get your attention."

"Oh, uh, yeah, maybe," said Derek.

William came walking up to them. He gave Rachel a smile, then said in concern, "How are you, my dear? Recover from last night?"

Rachel stared at him. "How did you— Oh, I remember! You're the man they were interviewing on television. Yes, thank you, I'm fine."

"Good," said William. He beamed at her, then said in a low voice to Derek. "We need to talk—"

Derek nodded. "I'm sorry, Rachel. I need to take care of this. I guess you can make it home by yourself all right?"

"So long as there aren't any purse snatchers," she said, smiling. She continued to stare at the man. "Excuse me, sir, but weren't you in the Hotel 71 the night—"

"Hotel 71? Me?" William chuckled. "Too rich for my blood."

Rachel was obviously about to pursue the matter and Derek was trying to think of some way to get out of this when a couple walked up to them.

"I beg your pardon, Derek," the man said. "If I could have a word with your friend . . ."

Derek groaned. It was the Cyruses, that couple from the other night. The couple William had berated—Jimmy Raye and his wife. Of all the bad timing! Rachel was looking flustered and ill at ease. Of course. She wouldn't want them gossiping about seeing her in the park, frolicking with the doorman.

Derek was about to say something, to try to get Rachel off the hook, but Mr. Cyrus ignored him and Rachel and walked up to William.

"Why, hello, Jimmy Raye," said William, smiling. "Fine day, isn't it?"

Jimmy Raye looked slightly puzzled at this, considering that it was once again raining.

"What can I do for you?" William asked.

Sheltering beneath his umbrella, which his wife was holding over their heads, Jimmy Raye began to fumble about in an inner coat pocket. He brought out an envelope, and handed it to William.

"I'm glad I found you. I was looking for you. You see, I got to thinking about what you said," Jimmy Raye told William earnestly. "And I want to do something for your people. People like you."

"The homeless," his wife clarified.

"Inside the envelope is a copy of a letter that I plan to send to my money manager instructing him to set up a trust fund to be used to provide food and shelter for the homeless. If you could specify where you'd like the money to go—if there's a soup kitchen or a shelter—all you have to do is provide me with the names and addresses. I'll make all the arrangements."

"Thank you, Jimmy Raye!" said William, pleased. He took the envelope and thrust it into his pocket. "Your granddaddy would be proud of you."

"It's the least I could do," Jimmy Raye said, red-faced. "You were right, you know. I couldn't sleep all night thinking over what you said. I'm going to try to fix things, though. I'm getting involved in the business again. A good thing, too. I found out . . . Well, never mind. Let's just say that I might have lost everything if it hadn't been for you reminding me of my responsibilities."

"And we have no problems with you visiting

your friend here," his wife added. She sidled over next to Derek and said quietly, "Though if you *could* persuade your friend to bathe—"

"Come along, my dear," said her husband hurriedly. He nodded in a friendly fashion to William and he and his wife walked off.

Rachel was staring at Derek. Her eyes were bright with admiration and astonishment. "I didn't know you were involved with the homeless! I think that's wonderful." She smiled at him, then said, "I guess I'll be going. Thank you for lunch. I had a good time."

"Thank you for coming," he said.

"Nice meeting you, my dear," said William, taking off his hat.

"Yes, nice meeting you . . ." Rachel gave him an odd look and then walked off, keeping one eye on the blue-black clouds massing overhead and the other on Derek as she passed. He and the homeless man were very quickly deep into conversation.

So on top of running down purse snatchers and walking crippled dogs and studying medieval history and being extremely handsome, he helps the homeless, Rachel thought. *Not only that, but somehow he convinced that old crab, Mr. Cyrus, to help the homeless! Who would have known?*

Still, she had to admit there was something strange about him. She was sure that homeless guy was the same one at the hotel. And the same guy who just happened to show up when her purse was being snatched. And now he was here in the park . . . odd. Very odd.

Rachel would have given it more thought, but at the moment the rain started falling in earnest—a cold rain, not suited to flip-flops. She increased her speed.

"Sorry to interrupt," said William contritely, wringing water out of his hat.

"That's all right," said Derek, shrugging. "We were just having a friendly lunch."

"Was that what it was?" William asked, concerned.

"Yes, that's what it was," said Derek. "I did what you asked. I'm trying to gain her trust and I think it worked. She apologized. I apologized. We're friends. By the way," he added, hoping to change the subject, "you were right about Zanus getting rid of any evidence of demons. The police called Rachel to tell her the kid who took her purse disappeared on the way to the hospital."

"I'm not surprised. So lunch went well?" William eyed the well-stuffed backpack. "Anything in there you'd like to share?"

Derek smiled and handed it over. "Now, what was it you wanted? Besides cheese and olives."

"Olives? I love olives! Black ones, I hope?" William unzipped the knapsack and began rooting around inside.

"William," said Derek, turning up the collar on his jacket and hunching his shoulders. "It's raining. What did you want?"

"Oh, yes." William zipped up the knapsack. "I

just wanted to let your know your partner has arrived. I'm not sure where or when or how he'll contact you. Michael was vague as to details. But he's here."

"Great," Derek said grimly. "Just great. I finally manage to gain Rachel's trust and now someone else turns up to complicate matters."

"I think you can trust us to manage better than that, Derek," said William soothingly. He patted Derek on the arm. "Thanks for the grub. You know where to find me if you need me."

He turned and trudged off through the rain.

Derek shook his head and continued on his way home. He walked slowly, despite the rain, reliving in his mind an afternoon that had been, for him, heavenly.

Rachel was still a few blocks away from her building, thinking what a fool she'd been to wear flip-flops in April. Her feet were chilled to the bone from sloshing through the puddles in the street. She was thinking that the first thing she was going to do tomorrow was go out and buy one of those little umbrellas you could stick in your purse, when she stopped to look around. She had heard what sounded like a child crying over the deluge of water pouring out a rain gutter.

There it was again—a long, plaintive wail. Rachel turned toward the sound and finally located it. The wail was coming from a bush near a two-story brick walkup. Rachel peered inside the bush.

A small orange cat looked up at her. When he saw her, he let out another wail. The cat was soaked to the bone, shivering, and skinny. Very skinny.

"For the love of . . ." Rachel whispered under her breath. "It's Sam!"

The cat was the spitting image of a cat she'd had when she was a little girl. This cat looked so much like Sam, the memories brought tears to her eyes. She'd loved that cat. He'd been with her through the bad teen years all the way through high school. She'd told Sam secrets she'd never been able to tell anyone else. When her mother wrote to her, while she was in college, that Sam had died at the ripe old of age of eighteen, Rachel had cried for two days straight.

She knelt down and hesitantly reached out her hand to him. She was afraid he would take off, but as soon as she came to the ground, the cat crawled out from under the bush to greet her. He shook the water from his head and gave her a meow and a lick on the hand.

"Where's your owner?" Rachel asked. She saw a woman coming down the stairs from the apartment building.

"Pardon me, ma'am, is this your cat?" Rachel asked, indicating the scrawny little thing.

"No," the woman said brusquely, barely glancing at it.

"Do you recognize this cat?" Rachel persisted. "Do you know if this cat belongs to someone in the building?"

"I'd be surprised if it did," the woman answered. "No pets allowed." She walked off.

Rachel looked back at the cat. He wasn't wearing a collar and he looked as if he hadn't been fed in days.

"Do you belong to someone around here?" Rachel asked the cat.

As if in answer, he jumped into her arms and crawled inside her jacket. He nestled close to her. She could feel him shivering.

"You poor cat, you must be freezing. Okay, kitty, I'll take you home, but tomorrow we'll ask around to see if you belong to anyone. We'll have to buy you some cat food and litter and a litter box. This is all temporary," she told the cat.

He winked his green eyes at her. They both knew he wasn't going anywhere tomorrow.

She really didn't need a cat, she told herself, even as she tucked the cat deeper into her jacket, then headed to the convenience store on the corner.

She had killed numerous plants, including a lucky bamboo plant Kim had given her, assuring her that you had to work really, really hard to kill bamboo. Rachel hadn't worked that hard at it. Within two weeks, the bamboo had turned yellow and all the leaves had fallen off.

But Rachel continued to keep the cat in her jacket. She remembered how comforting it had been to share her feelings with her dear old cat. A cat was not judgmental. A cat would love her unconditionally. A cat would be there to greet her when she came home and he would not want to talk about the Nikkei index or pork bellies. He would only want to sit in her lap and purr. She felt happy with this sopping wet little ball of fur pressed close against her. And it had been a long time since she'd been happy.

Well, no, that wasn't quite true. She'd been happy this afternoon with Derek. For the first time in a long while, she hadn't thought about her charts or the market or Freeman or making money. All well and good, but a girl couldn't live on happy afternoons in the park.

Rachel bought cat supplies, including liver treats and a catnip mouse. Once home, she fed her cat and gave him a bath, blow-dried him with the hair dryer (he didn't much like that), and wrapped him in some warm towels to make him feel more comfortable.

"Hmmm, you need a name," Rachel said. "I can't keep calling you 'cat.' "

An image came to her—a picture of a cat on the cover of a book. One of her favorite stories as a child had been about a cat that took it upon himself to watch over a group of church mice. She hadn't thought of that book in years. Yet, the name seemed oddly appropriate, somehow.

"Sampson," she said, trying it out.

The cat meowed loudly. Rachel wasn't sure if he was yowling in agreement or if he was just hungry.

"All right, Sampson," she said. "How about a liver treat?"

Sampson curled around her ankles and winked at her with his green eyes.

They were sitting on the couch together—the cat purring and Rachel relaxing with a glass of wine—thinking about the lunch and how much fun it had been, when her phone rang.

"Darling, it's Zanus, I just heard about your attack. Are you okay?"

How had he not heard about this until now? Rachel asked herself. *Was he living under a rock?*

"Yes, I'm fine. Everything is fine. Derek collared the thief and retrieved my purse."

"Ah, Derek the doorman. Of course. He's quite handy isn't he? Always around when you need him."

"The robbery *did* happen outside the front door. Where Derek works," Rachel said, annoyed. She couldn't help but add, "I'm surprised you didn't call to check on me sooner."

"I didn't find out about it until I picked up the paper a moment ago," Zanus explained. "I was out of town on business. I just came back. I thought I told you I was going to be gone. That's why we couldn't go out last night."

So he really had gone out of town. He wasn't mad at her.

"Yes, right," she said. "I forgot. I'm sorry."

"And I'm sorry I made that crack about Derek," Zanus added. "I'm thankful he was there to help. It's nice to know someone is looking out for my girl. Which brings me to the reason for my call. Would you have dinner with me tonight?"

Rachel looked down at Sampson. He was sound asleep, still purring. She didn't want to leave him alone tonight, but she was feeling a little guilty about her lunch with Derek. She'd had such a good time with him. She still felt a little thrill run through her when she remembered the way his lips had come so close to hers. But there was no future in this. None. She and Derek were from two different worlds. A night with Zanus would help convince her that Derek was simply a passing fancy and nothing to get worked up over. Yes, dinner with Zanus would be exactly what she needed to take her mind off of Derek.

"Dinner would be wonderful."

"I'll come round for you at eight."

Rachel hung up the phone and looked at the cat. She knew she was probably being silly, but she didn't like leaving him alone while she was gone. And maybe she wasn't being all that silly. He'd scratched about in the litter box, but she wasn't certain he would use it. And she'd caught him already digging his claws into the sofa.

"What you need," she said to him, "is a walk in the park."

At about ten minutes before eight, Rachel went down to the lobby and stopped at the front desk.

There was no one there. Behind the front desk was a closed door. A sign on the door read: "For Assistance After Hours, Please Ring Bell." Rachel pressed on the buzzer.

The door flew open.

"No, Mike," said Derek impatiently, "I am not going to cover while you go out for a smoke!"

He was not wearing a shirt, just blue jeans, and he held a towel in his hands. His hair was wet and rumpled; he'd probably just come out of the shower. He smelled good—of soap and aftershave, nothing fancy. Just smelled good. He looked good, too. Muscular, firm, and strong.

Rachel froze. "Oh," she said, staring.

"Hi," he said, smiling. "Sorry, I thought you were Mike."

"I'm sorry to bother you," said Rachel, feeling her cheeks grow warm.

"What can I do for you?" Derek asked.

"Oh, um, I'm going out for the evening and I was feeling nervous about leaving my cat alone . . ."

"Cat?" said Derek, raising his eyebrows. "I did not know you had a cat."

"I didn't until a couple of hours ago. I was on my way home when I found him. He'd been abandoned and he was so wet and cold and hungry—you could see his ribs, Derek! Anyway, I picked him up and brought him back. He's not quite used to things yet, so I was wondering if . . . someone could take care of him for me while I'm gone."

He was staring at her. The smile was no longer on his face. "You are going out with Zanus, aren't you?"

"Derek, don't start!" Rachel returned, irritated. "I have a perfect right to go out with anyone I choose. Have Mike or whoever is on duty walk my cat, please. Anytime this evening and around noon on weekdays when I'm at work."

She held out her spare key to him. The sight of him half-naked with water glistening on his bare chest and his wet hair falling over his face was doing terrible things to her composure. She had a sudden image in her mind of brushing up against his bare chest, kissing his lips that were still wet from the shower, brushing back the rumpled hair.

He didn't take the key. He just stood there, regarding her with a grim expression on his face.

"You walk JoJo every day," she said.

"That is different," he said coldly.

"I don't see how! Take my key! You'll find the leash and the harness on the counter." Rachel pressed the key into his unwilling hand, then turned and hastened away, almost running.

"You cannot walk a cat!" Derek called angrily after her.

"Yes, you can," Rachel shot over her shoulder. "I used to walk my cat all the time. You just have to be patient. Sorry, I have to go. My ride is here!"

She hurried out the front door to where Zanus and the limo were waiting.

Derek stood there with Rachel's apartment key in his hand, staring after her. Had she truly just asked him to walk her cat? Her cat! A blood vessel in his forehead started to throb and an uncomfortable warmth began to creep up the back of his neck. He was a knight, a holy warrior. He was here to guard and protect her. He was not Milady's curly-haired page boy mincing down the castle halls with a cat on a leash! This was it! Derek was no woman's cat-sitter.

He phoned his manager. "Sir, Rachel Duncan in twenty-two-fifteen just asked me to walk her cat. This will take me away from other more important duties here at the building." Derek paused to listen. "Yes, sir. One of my duties. I know I am supposed to walk dogs, sir, but a cat—yes, I understand. Sorry to bother you, sir. Goodbye."

He could have Mike do it. Derek was, after all, off duty this evening. Mike would probably welcome the task, for it would give him a chance to have a smoke. Derek didn't trust Mike all that much. If Rachel lost her newfound cat, she'd blame him.

Sighing deeply, Derek thrust her key in his pocket.

Later that evening, Derek steeled himself to his new job and headed up to Rachel's apartment. He unlocked the door and went inside. The first thing that struck him was the clutter and disorder. He himself lived with the Spartan simplicity of a soldier. Everything in its place and a place for everything. Rachel lived by a totally different philosophy—everything everywhere.

Her clothes were strewn around the living room, underneath and on top of charts, newspapers, books, and empty water bottles. Dishes were washed, but they'd been left stacked the sink. As he stood looking about, he had the feeling that something was missing. He couldn't quite place it, and then he realized that there was nothing of Rachel. Nothing personal to her. No pictures decorating the walls—just an ugly cork board. No flowers in a vase. No comfy pillows on the sofa. In her way, she lived much like he did. She didn't live here. She worked here. Which meant she didn't "live" anywhere. Her life was her work. Just as his life—now long past—had been.

He shook away the thoughts that brought back bittersweet memories. He wanted to get this over with. Time to find the blasted cat. He found the leash and what he supposed was the harness on the kitchen counter. He eyed the harness contraption in disbelief and shook his head. What was the world coming to?

"Hey, cat," Derek called irritably.

No response.

Seething, Derek looked behind chairs and under furniture, calling out, "Cat!" in increasingly annoyed tones. Then he glanced into the bedroom and there was the cat. He was curled up asleep on Rachel's bed.

Derek had never liked cats. People back in his time had thought cats were wicked animals who consorted with witches and were used in black magic rites. He'd never believed such superstitious nonsense himself, but he didn't like the way a cat looked you in the eye, as if the cat knew things about you that you didn't.

Just as he was thinking this, the cat woke up and looked at him with unnerving intelligence. Derek glared back at the creature. He had no idea how he was supposed to put the harness on. Then he reminded himself that he had harnessed horses back in the days of his training for the knighthood. Certainly he could harness this fur ball.

Derek held the harness with his right hand and reached for the cat with his left hand. He thought it might run (Derek was actually hoping the cat would run, then he could tell Rachel he hadn't been able to catch him). The cat stayed put on the bed, however, and Derek picked him up by the scruff of his neck. He eyed the cat and eyed the harness, then started to shove the harness over the cat's head.

"You're putting it on backward, sir."

He didn't hear the voice aloud. He heard it in his head. The voice had a familiar ring to it.

Derek stared at the cat.

The cat stared back.

"It's me, Commander." The voice sounded aggrieved. "Don't you recognize me? Not the way I look, of course. But my voice. You should recognize my voice, sir."

Derek looked at the cat, really looked at him. "I'll be damned! Sampson!"

"Such language, sir. And you call yourself an angel. I'm your partner," added the cat excitedly.

"Angel William put in the request and Archangel Michael sent me to help you!"

A cherub! And, on top of that, he'd sent a cherub known throughout the heavenly halls to be scatterbrained and unreliable. Eager and enthusiastic, perhaps, but unreliable. Derek was livid with fury.

His new partner, now comfortably ensconced inside Rachel's apartment, was a scrawny, orange-furred cherub, who winked at him with green cat eyes and talked to him in his head.

Of all William's harebrained schemes, this was the worst.

Cherub were serene, joyful, adolescent angels, whose main duties consisted of opening the gates of Heaven and intervening gently in the lives of humans to increase their happiness. Over the centuries, humans had portrayed cherubim as fat-cheeked, chubby little urchins armed with bows and arrows who shot darts of love into the human heart. Cherubim could assume that image, if they wanted to, though Derek couldn't imagine why any of them would. They could choose any image, such as that of a cat. Their interactions with humans were strictly limited. Generally they touched human lives only briefly, doing small acts that left a smile or joyful feeling behind.

The situation in Heaven and on Earth must be very dire, indeed, if Archangel Michael had been forced to resort to using cherubs to help battle the forces of darkness. To Derek's mind, cherubs were not equipped to handle such a dangerous job. They were not capable of comprehending such evil. This was one reason he'd never permitted Sampson to become a holy warrior, no matter how hard the young cherub had begged him.

He had first met Sampson when he was posted at the gates that led from Purgatory to Heaven. A heavenly doorman. Though Sampson wasn't supposed to leave the gates, he would often slip away from his position to watch the battles between the demons and the angels that raged throughout Purgatory. Derek was always having to send him back to his duties.

And now, young Sampson was his partner!

Derek was so angry he would have walked to the Fullerton Street bridge and personally throttled William, but he couldn't leave his post.

Derek squatted down to look the cat in the eye. "You go back and tell Archangel Michael I don't need a partner. And, above all, I don't need a cherub for a partner." He stood up and started to walk out.

"Rachel's with him right now, sir," Sampson stated.

Derek stopped moving.

"Wouldn't you like to know what happens tonight when she comes back, sir?" Sampson said, adding slyly, "She tells me everything. For example, she told me all about how much fun she had in the park today. I can tell you what she said . . ."

"All right," said Derek grudgingly. "How the devil does this contraption go on?"

Derek wrestled the cat into the harness and they rode down the elevator and walked out through the lobby doors. A couple of guys playing Hacky Sack in the street snickered as Derek walked past with the cat on the leash. Derek glared at them and they wiped off their grins and went back to their game. He took Sampson to a small park nearby that was mostly empty this time of evening.

Once there, Derek found a bench that was out of sight. He picked up the cat, plopped him down on the bench.

"All right," he said, "what'd she say about me?"

"Nothing, sir," said Sampson, and if cats could grin, he was grinning. "I lied. Hey, I'm a cat. That's what we do."

"You're also an angel," said Derek dryly. "In case you'd forgotten."

"It's not easy being in this body," Sampson said defensively. "Not all tuna and catnip. But then I guess you know how it feels to be a living being after all these centuries. Takes some getting used to."

Derek could sympathize, but he didn't want to discuss his human frailties with a cat. Plus he needed to know about Rachel. "So what did she talk about?"

"Zanus, Zanus, Zanus. That's all I heard about today." Sampson was suddenly serious. "He's playing her, Commander. Using her."

"Why? What for? What does he want with her?"

"Beats me, sir. That's what we're supposed to find out. Say, Commander, could you scratch me behind my right ear? I've got this itch . . ."

Derek regarded the cat in grim silence and made no move to scratch him.

"Come on, sir," said Sampson, pawing at him. "You've got to admit that I can be useful to you. I can find out all sorts of things you can't. She tells me everything. We'll make a great team, you and I, sir."

Much as he hated it, Derek had to agree. He reached out and gave the cat a quick scratch behind the ear.

"Ah, that's the spot!" Sampson purred and began to rub his head against Derek's hand.

Derek snatched his hand away. "Stick to business," he ordered sternly.

"Yes, sir," said Sampson, and he winked his green eyes.

Thirteen

Dinner with Zanus was fantastic as usual. He had rented a private yacht and instructed the crew to cruise around Lake Michigan so they could admire the city skyline. After dinner, they had their brandy on the aft of the yacht outside. Zanus fetched a blanket for Rachel and draped it over her legs.

"Do you like the view?" he asked.

"It's wonderful," she said.

"We have champagne." Zanus gestured for the waiter to pour her a glass. As he arranged the blanket, he took hold of her foot and slowly and sensuously slid off her shoe. He then began to massage her foot. Rachel squirmed. His hands were cold and he was really very bad at giving massages. He probably didn't realize it, but he was hurting her.

She managed to draw her foot away, tucked it under the blanket.

"Okay, now the other shoe."

Rachel forced a laugh. "If I'd known you were going to be giving me a foot massage, I would have gotten a pedicure."

She drew this foot in, too, under the blanket.

"What? You don't need a pedicure." Zanus didn't press her, however. He added teasingly, "Your foot is perfection. There is no improvement needed. It is said that feet are the windows to the soul. And Rachel dear, you have a beautiful soul. No pun intended."

Rachel shook her head. "I think the quote goes 'eyes are the windows to the soul.' "

"What? Eyes, no that's wrong. It's feet, I know it," Zanus said gallantly. He paused, then added, "Rachel, I know I promised I wouldn't talk business, but I can't thank you enough for all the work you've done for me these past few months."

"Oh it's nothing—"

He cut her off with a shake of his head. "Without your skill and expertise, I would have failed miserably trading on my own. You've made me a lot of money. But there is something better."

"Better than money?" She laughed.

"I'm serious." He gave her hand a playful swat. His eyes, looking at her, were warm and soft. "You, Rachel. I've enjoyed working with you. You are the perfect mix of intelligence and radiant beauty."

Zanus reached up with his hand and stroked her hair. Then he gently took hold of the back of her head and pulled her into a kiss. She tried to tell herself she felt something for him, but his lips were as cold as his hands.

When he pulled back from the kiss, Zanus looked into her eyes.

"Just imagine the things we could do together." His voice was gruff, low.

Rachel smiled at him. "Just what kinds of things are you imagining, Mr. Zanus?"

His answer was unexpected. "I'm imagining the two of us as the most influential people in Chicago. The city is yours, you know. You and I together will make it ours. It's all there for the taking." He looked at her and smiled. "Did Freeman talk to you?"

"Oh, yes," said Rachel. "I meant to tell you. That was quite clever, the way you handled things. I'll be able to spend time with you and no one will think anything of it."

"So we can start those trades on Monday, the ones you agreed to make," he said quietly.

Rachel started to laugh, but his expression stopped her. "You're serious, aren't you?"

"I am always serious about business, Rachel," he said. "I didn't rise to where I am by being timid—in business or pleasure." He touched her hand again, running his fingertips up her arm, then sliding his hand back down.

But she didn't feel any pleasure in this. She had the sudden impression that this evening had been staged for one purpose, to get her to perform the trades.

"And you are not timid either, Rachel. I know that you didn't get to be one of the best traders on the floor by being a delicate flower, did you, my dear?"

"Well, no, I suppose not," Rachel agreed. His ambition was becoming infectious.

"I imagine a penthouse with a spectacular view, lavish weekends in Paris, Christmas on St. Thomas. And I imagine you sharing them all with me."

He paused, regarded her intently. "You are the key to the plan, Rachel. I can't do this without you. I don't have your knowledge. All I have is money. I need your knowledge of the markets and your ability to make trades."

"Just what exactly are you proposing?" Rachel asked.

"Don't look at me that way, Rachel. What I'm asking is not illegal. Just some convenient swapping of trades with a friend of mine."

"Meaning your friend would trade through me? Zanus, I can't do that. It's against the rules." She wanted to put him off this subject for the last time, not because she didn't want to do it. It was because she *did* want to make the trades. He'd sent her the information last week and she'd ignored it, hoping he'd would drop the subject. It seems, though, he wasn't going to, and Rachel always felt like she had no will of her own in his presence.

"He wouldn't be trading through regular channels. He would be using the Globex trading system. He would be someone who is silent and faceless. The exchange would never know."

Rachel found herself actually considering this deal and she was shocked. This wasn't right. She knew it. Her actions at work had always been above reproach. Oh, she'd heard plenty of stories of corrupt activities on the floor. She knew that the offenders were rarely caught. Unethical deals such as the subtle one he was proposing took a long time to be discovered by the exchange officials—if they ever were.

The Globex electronic trading system offered computerized order entry and trading virtually twenty-four hours a day to people around the world. It was extremely fast. In the ordinary way of doing business, a client usually phoned a broker, who then called the order desk at the Merc where a phone clerk took the verbal order and then entered the order into an electronic order routing system and from there to the pit. Globex bypassed all that and went straight to the trade, which could happen in as little as five seconds. But you had to know what you were doing, which was one reason why Zanus needed her help. Rachel had heard of Globex traders who accidentally hit the wrong key and lost millions.

Not that you needed computers for illegal or unethical practices. Those had probably been around since 1898, when the Merc was the Chicago Egg and Butter Board. Trades were handled so rapidly now that by the time the illegal traders were discovered, people had made their fortunes and gotten out. Either that or they'd gone bust and jumped off the top of a high-rise. Rachel was still haunted by the tale of a young woman who had done just that. She and Rachel had not been friends, but they'd say "hi" to each another in the ladies' room and sometimes saw each other in the bars after the close of the market. The news of Belinda's tragic death had come as a shock to Rachel. Still, scared money never wins, as the saying went on the poker tour.

"I suppose we could discuss the quantities and details," Rachel said, stalling. She still felt uncomfortable about this. That was one reason she hadn't brought up Freeman's talk with her.

"We can, and we will," said Zanus.

There was something odd about his voice. It had a hard quality to it. Rachel was suddenly chilled. She reached down and started to pull up the blanket.

"Allow me, darling." Zanus took the blanket out of her hands, arranged it around her shoulders. He eyed her. "You're not having second thoughts about this, are you?"

"You do know that what you're wanting me to do isn't ethical," she said.

"Bah! People do this everyday and they almost always get away with it, right?" He seemed to have read her thoughts.

"Well, yes," she admitted slowly.

"And these people make lots of money, don't they?"

"Yes, but—"

"And you want a seat on the exchange, right? You want to be on your own. Or do you want to continue working for Freeman? Making money for the firm so that he looks good, while he threatens to have you fired every other week. You know he claims you are his protégé, that he taught you everything."

"No!" Rachel was indignant.

"He says he is your mentor. Everything you do, you ask his advice first."

"Ask his advice!" Rachel sat up, threw off the blanket. "He's a moron! I wouldn't ask his advice on what to have for lunch, much less anything to do with commodities—"

"There, there. Calm down," Zanus said. "I wouldn't have brought it up if I'd known how upset it would make you. Of course I don't believe him. After all, it's you I'm offering to purchase a seat on the exchange for. Not him."

Rachel calmed down and was even able to laugh at herself. But she was now determined to leave the firm and Mr. Freeman and set up on her own.

"I get a seat on the exchange," said Rachel, reaching out to caress Zanus's hand. "What do you get?"

"Besides lots of money?" he asked, teasing.

"Yes, besides that. You don't need me to make money for you, after all," said Rachel and she was suddenly serious.

"You've done very well for me, my dear. But as for what I get, I can claim that I discovered you. Freeman and those other idiots on the floor work with you everyday and they missed what I didn't. I found you. And I'll take my finder's fee, as well."

This is more like it, Rachel thought. She felt comfortable and very *un*confused with Zanus. No sudden lurches of her heart. No twisting of the stomach. Just a mild flutter of the pulse now and then. No mystery. Zanus was ambitious and decisive. She liked that about him.

"So, we start Monday," Rachel said. "I don't have a Globex system at my apartment, so I'll have to use those on the floor of the Merc. I'll stay after the market closes."

"That won't draw attention?" Zanus asked.

"No, lots of traders do it," said Rachel, shrugging. "And if Freeman says anything, I'll tell him I'm doing what he asked—taking care of his favorite client."

Zanus smiled and kissed her.

After the brandy, he took her home. They kissed again in the car and she could tell he was hoping she would invite him upstairs.

She thought she was going to, but when they pulled up in front of the building and he exited the car to help her out, she realized that she didn't really want to go to bed with him again, not until she was certain of her feelings about him. She couldn't think of any way out of it, however, without hurting his feelings and she didn't want to hurt him.

"Would you like to come up for a drink?" she asked, then gave him an out. "I'll understand if you're too tired. I'm kind of tired myself—"

"On the contrary," he said. "I feel exhilarated."

He told the limo driver to go home. Oh, well, Rachel thought. So you have meaningless sex and he makes you a delicious high-calorie breakfast. It's only one night . . .

They walked up the stairs together, Zanus holding her hand.

"Will Derek be here tonight?" he asked, and his voice had that cold, hard quality to it again. He was looking at her very strangely as he asked the question.

Rachel started to say no, he had the night off, but then realized that she should not seem to be quite so knowledgeable about the doorman.

"I don't know," she said airily. "I don't think so. He wasn't on duty when I left."

"We shall see," said Zanus.

But Derek wasn't around. Mike was on duty, if you could call it that. He was slumped over with his head on the desk. Rachel had to use her key to let herself and Zanus in. They walked past Mike, who continued to snooze, and entered the elevator.

"Oh, I have to tell you," said Rachel, "I now have a cat. I hope you're not allergic." She was almost hoping he was. She was feeling less and less eager to go through with this.

"On the contrary," said Zanus. "I adore cats."

As she unlocked the door, Rachel called for Sampson, but didn't hear a reply. She walked to the kitchen to fetch the brandy and Zanus entered the living room.

"Is Sampson the cat?" he asked.

"Yes, I named him after the story about the cat and the church mice. He's a stray I picked up today. He appears to have made himself quite at home here. I think I'll keep him."

Rachel brought out the brandy and sat on the couch with Zanus beside her. Relaxing, he put his arm around her.

"It's strange of him not to come—" she began.

Like a shot out of the dark, Sampson leapt up from the back of the couch. Spitting and hissing, he landed on Zanus's head and dug in his claws.

Swearing, Zanus seized hold of the frenzied cat, dragged him off him, and tossed him halfway across the living room.

Sampson landed hard on his side, skidded into a table leg.

"Oh, my god!" Rachel cried.

She ran over to the cat. Sampson lay still a moment, stunned.

Sick with worry, Rachel went to pick him up. Before she could reach him, Sampson was back on his feet, hissing and glaring at Zanus with narrowed eyes, his tail puffed up and his back arched.

Rachel eyed him. He didn't look as if he was hurt. She looked back at Zanus, saw him wiping blood off his forehead. Rachel felt a sudden wild desire to burst out laughing. Here, she'd been worried about the cat!

"Sampson, you bad cat! I'm so sorry." Rachel gasped, embarrassed. She caught hold of Sampson by the scruff of his neck and, ignoring his yowls of indignation, picked him up. "I can't imagine what got into him! Are you okay?"

She hauled Sampson, hissing and growling, into in the laundry room, where he had his food and litter box, and shut the louvered doors. "There. He can't get out."

Nothing daunted Sampson; he could still be heard growling and scratching at the door.

Rachel hurried back to the living room.

"I have some ointment," she said. "Do you need a bandage?"

Zanus frowned. "No, I fought him off in time. I do think he meant to kill me, though."

He was silent while drinking his brandy. Rachel sipped at hers. When he reached out for her, she stiffened in his arms. "Uh, maybe we shouldn't tonight. I think I'm coming down with a cold. I feel feverish."

He put his hand to her forehead. "You do feel a little warm. I will say good night to you here. Have a good night, sweet dreams. I hope you feel better. I'll let myself out."

Zanus rose to his feet and walked out of her apartment, shutting the door behind him.

Rachel wasn't really coming down with a cold. She had told the fib because she hadn't wanted to hurt his feelings. But now she was afraid she'd made him mad.

She couldn't imagine that he was upset about Sampson. But then, the cat had made him look foolish. Zanus didn't have a sense of humor; she already knew that. And he really shouldn't have been that rough. Sampson hadn't hurt him all that much.

A pitiful wail came from the laundry room, along with a drumming sound. She went to the laundry room, opened the door.

Sampson came dashing out, all furred up, and ran straight to the living room.

"Don't worry," she called after the cat. "He's gone. The only guy I'm sleeping with tonight is you. And, what have you got against Zanus anyway?" she demanded, as Sampson came dancing back to her. "Don't look so proud of yourself. What you did was very bad."

She kissed the cat on his head. Then she sighed and held him close.

"I'm about to do something *I'm* not particularly proud of, Sampson, but it means I'm going to be independent. I won't have to work for anyone anymore. Especially Freeman."

She cuddled the cat and rocked him.

"I've been a good girl for a long time. And where has it got me? Making lots of money for other people who don't appreciate it. So now I'm going to give being bad a try."

The next morning, Derek reluctantly went to take Sampson for his walk while Rachel slept. Opening the door, he found the cat limping but triumphant.

"What happened to you?" Derek asked.

"I got a piece of him, Derek!" Sampson announced proudly. "Did you see those claw marks on his cheek? Oh, I forgot. You weren't on duty last night." Sampson looked disappointed.

"I saw Zanus and the bloody marks." Derek smiled. "I thought maybe he'd cut himself shaving."

"That was me!" Sampson purred and then winced. "He paid me back, though. He pulled me off him and launched me. I banged into the cabinet and bruised my leg. My ribs hurt on one side, too."

"And Rachel? How did she react?"

"She was upset," Sampson said. "But Zanus was all smooth." Sampson snorted. "I nearly tossed up a fur ball."

Derek was grim. "What did Rachel say when he hurt you?"

"She wasn't happy. You notice he left early? She told him she wasn't feeling good. And I got some extra tuna after he left. I did find out one thing," the cat added more somberly. "He's asked her do some illegal trades for him. Well, not totally illegal. That's what Rachel keeps saying."

"I don't know what that means," said Derek, frustrated.

"Me neither. But the archangels will. Tell William I'll have the info for him tomorrow. Rachel's doing the first one today."

"I'll let William know."

Then Derek did something he never thought he'd ever do. He reached out to pet Sampson on the head.

"For a cherub, you're pretty gutsy," he told the cat in admiration. "I might consider recommending you for promotion to warrior angel."

"That would be great! Thanks," said Sampson, pleased. He nuzzled Derek's hand, then winced again. "Uh, go easy on the ribs . . ."

Sunday night Rachel had gone to bed eager and excited to make this daring and risky venture. Gambling with money wasn't new to her; buying and selling futures was always a gamble.

In the morning, after a restless night's sleep, she was less enthused. She wasn't just gambling with money, she was gambling with her career, maybe even her freedom. She told herself over and over that the trades weren't exactly illegal; they were just frowned upon. The likelihood of her being caught was low and that was balanced by the fact that the likelihood of her making lots of money was high.

She waited nervously all day for the phone call from Zanus's friend. When an unfamiliar number came up on her cell phone, she hesitated, and then answered. A strange-sounding male voice discussed some trades with her and told her to proceed. After the market closed, she went to the bank of computers and made the trades.

There. She'd done it. There was no going back now.

Zanus called her the next night and invited her out to dinner. He took her to a fabulous restaurant, but all he talked about was how much money she had made for him. He invited himself up to her apartment for a drink, but he didn't send away the limo. He stayed about an hour, talking about the financial markets, especially foreign markets, and the deals she was making for his "friend." Then he gave her a kiss and left, saying something to the effect that they both had to be up early in the morning.

He took her out again the night after and the night after that and this developed into a routine. They would go out to dinner, return to her apartment, discuss what she would do for his friend the next day, and he would leave. He would always kiss her goodbye, but he never moved beyond that. She came to realize that he was leaving their sex life up to her. She was glad, in a way, but again she couldn't help but feel he was using her.

And as if this wasn't tense enough, her cat made it clear that he detested Zanus. Every time Zanus came up to her place, Sampson never lost an opportunity to scratch, bite, hiss at or otherwise maltreat the man. Rachel was amazed at the creative lengths Sampson went to in order to get at Zanus. One night, after Rachel had shut him up in the laundry room, Sampson leaped up, pulled down on the door handle, let himself out, and went straight for Zanus.

Zanus never hurt Sampson again, but Rachel could tell he was starting to run out of patience. She had to buy a lock to install on the laundry room door.

She didn't see much of Derek. There was time for nothing more than a quick "good morning" as she left for work, and she was worn out and too weary to indulge in flirting with the handsome doorman when she came home. She would give him a wan smile and ask about Sampson. He would tell her they'd had a nice walk in the park and that would be that. She did notice that he seemed to be concerned about her and several times he tried to move the conversation beyond walking her cat, but she feared they were heading in dangerous territory and she excused herself and hurried off. He and Zanus exchanged baleful glances when Zanus went up with her to her apartment, but, fortunately, neither said anything, at least in her presence.

The following Sunday night, Rachel dined with the ladies. She hadn't felt like going, but Kim had persuaded her. Well, to be honest, Kim had practically forced her.

"We're all worried about you," Kim had told her. "You've skipped out on us the last two weeks. We want to know what is going on."

The problem was, Rachel couldn't tell them.

"Well, so what is new in the Derek-Zanus-Rachel love triangle? Any more brawls?" Lana asked as she poured the wine.

Rachel picked up her glass, but she didn't drink. "I don't suppose we could change the subject?"

Her friends exchanged glances.

"What is it, honey?" Beth asked. "What's wrong?"

"I'm starting to have second thoughts about Zanus," said Rachel.

"I knew it! It's Derek. Did you sleep with him?" Lana asked eagerly.

"Any man who takes you to lunch in the park and talks to you about courtly love is a man you should not let get away," Beth added.

They waited for Rachel to laugh and she did manage a smile, but it didn't last long. Again, they exchanged glances.

"So what's the matter with Zanus?"

"His teeth are too white? His shoes too shiny?"

"Third nipple. He's got a third nipple?" Beth quipped.

"No, it's the diamond bracelet he gave you. It's too heavy. It makes your arm hurt holding it up. Wait! I've got it! His sheets are only six hundred thread count, instead of a thousand?"

Rachel said nothing.

"We're working hard here, honey," said Beth. "You need to give us something."

"We're starting to really get worried," Kim said.

Rachel had to tell them something. "Look, I know it sounds silly, but Zanus doesn't show any interest in me. Not really. He's never once asked me anything about my family. Sometimes I wonder if he really cares about me at all."

Or if he's just using me, she added silently.

"Men have a habit of giving expensive gifts to women they don't care about," said Beth. "They plan romantic dinners for them and take them out almost every night of the week. I'd like to have a man not care about me like that."

Rachel sighed. "I said it sounded silly." She gulped down the glass of wine in one swallow.

Lana, Beth, and Kim all looked at her, then at each other.

"You haven't had anyone in your life for a long time now, Rachel," said Lana, pouring more wine. "Maybe you're just scared. You're searching for something to be wrong with him."

"Yeah," Kim agreed. "Maybe you should just let it be what it will be for a time. Don't analyze the poor man too much."

"Maybe you're right. I don't know. I guess I'll just wait and see what happens."

She wished she could tell them about the unethical trades. But she didn't want to and that in itself made her uncomfortable. They always shared everything—good and bad. Never any secrets. Why didn't she tell them? She told herself it was because they wouldn't understand. Whenever Rachel started talking business, they rolled their eyes and teased her. But she knew, deep down, it was because she was ashamed. They would be shocked and they'd try to talk her out of it.

"Hey, sweetie, I'm talking!" Beth waved her salad fork at her. "I think Lana's wrong. I think you should listen to your intuition. I mean, really, how much do you know about this guy? Do you even know how he made his money?"

"No, not exactly," Rachel admitted. "He keeps his business very private. Not just from me, but from everyone."

"But he should tell you. You should be his confidante," Beth argued.

"Aren't we jumping the gun a bit here?" Lana chimed in. "Maybe he's just one of those people who likes to keep his business and private life separate—at least in the beginning of a relationship? I mean, what's the rush to reveal every little detail right away? Rachel will learn all of that stuff soon enough. I, for one, wouldn't be all that eager to find out all of his bad habits and neuroses."

"Can we talk about something else?" Rachel pleaded.

"Fine," said Beth with a wink and a wicked grin. "Tell us more about the dreamy doorman who saved you from a fate worse than death!"

"He saved me from a teenage purse snatcher," said Rachel.

"Whatever!" Beth waved it away with a dinner roll.

Rachel shook her head. "He's still the doorman so I see him everyday. We don't talk much, though. He walks my cat."

"Wow! Courtly love and a cat walker. He's a keeper," Kim said. "Especially after you tried to get him fired for saving your life."

"He didn't save my life! And I apologized . . ."

"Maybe you have repressed feelings for Derek and Zanus knows this subconsciously and that's why he's gone all cold and businesslike," said Beth.

"I don't have repressed feelings for Derek," Rachel began and then she stopped.

Sometimes, when she came in late after a wearing and nerve-racking day at work, the way he looked at her—so kind and gentle and concerned—made her want to lay her head on his chest and let him put his arms around her and hold her tightly, until all the bad things in her life went away.

The thought made her eyes fill with tears and she took another drink of wine.

"Thanks for your help," said Rachel. "Let's talk about someone else for a change. Kim, tell us more about these salacious faxes you stumbled on at work."

Her girlfriends once more exchanged glances and, by nonverbal agreement, Rachel was off the hook for the evening. They started talking about Kim.

Rachel knew her friends meant well. They were very protective of each other and they all enjoyed analyzing each other's relationships. Sometimes, though, Rachel just wanted someone to listen and not offer an opinion. Someone like Sampson.

Thank god, cats can't talk.

Fourteen

A week passed. Rachel had a sick feeling in the pit of her stomach about her trades. She was making money, lots of it, but it wasn't right, and she knew it. She guessed Zanus and his "friend" were acting on inside information or manipulating things somehow. She asked no questions. The less she knew, the better. Zanus's excitement and his talk about her future kept her making the trades. Of course, she couldn't neglect her firm or the trades she made for their clients. She also kept making trades for Zanus through the firm, and these also made money.

Rachel always did her floor trading first, then she would grab a computer at the Merc to trade in whatever markets the strange voice on the phone communicated to her that day. After that, she would go to the office. It made for a long day.

On Thursday Rachel stayed even later at the office. She was feeling increasingly guilty over the trades and she had decided to talk to Freeman. She wasn't sure what she hoped to accomplish. Maybe he could provide some guidance as to how she should proceed with Zanus. Or maybe this way they'd both go to white-collar prison together. If Freeman shared her concern, then maybe she could come out of this situation clean and still keep her job and her relationship with Zanus. If that was what she wanted. She was so upset and confused, she didn't know anymore.

It was after seven. Everyone else had gone home long ago. Freeman always stayed late, however, so Rachel knocked on his door.

"Mr. Freeman," she said. "Can I have a moment?"

"Yes, of course, Rachel," Freeman called. "Come in."

"Thank you, sir. I wanted to share some concerns I have regarding Mr. Andreas Zanus." Rachel paused, searching for the right words.

"Yes?" Freeman regarded her gravely. "What's he done? Has he been rude to you?"

"No. On the contrary, he's been quite nice—"

"Then what's the problem, Rachel? Has he been unable to cover his trades? Is he short on funds?"

"No, nothing like that. He's been . . . uh . . . hinting at some unethical activity."

"Do you have any evidence of this? Did he say something on our recorded phone line?"

"No, we were . . . we were at a social gathering."

Rachel looked at Freeman closely, hoping he would read between the lines, hear what she wasn't saying.

Mr. Freeman leaned back in his chair. "You were at a social gathering with Mr. Zanus, a very wealthy businessman, and he dropped a hint that he might want to do something unethical. But you have no proof of what he was asking or even that he was planning to do anything about it."

"Well, I guess . . . No, I don't."

"Could Mr. Zanus have been teasing you?"

"He's not the type to tease, sir," said Rachel wearily.

"I think he was making a joke, and you were just being overly cautious. No harm done."

Rachel sighed. Freeman was so dense. "Mr. Freeman, what if Mr. Zanus did ask me to do something unethical. What should my answer be?"

Freeman eyed her, frowning. Then he got up, walked around her, opened the door, and looked out. He shut the door, walked back to his desk, and sat down.

"You should tell him no, of course. *But* Mr. Zanus is our best client, Rachel," he said carefully. "We make a lot of money off of his trades, not to mention the referral business that he could bring to our firm. I'm counting on you to ensure that his relationship with us stays firmly intact."

"Yes, Mr. Freeman. I understand."

Damn the man! He'd implied that it was her job to do whatever it took—legal or illegal—to hang on to a money machine like Zanus. But he hadn't actually come out and said she should do anything unethical for Zanus, and he would deny it force-fully if she claimed he had. Yet she knew that her job was riding on this. Lose Zanus and that was it.

Rachel should have expected as much. Freeman was old school. It was rumored that he'd built his business on a few shady trades, if not a few out-right illegal ones. He was part of the old guard who believed a trade dispute should be solved with a fist fight in the pit, and that firms should bail out the traders by paying the fines they lev-ied for throwing punches.

What am I going to do now?

Derek was forced to admit that having the cherub around had been a good idea on William's part. Rachel told Sampson everything she was doing, and, even though he was shut up in the closet, the cat was able to eavesdrop on her evening conver-sations with Zanus.

Derek took Sampson for his daily walks in the park and they would stop at a bench to hold their conversations. Thank goodness they could ex-change thoughts and Derek didn't have to speak to the cat aloud. People gave him enough amused glances as it was.

"Just what Angel William figured, Commander," Sampson told Derek. "Something to do with the world economy. That's all they talk about. I don't understand it. Do you?"

"No," Derek admitted, "but apparently Archangel Michael does. I pass along what you tell me to William, who passes it to Michael. And, no, you are not going to sit on me!"

Derek picked up Sampson, who had jumped up on the bench and was making his way into Derek's lap, and deposited him in the grass.

"Ah, c'mon, sir, it's cold today!" Sampson pleaded.

"No." Derek was firm.

"I'm worried, sir," Sampson said, sitting down and facing him. "Rachel is growing increasingly nervous about what he's making her do. She doesn't eat and she can't sleep. She tries to object, but he always has some slick answer for her. Why don't we take him out, sir? Put an end to this?"

"I would love to, believe me," Derek said grimly. "But Archangel Michael keeps saying we do not yet have enough information about the big picture—whatever that means."

The cat licked his paw and made a swipe at his ear.

"Yeah, right. Rachel was so depressed and unhappy she forgot to feed me my liver treats before bed last night. I've really come to love those liver treats," Sampson added dolefully. "They're shaped like little fish. I don't suppose you could buy some for me?"

"No, I could not," said Derek, preoccupied.

Angel William had reported some strange doings in the worldwide financial markets, but nothing that couldn't be explained. Yet he and Derek both had a feeling that this was just the lull before the storm. Something dire was in the works.

"Rachel would think buying me a treat was a nice gesture, sir," said Sampson slyly. "She was saying just the other day she was glad we were bonding."

"Did she really say that?" Derek demanded.

"Well, no," Sampson admitted. "But if you bought me the treats, she might."

Derek bought the liver treats.

Two more weeks passed. Rachel performed a number of trades for Zanus's "friend." She came to dread the phone calls from the unknown voice and always walked away from the computer with sweaty palms, a queasy sensation, and the determination to tell Zanus that she wasn't going to do this anymore.

One night, as they were dining at the famous Nick's Fishmarket, and Zanus was going on about how much money they'd made that day, Rachel drew in a deep breath, gathered her courage, and said, "We have made a lot of money. And no one's caught on yet, but it's just a matter of time. Let's stop, right now, while we're ahead."

"Stop?" Zanus smiled at her. "You're not serious."

"I am serious," said Rachel. She took a gulp of wine. "I don't think I can do this anymore."

"My dear," said Zanus, reaching out to stroke her hand. "Am I going to have to make a complaint to Mr. Freeman? Do I tell him that you're not treating me right?"

Zanus continued stroking her hand. She shivered at his touch and tried to slip her hand away, but he caught hold of her, held her firmly in his grasp. "What do you think he would say to that, my dear?"

Rachel knew perfectly well what he would say and she dropped the subject. For they were making money. Lots of money, not only for Zanus and his friend, but he saw to it that she was doing quite well for herself *and* her company. Mr. Freeman had practically hugged her the other day when he passed her in the hall. He would be furious if Zanus complained about her.

She would keep going for a little while, at least.

The next day was Monday. Rachel did her time in the pit and then headed back to her office to go over the day's trades.

Her assistant stopped her before she went inside her office.

"Head's up, Rachel, Mr. Zanus is inside your office. Freeman told him he could wait there until you came back."

Rachel tensed. That was unusual. Zanus never came to the office. He always called her. She wondered what was wrong.

Opening the door, she found Zanus seated at

her desk in her chair. For some reason, that irritated her.

"Hello, Kitten," he said. "Rough day at work?"

Rachel quickly closed the door behind her.

Zanus walked over to her. He removed her briefcase from her shoulder and set it on the desk, then pulled her into his arms, almost lifting her from the floor, and kissed her. Rachel stiffened in his arms. Zanus released her from the kiss, but continued to hold her, though she tried subtly to break away.

"What was that for?" Rachel asked nervously.

"This is me showing my gratitude for having such a wonderful woman in my life," he replied.

"Really?" She gave a forced laugh. "If I didn't know better, I'd say you came here to ask me to do something."

This time, she made no pretense. She broke free and walked behind her desk. She did not sit down, however. Sitting while he stood made her feel vulnerable. She faced him, equal, eyes on the level.

Zanus smiled. "Of course, you're right. You've seen right through my surprise visit. There is something I wanted to talk to you about."

Rachel tried to sound casual. "Okay, ask away."

Zanus leaned near her and said in a low voice, "Rachel, what if I told you that tomorrow the value of the Euro is going to drop fifty percent?"

Rachel drew back away from him. She didn't like the sudden cold, hard glitter in his dark eyes.

"You couldn't possibly know that!" she said, and she tried again to laugh it off. "No one could."

"I don't need you to believe me, Rachel," Zanus said coolly. He placed his hand over her hand. "I do, however, need you to be there first thing tomorrow morning to trade for me."

"I can't do that!" Rachel gasped. "It's illegal. You know I can't do that." She tried to move her hand, but he kept firm hold of it. "Even if I did believe what you're telling me, I can't make trades on nonpublic information or even a rumor of such information—"

Rachel stopped and stared at him. She *did* believe him. It was ridiculous, but she suddenly realized that Zanus knew what he was talking about.

"Dear God!" she breathed. "It's true, isn't it? But how do you know? What—"

"That is my business, Rachel," he said, pressing down firmly on her hand. "And I'm not asking you to do this, my dear. I am telling you. This is not open for debate."

He gave her hand a pat, then walked past her and resumed his seat in her chair. He looked at his fingernails, frowning, as he though he'd had a bad manicure.

"Considering what you've already done for me, Rachel," he said smoothly, "I didn't think this would bother you. You'll get your share of the money, of course, if that's what you're worried about."

Rachel couldn't believe what she was hearing.

"What I did for you before wasn't like this," she told him. "What you want me to do now is totally different. Not only is it against the law, it could affect the world's financial markets. This could cause economic damage worldwide. Not to mention the little matter of me going to jail for thirty years."

Zanus looked up at her. The dark eyes were cold, so cold that she felt her blood freeze to prickly needles of ice.

"Rachel, my dear, I find that I am running out of patience with this discussion." He shrugged. "I don't want to go to your boss and explain to him that I believe that your ethics are compromised. I don't want to show him the evidence of the trades you placed with my friend, evidence that I've kept very carefully. That would most certainly get you fired, and probably blacklisted from the industry. A smear like that could ruin your career."

Rachel staggered, came near to falling. She clutched at the edge of the desk for support. She couldn't believe what she was hearing. This was dreadful, some sort of nightmare.

"Why are you doing this?" Rachel stared at him, horrified. "I don't understand! You come in here and kiss me and now you're threatening me?"

Zanus rose from the chair and walked toward her. He tried to take her in his arms, but she backed away.

"Don't touch me," she said hoarsely.

"Rachel, darling," he said, and his voice was

black velvet, only now it seemed to be smothering her. "You're making this too hard for yourself. Relax. Just do as I say and everything will be fine. It will be better than fine, I promise. This is worth millions. I'm trying to make you one of the wealthiest women in Chicago!"

Rachel turned her head away, avoiding his gaze. She could feel tears welling up in her eyes.

"I know this has been a shock," he said. "I'll let you think about it for a while. I'll pick you up for dinner tonight at seven."

And with that, he strolled out of her office, closing the door behind him.

Rachel collapsed, shaking, behind her desk. How was she going to extricate herself from this mess? She gave a sob, let herself lose control for a moment, then clenched her fists, and tried to pull herself together.

She picked up the phone, called her manager's assistant. "Tell Mr. Freeman that I'm not feeling well. I'm going home for the day."

That wasn't a lie. She'd never felt so sick in her life and that included a bout with double pneumonia. Rachel took her mirror out of her purse, dabbed powder on her red and swollen nose, and wiped off the ruined mascara. She didn't want to look as if she'd been crying when she left the office. Rumors would certainly fly then. First Zanus leaves, then Rachel comes out crying. Everyone would think he'd dumped her.

If only he had!

Rachel drew some deep breaths and prepared

to leave. She made it all the way out the door and into a cab before she broke down again. She stammered out the address of her building to the cab driver, ignored his, "Hey, lady, are you okay back there?"

When he pulled up to her building, Rachel paid him and hurried into the building. Derek was on duty. He rose to his feet, startled that she was home from work so early.

"Rachel, what is it?"

She swept past him without a word. She took the stairs, not wanting to wait for the elevator. Not with him looking at her like that—so caring, so concerned. There was nothing he could do. Nothing anyone could do.

She breathlessly reached her apartment and then stood fumbling with the keys. She couldn't see the lock for her tears. At last, she managed to open the door and stumbled inside. Slamming shut the door behind her, she ran to her bed and collapsed.

She felt something soft touch her shoulder. Looking up, she saw Sampson. He touched her again with his paw, claws retracted, and licked the tears from her cheek. He was so sweet and he was looking at her with such compassion that she sobbed out everything.

Derek had heard Rachel sob as she fled into the stairwell. He guessed immediately that Zanus had done something to her. But what? He had to find out.

"If he has harmed her in any way, I'll kill him,"

Derek muttered. "Orders and Archangel Michael be damned."

Derek was tempted to rush up to her apartment and demand to know what happened. He forced himself to calm down. The most dangerous thing a warrior could do was rush headlong into battle in a rage. Anger blinded a man, left him open to the enemy. Derek had to go about this cool, level-headed, disciplined. He had to have a plan.

Derek stared at the clock, gave himself a half hour, long enough to make it seem plausible, then he went to Rachel's door and listened for a moment, to find out if he could hear anything from inside.

Only silence. That was worse than objects smashing and hysterical weeping. He had to know if she was okay.

Derek knocked gently on her door. At first he was afraid she wouldn't answer, but then he heard her.

"Who is it?" Her voice was muffled.

"It's Derek. I'm sorry to bother you, Rachel, but it's time to walk the cat."

There was a moment's pause, then the door opened. Rachel stood behind the door, so that he had trouble seeing her. What he could see of her looked terrible. Her face was puffy and her eyes were red and nearly swollen shut. She had gone to fetch Sampson and now she thrust the cat and his harness out the door and into Derek's arms.

"Are you okay?" Derek asked, grasping Sampson awkwardly.

"I'm sorry, Derek, I can't talk right now." Rachel slammed shut the door.

A moment later, she opened it and flung out Sampson's leash. She shut the door again.

Derek didn't bother with the leash. Holding the cat in his arms, he headed for the elevator. He noticed that Sampson's fur was wet and he guessed it was from Rachel's tears. He walked the cat up and down in front of the building, so he could keep an eye on things.

"She told me everything, sir," Sampson said, spitting with indignation. "Zanus is blackmailing her. He wants her to do something really bad in the pit tomorrow. Something to do with Euros. I don't understand it, but here's what she told me."

Sampson gave Derek the details, then added, "From what Rachel says, it could have a devastating effect on the world economy! Might touch off riots, rebellions. Even full-scale war—"

"You don't mean bad," said Derek. "You mean apocalyptic."

"I think this is it, Derek. This is the big one. She told him she wouldn't, but he talked about terrible things happening if she didn't cooperate. I don't know what she's going to do. She's supposed to see him tonight to give him her answer."

"This is what he's been leading up to," said Derek. "The other stuff was just to suck her in, give him something on her. Damn it, Archangel Michael let this go too far!"

"We can take him out, Commander," said

Sampson. He unsheathed his claws and bared his fangs.

"I have orders," said Derek glumly. "I have to report this to Angel William. He'll decide what to do."

"That's all, sir?" Sampson glared at him. "You're going to go running to your superiors? Now's the time to fight, not talk. I thought you were a warrior!"

"Not anymore apparently," said Derek bitterly. "Come on. You better go back. At least one of us should be with her. And I've got to go tell William."

"Right, sir," said Sampson.

Derek carried the cat upstairs but paused outside the door.

"Sampson, promise me something."

"Cats don't make promises, but I'll take it under advisement. What do you want, sir?"

"Notify me immediately if anything goes wrong. Even if you don't know what it is. I need to know if she's in danger."

There was a long pause, then Sampson said somberly, "Derek, Rachel's in danger *now*."

Rachel didn't answer when he knocked, so he quietly opened the door. She was asleep on the couch, still clutching soggy tissues in her hand. Not wanting to disturb her, he let Sampson in and placed the leash on her counter. Sampson jumped onto the couch, keeping vigil over Rachel as she slept.

"You take care of her and yourself," Derek warned the cat. "Zanus will stop at nothing."

Sampson curled up inside Rachel's arms.

Derek left to find William. He'd probably be fired if the manager discovered he'd walked off the job, but that didn't matter now. After a long walk through parts of Chicago that no one liked to admit existed, he found William under the Fullerton Street bridge with a lot of other homeless people.

The angel was playing craps.

Fifteen

"I feel a pair of deuces comin' up next, boys! Whaddya say, double or nothing?" William shouted.

Several ragged people in the crowd placed their bets, tossing coins and dollars onto the pavement. Then they all gathered around to watch William's throw.

Lifting his right hand in the air, William shook the dice and then threw them against the wall. He gazed at them expectantly as they bounced to the street.

A pair of fours came up.

William groaned and shook his head. Cheers came from the crowd.

"William?" Derek exclaimed, amazed.

The angel jumped and whipped around.

"Oh, uh, hullo, Derek." William gave a sheepish grin and stuffed his hands in his pockets.

"Are you gambling?" Derek asked.

"Well, yes, you did catch me indulging in a game of chance or two. But I'm not really gambling," William hastened to assure him. He edged closer to Derek, grabbed him by the collar and whispered, "You see, the dice are loaded."

"You're cheating these people?" Derek said, shocked.

"No, no, no," said William hurriedly. "It's not like that." He smiled proudly. "I always lose! People hate charity, but they love losers. Besides, I do so enjoy craps," he added wistfully. "And it's been years since I played. Not allowed up there, you know." He cast his gaze heavenward.

"If I could tear you away from your game for a moment, I need to have a word with you. There's news," Derek said.

"Yes, of course." William pulled some money out of his pockets, tossed it on the ground, and followed Derek down the alley. "What have you heard?"

"Zanus is making his move. He's blackmailing Rachel, asking her to do something in the market tomorrow. I don't understand it—"

"Tell me everything you know," said William.

Derek explained what he'd heard from Sampson. William nodded and looked very grave.

"This is serious, Derek. You were right when you said it was apocalyptic. Will she do it? Do you know?" William asked urgently.

"She doesn't know what she's going to do." Derek shook his head. "He told her he'd expect her decision tonight. William, it's tearing her apart. We've got to do something." Derek's fists clenched. It was obvious what he wanted to do.

"We *are* doing something, Derek," William said severely. "You and Sampson will maintain your position of surveillance. We can't intervene. Not at this moment. She must make this decision herself. It's critical." William scratched his beard and sighed deeply.

Derek glared at him. "What do you mean, we can't intervene. I have to stop him. I have to stop her."

"Derek, calm down," William said sharply. "Listen to me. Our mission here is not to win this battle, but to win the war. We need to know who else is involved. A single archfiend didn't bring this about on his own. There's a worldwide network here. We need to know who Zanus is working with and then we can take them all down. Do you understand?"

"No, I don't understand!" Derek returned angrily. "Rachel is in danger. What if she does refuse, William? She'll lose her job, maybe even go to prison or worse. Zanus won't take no for an answer. He might kill her, for God's sake—"

"Use your brain, Derek!" William admonished. "He won't harm her physically. He needs her cooperation and he knows she would never help him if he carried out his threats. He's trying to scare her, coerce her."

Derek shook his head, unconvinced. "We should destroy him—"

"We can't. Not now. You're not seeing the whole picture, Derek. You just see one little part of it. Heaven *does* know what it's doing."

"I've heard that before!" Derek retorted. "When the Inquisition was breaking my bones on the rack!"

"Derek, you have let yourself get personally involved," said William sternly. "I warned you about that. Am I going to have to remove you? I don't want to." His voice softened. "Your work so far has been invaluable, the information we've gained . . . But I will if you force me to do so."

Derek eyed him grimly. His fists were still clenched. He was looking at William, but all he was seeing was Rachel, so miserable and unhappy. He could still feel her tears on Sampson's fur.

"Yes, I'm personally involved," Derek said with quiet dignity. "Yes, I love her. But isn't love what Heaven's supposed to be all about?"

He turned on his heel and walked away. He could feel William staring after him. He could feel the angel's sympathy and also his worry.

"Don't worry," Derek shot back over his shoulder. "I'll obey. I've obeyed for several hundred years. I'm not going to stop now."

Frustrated, he walked back to the building and returned to his post. He couldn't do anything but sit and watch and wait. He felt as if he was being stretched on the rack all over again.

* * *

The familiar black limousine pulled up in front of the building. Derek waited tensely for Rachel to walk out of the elevator, but she didn't appear. His heart swelled with admiration and pride. *She's not coming. She's not going to go through with it. So you can just drive away, Mr. Archfiend. Go back to your seat by the fire . . .*

The door of the limo opened. Zanus stepped out. His face was dark and ugly, his lips compressed.

Zanus entered the building and walked up to Derek's desk.

"Call Ms. Duncan and tell her I am here," Zanus ordered him.

Derek was tempted to take the phone cord and wrap it around the fiend's neck and choke him to death—slowly. He had promised to obey orders, and, like a good soldier, he would. Besides, he had a feeling he was going to enjoy this.

"Who should I say is calling?" he asked pleasantly.

"You know who is calling," said Zanus coldly. "And if you know what is good for you, you'll do as you're told."

Derek put in a call to Rachel's apartment.

"Ms. Duncan, this is Derek. You have a guest waiting for you in the lobby."

He heard her make a choking sound. Then she drew a ragged breath and said, "Tell Zanus I'm not feeling well. I won't be able to come to dinner with him this evening."

She hung up the phone.

Derek had to fight back a grin as he delivered the message.

"Mr. Zanus, Ms. Rachel sends her regrets, she is ill and will not be able to go to dinner with you this evening. I suppose you'll be on your way, then?" Derek added, rising to his feet. "Here let me hold the door for you—"

Zanus's face darkened. "The hell she will!" he muttered. He shoved his way past Derek, stepped outside the building to stand under the awning. Zanus deftly flipped open his cell phone.

He spoke briefly into the phone, then hung up and returned to the car. Derek expected it to pull away, but it remained.

He began to get worried. Fifteen minutes later, Rachel emerged from the elevator. She looked pale and ill.

Derek rose to his feet. He wanted so much to tell her she didn't have to do this. She just had to say the word and he would defy Heaven itself for her.

"Rachel . . ." he said softly.

She just shook her head and strode past him, walking more quickly now, as though she feared if she slowed down, she would not make it at all.

We'll get you out of this, Rachel, Derek promised her silently. *Just be strong. It'll all turn out okay.*

He remained at his post until they returned, determined to make certain that Rachel arrived home safely.

The limo pulled up earlier than usual. Rachel

stepped out and walked to the front door of the building. She didn't look behind her and so she didn't see Zanus emerging from the other side. Derek walked over to the door and held it open.

Zanus came up behind her and grabbed hold of Rachel's arm. "I think you should reconsider—"

Rachel turned around. She was extremely pale, but she was in control. "We've already gone through this. I don't plan to continue this discussion. Please let go of me. I'm not feeling very well and I have to be up early in the morning."

Zanus continued to hold on to her. His expression was grim. "Then let me come up with you. I want to make sure you're all right."

"I am quite capable of taking care of myself," Rachel returned. Her eyes glimmered with tears, but she blinked them back. "Please let go of me."

Her eyes connected with Derek's. That was all the signal he needed. Derek stepped outside and laid his hand on Zanus's arm.

"Ms. Duncan asked you to let go of her," said Derek.

"Rachel, I insist—" Zanus was saying, talking past Derek to Rachel.

"I believe Ms. Duncan asked you to leave, sir," Derek said again. Then he gave Zanus's arm an expert twist. Zanus grunted in pain and released his hold on Rachel. She escaped inside the door. Zanus's gaze focused on Derek. The fiend's black eyes fixed balefully on him.

"This is none of your business, boy," Zanus said curtly and he started to shove Derek out of the way. "Trust me," said the fiend. "You don't want to make this your business."

"On the contrary," Derek stated calmly. "My business is protecting the inhabitants of this building. One of those inhabitants has asked you to leave. Now either you do so on your own or I will be glad to assist you. More than glad."

Rachel was now in the building. She hadn't gone up to her apartment yet, however. She was standing near in the lobby.

Zanus paused for a moment as though he was reevaluating the situation. He gazed intently at Derek, then called past Derek's shoulder, his words meant for Rachel.

"Darling, I'm sorry I upset you. Please get some rest tonight. Tomorrow is a big day," he said, his tone fraught with meaning.

Zanus then turned his gaze to Derek, who still had fast hold of him.

"I know who you are, Commander," Zanus said in a soft voice, his words meant for the two of them alone. "And you should consider working for our side." He glanced with scorn at Derek's uniform. "The expense accounts are better."

He broke free of Derek's grasp and walked down the stairs toward the limo's open door. Derek stayed where he was until the car drove off.

"He's gone," Derek said. He turned around and walked over to her, touching her shoulder gently. "Don't be afraid. I'll stay here all night. He won't bother you."

"Thank you," Rachel said brokenly.

She looked ready to crumple, so Derek swept her up in his arms. "I'll take you to your apartment."

"I can walk," she protested. "You don't have to carry me—" She gave a wan smile. "That's not really part of the duties of a doorman."

"How do you know?" Derek asked, tightening his grip on her. "Have you read the doorman's handbook? 'Carrying fainting women to their apartments.' It's on page ninety-six."

She tried to smile, but her lips quivered. "Oh, Derek, I've done something terrible, and I'm in such trouble, and there's no way out of it." A tear slid down her cheek.

"Yes, there is," he said, his heart aching for her anguish. "Tell me what I can do."

"You can't do anything," she returned in hopeless, despairing tones. "No one can. I've done this to myself."

She closed her eyes and rested her head on his shoulder. She did not sob. She cried silently and that was worse. He watched the tears slide down her cheeks. He felt her warmth, felt her body tremble against his. He smelled the fragrance of her hair that brushed his cheek and the softness of her breasts pressed against his chest. He was overcome by desire and love and pity and anger, so that for a moment it seemed his heart would burst from the pain. The pain of longing. The pain of love. The pain of frustration.

He had not felt this angry at God since He had abandoned him so long ago. If he could have, he would have stormed into Heaven this moment, gone raging to stand at the throne of the Lord, and railed against Heaven.

He couldn't, however. That would only make things worse. And, besides, he couldn't leave Rachel.

She insisted on walking on her own. He accompanied her to her apartment, keeping his arm around her, holding her close, letting her lean on him. She didn't speak, but she seemed to find comfort in his nearness. When they came to her door, she looked up at him.

"Thank you, Derek. You've turned out to be a true friend. I want you to know I appreciate it."

She put her key in the door.

"Let me help," he said.

She turned around, faced him. "You are," she said. "Just by being here."

She opened the door. Derek waited outside to make certain nothing was amiss.

Sampson was there, claws out, back arched, tail puffed up like a bottle brush, ready to attack.

"It's okay, Sampson," said Rachel, bending down to pick up the cat. "It's Derek. Not Zanus."

She rubbed her cheek against Sampson's head. "They say animals are good judges of people. Sampson never has liked Zanus. I should have known."

"Try to get some sleep," Derek advised.

Rachel shook her head. "I'm so wired I'm not sure I can. Besides, I have a decision to make. Good night, Derek. Thank you again."

She shut the door.

Sampson's voice rang in Derek's head.

"Will Rachel be safe tonight?" Sampson asked anxiously.

"I hope so," said Derek, and he sighed. "I don't know, though. She told Zanus she wouldn't go along with him, but he has a pretty strong hold on her. I'm not sure what she'll do."

"What do *we* do?" Sampson asked.

"Our orders are to do nothing," Derek said grimly.

"Well, then, if *we're* not supposed to do anything, is somebody up there doing something?" Sampson demanded.

"I hope so," said Derek. "I certainly hope so."

Sixteen

When Derek returned to the lobby, the night man was on duty. Derek told him that there'd been a problem between one of the tenants and a man who was harassing her. On no account was this man to be allowed into the building. Derek gave the night man a description of Zanus, then went to his apartment. He paced back and forth, thinking through the situation and he came to the unfortunate realization that while Zanus wouldn't be likely to harm Rachel because he needed her to assist him in his nefarious schemes, Zanus didn't need Derek at all. And he undoubtedly considered Derek a serious threat. He wondered what Zanus would do to him, suspected it would be something nasty.

Derek was still pacing when his phone rang.

He stared at it. He'd been thinking so much about Zanus, he had the strange feeling this had something to do with the archfiend. Derek glanced at the clock on the wall. It was past midnight.

He picked up the phone. "Yeah," he answered warily.

"Derek, it's William."

"What is it?" Derek asked, alarmed. William never called him.

"I was going to ask you the same question?" William sounded upset. "What did you do tonight?"

Derek shrugged. "Me? Nothing."

"Derek," William returned, "you can't lie to me. I'm like Santa Claus. I know if you've been bad or good—"

"I may have had a little altercation with Zanus," said Derek.

"*May* have?" William repeated.

"All right. I twisted his arm," Derek admitted. "He knows I am a heavenly warrior. He called me 'Commander.' But I didn't have a choice. He was trying to force Rachel to let him come up to her apartment. She asked me to stop him and I had to do what she asked. It's my job—"

"It's not your job to twist the arm of an archfiend!" William groaned. "I might have known you'd do something bone-headed like this. I've received information from Archangel Michael that the Dark Angels are meeting tonight, and I think you and Rachel are the reason. Zanus is afraid you're going to try to influence her."

"He's right," said Derek grimly. "Where is this meeting?" he asked in casual tones.

"Some bar called Apokalypse. Nice name, huh? Don't worry. We'll take care of it. I just want you to remain alert and from now on—"

"I'll do that." Derek started to hang up the phone.

"Don't you hang up on me!" William was practically shouting into the receiver. "I know what you're thinking and don't even consider it. You keep out of this, do you hear me? Derek, I'm ordering you to stay out of this—"

"William, this isn't something I'd ordinarily say to an angel, but—go to hell!"

"Derek!" William cried urgently. "Listen to me. I didn't want to say anything, because I know how you'll react, but I'm beginning to suspect that something's not right in Heaven and that you could be walk—"

Derek slammed down the phone. He felt good, better than he had in a long time. At last he could take action and help Rachel make her decision.

Derek quickly dialed her apartment. The phone rang several times. She wouldn't recognize his number and she'd be afraid to answer. He hung up, dialed again.

"Pick it up!" he urged her mentally.

"Hello?" Rachel answered in trepidation. "Who is this?"

"Rachel, it's Derek."

"He's not here, is he?" Rachel said, frightened. "Zanus? He didn't come back?"

"No, but this is about him." Derek wondered how he was going to explain. He decided a little lying was in order. What she had said the other night in the coffee shop gave him an idea. "Listen, Rachel, I have not been exactly honest with you. The truth is I belong to an organization that sent me here to keep an eye on Zanus . . ."

He waited for her reaction. There was silence, then she said quietly, "I knew it . . ."

"Zanus is a really bad man, Rachel, and I can prove it to you. I need you to put on some jeans or something inconspicuous and some sensible shoes"—he emphasized this—"and meet me downstairs by the back door so the night man doesn't get curious. I have something to show you tonight, something that might help you . . . figure out some things."

There was another moment of silence, then she said, "Give me five minutes."

"Oh, and do what you can to disguise yourself," Derek added. "He must not recognize us."

Derek grabbed the only street clothes he owned—jeans, a white tank top, leather jacket, and boots. He looked up the address for the Apokalypse in the phone book, consulted a map, located the street, and then waited for Rachel by the back door, where the deliveries were made.

She came out of the service elevator and Derek went to meet her. She was dressed in blue jeans, a sweater, a hoody and tennis shoes, and she had suddenly acquired long red hair and smoky-lensed glasses.

"Halloween," she said in reply to Derek's startled glance. She looked at him and her gaze was serious. "I think you should tell me what's going on."

"I am sorry," he said. "I cannot. I have already broken the rules as it is by letting you in on this much." He shrugged. "They are probably going to take me off this assignment anyway. The truth is . . ." He drew in a deep breath, gazed down at her. "I've become emotionally involved."

They were standing beneath the bright security light in the back of the building. He smiled to see a blush spread over her cheeks.

She reached out and took hold of his hand. "I hope they don't take you off this assignment."

"You have to trust me, Rachel. Can you do that?"

She regarded him steadfastly, gazed at him intently. "Things like this only happen on television."

"I wish they did," said Derek earnestly. "I truly wish they did. We should go now. We do not have much time to lose."

"I do trust you," she said and her grip on his hand tightened.

"And I accept your trust as a sacred responsibility. I will not let anything happen to you. I swear on my honor as a . . ."

"As a what?" she asked, as they were walking through the parking lot.

"As your doorman," he said, smiling at her. "Here is the address. I don't know the city that well. Do you know how to get there?"

Rachel looked at the note. "Yes, I know the street. It's not far. You know," she added, as they headed down the sidewalk. "I guessed you were ex-military. You are, aren't you?"

Derek was startled. "You did? How?"

Rachel shrugged. "The way you carry yourself. Strong and proud and unafraid." She bit her lip and blinked back sudden tears. "I've been a fool, haven't I?"

"It was not your fault," said Derek. "You could not know."

"I don't suppose you can tell me the truth about Zanus?"

"I cannot," said Derek grimly. "But he can."

At Rachel's direction, they headed for the nearest el train station, there wasn't time to wait for a cab. The train was almost deserted. They sat in silence, Derek thinking how much trouble he was going to be in. He wondered what Rachel was thinking. She appeared dazed, as though she couldn't believe this was happening.

"This is our stop," she said, shepherding Derek off the train.

They located the street, which wasn't a street so much as an alley. There was no sign of a bar. No neon lights, no door, no windows. Nothing showing any sign of life anywhere. Just a bunch of closed and boarded-up shops. Yet, this had to be the place. And, of course, the bar would be hard to find, out of the way. You couldn't expect the Dark Ones to be holding a secret meeting in the Ritz Carlton.

Rachel was starting to look dubious. She glanced at Derek and frowned. "Are you sure this is the right address?"

"I'm sure," he said.

Derek waited. If he stood here long enough, he would see or hear something.

"Derek, this isn't the best neighborhood—" Rachel began.

"Shhhh, just wait another couple of moments."

"Wait for what?"

His patience was rewarded.

A door slammed.

"For that," he said.

The sound had come from an alleyway behind them. He heard two voices, those of a man and a woman. Derek walked toward the opening of an alley, keeping Rachel behind him, both of them staying in the shadows. The man and woman were headed in their direction, walking toward the street.

The woman had bright purple hair and wore a black leather jacket adorned with chains. The man had jet black hair, done in spikes, and also wore a leather jacket and boots. The two were in their own world, discussing a new band and speculating on the odds of finding a taxi at this time of night. They didn't notice Derek or Rachel. He waited for them to pass, then continued on down the alley.

He spotted the door and a sign above it: Club Apokalypse. The sign had apparently once been lit by a floodlight, but the lightbulb had burned out and had not been replaced, so that was the reason they hadn't seen it earlier.

They came to the door, but there was no way to open it.

"What kind of bar is this?" Derek asked, frustrated.

"It's a private club," said Rachel. "Members only. They probably won't let us inside unless we know someone."

"Well, we do know someone," said Derek. "Wait a moment. I don't want him to recognize us."

He scruffed his hair, dragging it over his face, and turned up his jacket collar. Rachel messed up her red hair and shook it in her face. Reaching into her purse, she brought out a tube of lipstick and smeared it over her lips. She drew the hood of her jacket over her head and slouched down, hunching her shoulders.

"Okay, follow my lead," Derek said.

He knocked on the door.

A man opened it. The man's face was covered with tattoos. There were tattoos under his eyes, above his eyebrows, and down his neck. As an odd contrast, the tattooed man was dressed in a tux. He eyed Derek and grunted.

"Yeah?"

Derek raised his eyebrows, as though startled by the question. "Can we come in?"

"Members only," said the man. "How'd you hear about this place?"

"Zanus told me," said Derek. He could see

lights and hear the sounds of laughter in the background. "He's having a meeting here tonight. He told me to meet him here."

"Zanus." The man grunted. "Never heard of him."

"Well, if you do hear of him, you can tell him I came like he ordered. And you can also tell him that you were the one who wouldn't let me inside."

Derek thrust his hands in the pockets of his leather jacket and motioned to Rachel for them to leave. They started to walk off.

"Hey, wait. Don't get your shorts in a knot," the guard grumbled. "You are a little on the grubby side to be one of us, but I guess Mr. Zanus knows what he's doing. They're in the back. You're late."

He stepped aside to let Derek pass. The doorman stopped Rachel.

"Who's she? No one said anything about a woman."

"She's the reason I'm late. She's with me." Derek winked at the doorman.

The doorman looked her up and down. Rachel stared right back. "Like what you see?" she demanded.

"Not particularly," said the tattooed man, and he let her pass.

They walked into the bar and both of them came to a stop and stared. Judging by its back-alley location, Derek had expected a dive, a low-life hangout. What he found was an upscale jazz club. The place was lit with soft blue and purple light. The waitresses, dressed in elegantly revealing satin dresses, moved quietly among the patrons seated in comfortable chairs. A trio of sax, bass, and piano occupied a raised dais, playing music that made the soul ache. Smoke hung in the air. Quiet laughter blended with the music.

A waitress met Derek, offered to show him and Rachel to a table. "I'm meeting someone," he told her.

"Mr. Zanus?" The waitress smiled. "He's over there."

She indicated the back of the room, gave Derek another smile and an arch glance. "If you're interested, I get off work at four A.M." she said, adding to Rachel. "You got lipstick on your teeth, honey."

Rachel took out a tissue and rubbed her teeth.

"Now what?" She looked suddenly afraid. "You're not going to confront Zanus here, are you? He mustn't catch me here."

"He won't know you're here. We're going to do a little eavesdropping, that's all. Keep close to me."

Zanus and several other men were seated in high-backed black leather chairs around a table. Each man had a brandy glass in front of him and all were smoking cigars. Zanus was speaking; the others were listening intently.

Blessing the smoke and the dim lighting, Derek led Rachel among the tables, heading for the back of the room. They kept their faces lowered. People stared at them as they passed. They did look out of place. Everyone else was wearing evening clothes, with the exception of two guys packing up instruments on the stage. The couple they'd seen must have been band members.

Derek chose a booth near the table where Zanus was sitting. This suited his purpose perfectly. The booth was positioned so that their backs were to Zanus. The man's deep voice carried well. Derek and Rachel could hear every word and remain hidden from view. The waitress came by and they ordered drinks, just to keep up appearances. When she brought them, neither of them touched them.

Derek settled back to listen, then he noticed that Rachel had gone extremely pale. He reached out and took hold of her hand. She squeezed his tightly.

". . . and, Sebastian," Zanus was saying, "I want you to report back to my office to keep watch as soon as we're finished here. Now, to business. The female is completely under my control."

"You're sure about that?"

"I'm sure," said Zanus and he smiled and blew a smoke ring.

Rachel's face had been pale, but now it was flushed with anger. "That bastard . . ."

"Shhh!" Derek warned.

"She will execute the trades tomorrow. The Eurodollar's price will skyrocket on false data supported by the female's trades and then when our partners in Europe make their move, the bottom will drop out. There will be worldwide chaos."

"What about the female?" someone asked. "She can't be permitted to talk."

"She will be so distraught over what she has done that she will kill herself." Zanus spoke matter-of-factly, without emotion.

"Are you sure?" the man sounded dubious. "You can't trust these humans."

"I am sure," Zanus replied, adding coldly, "we will make sure."

Rachel gave a little gasp and covered her mouth with her hand. She rose quickly to her feet. "Let's go!" she said shakily.

Derek stood up. They'd heard enough.

They wended their way among the tables, Rachel taking the lead and Derek following, keeping one eye on Zanus. None of his group had noticed them. They were almost at the door when the waitress cried, "Hey, stop those two! They didn't pay their bar tab!"

"Run!" Derek told Rachel, giving her a shove.

She looked back at him, her face strained.

"Get out of here!" he ordered. "He can't see you!"

Rachel hesitated a moment, then did as he ordered. She ran. The tattooed bouncer made a move to stop her. As he put his hands on her, Rachel kneed him in the groin. He doubled over with a groan, grabbing at himself.

Rachel darted out the door.

A blow on the back of Derek's right knee

knocked his leg out from under him. He stumbled and fell flat on the floor.

"He's drunk!" said a woman in disgust.

Derek twisted around to see the man who had kicked him, one of Zanus's associates. He looked down at Derek and smiled.

"I think we should take a walk to help you sober up, Commander. These gentlemen will be happy to assist you."

Four men stood over him, staring down at him as he tried to pick himself up off the floor. He cursed himself for a fool. Now he realized what William had been trying to tell him if Derek had taken the time to listen.

You could be walking into a trap!

Zanus caught Derek's eye and raised his cigar to him.

"What about the red-head, boss?" the man asked over his shoulder. "Do we go after her?"

"What do you think, stupid?" Zanus asked, putting his cigar to his lips.

One guy ran out of the bar in pursuit of Rachel. She had a good head start and Derek could only hope she got away safely. There was nothing he could do for her now, except put in a prayer to those Higher Up. He wouldn't pray for himself; he'd tried that before and God had spurned him. But Heaven might be more disposed to look out for Rachel.

Two of the four guys seized hold of Derek,

grabbing him by the arms. They jerked him off his feet and hustled him out the door, held open by the guy with the tattoos, who was standing all hunched over. He glared at Derek. "Tell your girlfriend she'll pay for this."

Derek just grunted.

"Work him over, boys, enough to take the fight out of him, then haul him off to headquarters. Mr. Zanus wants to finish the discussion in person," the tattooed guy ordered and slammed shut the door.

Derek struggled to free himself, but the four men were big and strong and knew their business. They carried Derek out into the alley, and pitched him up against the wall.

He landed hard and fell to the street. One of them came at him, ready to kick him. Derek rolled away, flipped over onto his stomach, and jumped to his feet. He put his back to the wall and considered his options.

There weren't many.

The alley was a cul-de-sac, only one way out, and Zanus's minions were between him and the exit. He had no weapon, only his fists. At least, he thought, they're not armed. But they were eight fists to his two. He needed something to even the odds. His gaze fell on a beer bottle that had rolled up against the wall.

He wondered why the thugs hadn't rushed him yet. Looking back at them, he saw the reason and his heart sank.

He'd been wrong. They did have weapons. They had the weapons of the damned.

The thugs were no longer thugs. They were demons who had crawled up from depths of the pit. It was as if he could see them burning in the flames. Their flesh blackened and withered on their bones. Dark wings sprouted from their backs. Their teeth sharpened to fangs, their fingernails lengthened to claws.

He recognized them—demon minions who served the archfiends. For centuries, he'd fought their kind in Purgatory. But then he'd had his flaming sword and the power of Heaven in his arms and hands. Here he had nothing but a beer bottle. And, somehow, he didn't think God was going to bless that beer bottle.

The fire of their rage burned bright in their red, slit eyes.

Work him over, then take him to headquarters.

Headquarters. Their headquarters. Known by various names: Hades, Sheol, Gehenna, Tophet, Abaddon, Naraka . . .

Hell.

Imprisonment. Torture. Just like the Inquisition. And, just like the Inquisition, God wasn't going to give a damn . . .

Slavering and gibbering, the demons leapt on him.

Derek gave a sideways lunge, grabbed hold of the beer bottle, and came up swinging. He struck one of the demons in the face. The bottle smashed. The demon howled and staggered backward, clutching at the socket where its red eye had been. The other three fell back.

Derek faced them, swinging the broken beer bottle, holding them momentarily at bay.

The Dark Ones watched him warily and he wondered almost angrily what they were waiting for. Then he knew. They were waiting for him to use his angelic powers! They, too, had fought in Purgatory. They feared him, feared the dread warrior angels. They didn't know he wasn't permitted to use those powers. They were waiting for that beer bottle to change to a silver sword, for his face to glow with the radiance of Heaven, and his hands to fling lightning bolts.

Are they ever gonna feel stupid! Derek thought. His face was glowing, but only with sweat. The beer bottle was nothing but a damn beer bottle.

The demon who'd lost an eye said something in its horrible language to its fellows. One of them cackled. They were starting to get the idea.

Why not use my powers? Derek wondered, suddenly tempted. He could hear Archangel Michael's sonorous voice.

It is too dangerous. We cannot risk being discovered.

They don't care about being discovered. Why should I?

Because you are different. And now it was William's voice he heard. *You swore an oath of obedience and you are a man of honor.*

"I died once a man of honor," said Derek grimly. "Looks like I might do the same again."

The demon who'd lost an eye charged Derek. He jumped to the side, dodging the creature's fangs, only to feel its clawed feet swipe at his legs. He staggered back, right into the arms of a second demon coming at him from behind. Lifting Derek in its clawed hands, it slammed him against the wall of the alley.

Derek heard ribs crack and felt searing pain in his chest. He slumped to the ground, gasping painfully for breath. One of the demons grabbed him by the hair, lifted him up. Its claws raked across his chest, slicing his shirt and his flesh to ribbons. Blood streamed from the wounds. He gasped and moaned from the burning pain.

Dear lord, he wouldn't last long like this! He was a warrior. He would not disobey his orders and use his powers, not to save himself.

But to save Rachel . . .

One of the demons kicked Derek in the stomach. He doubled over, groaning. Another smashed him in the head and drove him to the ground. He tried to get up. The demons began to rain blows on him. He was starting to lose consciousness and then, suddenly, a dazzling white light was in his eyes.

God had not forsaken him.

The blows ceased. The demons let go of him.

He heard the Dark Ones chattering in anger and then he heard the sound of an engine and smelled diesel fumes. The light wasn't shining from the bright halos of a heavenly host. It was shining from the headlights of a garbage truck that was pulling into the alley.

Immediately, the demons shifted form, changing back into ordinary humans. They bent over Derek, as if they were helping him. The driver rolled down the window. Leaning out of the truck, he called, "Everything okay here, boys?"

"Our friend's had a little too much to drink," one of the thugs said and he took hold of Derek's arms, apparently with the intention of dragging him back into the club.

And then a voice rang out with the fury of a heavenly trumpet. "That's them, boys! They're the ones who have been beating up our friends. Let 'em have it!"

Derek lifted his head in wonder. The voice was William's!

Suddenly the night was filled with shouts and curses and flying objects. Leaping off the garbage truck, William's cavalry of homeless warriors charged into battle, flinging rotten tomatoes, old shoes, rocks, cans, and cabbages at the disguised demons. The attack took the thugs completely by surprise. They tried to run for the safety of the bar, but the barrage momentarily pinned them down. All they could do was raise their arms over their heads, try to protect themselves.

Derek glanced over at the bar, saw the door open. Zanus stood there, staring out. His face was dark, his expression grim. His eyes caught Derek's.

Bring it on, you bastard, Derek fumed.

The thugs finally ran for the safety of the bar. Zanus waited until they had ducked inside. He gave Derek one last baleful look. His lips moved.

Derek couldn't hear him, but he knew what Zanus was saying.

"This is not over between us."

Zanus slammed the door shut. The homeless kept up the barrage, flinging garbage and vegetation at the door and yelling for the cowards to come out.

Then came the distant wail of police sirens.

"Come on, boys!" William ordered, taking charge. "You best get out of here! Go ahead. I'll stay with my friend. Don't worry! And don't forget to return that truck like we promised!"

"We won't, boss!" shouted the driver.

The ragged warriors gave a whoop of triumph, leaped onto the truck, and it backed down the alley, turned around, and went careening off down the street.

William knelt beside Derek.

"Are you hurt badly? I can't tell through all the blood," William asked anxiously.

"Just help me stand," Derek gasped. "Did Rachel get away?"

William grabbed his arm, assisted him to rise.

Every breath sent pain shooting through Derek. He gasped and staggered, nearly fell.

"You're going to have to heal yourself," said William.

Derek looked at him in astonishment. "That is against the rules."

"Yes," said William. "I can't explain now. Just do it, will you? Be quick about it and don't let anyone see you!"

Derek turned his attention to the human body that had been so maltreated. He had broken ribs, a punctured lung, damaged internal organs, a broken arm and wrist.

"Bastards," he muttered, as he worked, sending warmth and healing power throughout his battered frame.

Once he was feeling more himself, he looked at William. "Did Rachel get away?" he asked again, insistently.

"Yes, she caught a taxi. The last I saw of her, she was dialing nine-one-one to send the cops in to rescue you. Of course, that couldn't be allowed. She's safe. No thanks to you."

William was extremely angry. Derek had never seen an angel so mad. His eyes blazed. Derek understood now what was meant by the "wrath of Heaven." He was facing that wrath right now.

"What were you thinking?" William raved. "You put her and yourself in terrible danger."

"I had to make her see Zanus for what he was," said Derek stubbornly. "She knows him now. He talked about how he planned to use her and then murder her."

"And so what will she do now that she *does* know?" William demanded. "Let's say she refuses to make the trades. Zanus will want to know why. What does she tell him? That she was here tonight? That she found out everything he was plotting? What will he do to her then? You've put her in more danger than she was before, Derek! He *has* to kill her now."

Derek stared grimly at William. The Angel was right, of course. Derek didn't know what to say.

"I told you we would take care of this, Derek. Next time, maybe you'll listen to me."

"The solution is simple," Derek argued. "Zanus knows we are on to him. We bring the fight to him, stop him from affecting the world economy."

William shook his head. "It's much more complicated than that, Derek. He's just a small part of this."

"What do you mean? How is it complicated?" Derek demanded.

"I can't explain. Not yet. I have my suspicions, but I have to make absolutely certain. If what I think is true, it will shake the very foundations of Heaven."

William sighed deeply, then rested his hand on Derek's arm. "You came very near destroying everything we've worked for, son. For once, just do as you're told. Go back and keep an eye on Rachel."

"What about Rachel?" Derek asked stubbornly. "What if she is so scared she goes along with Zanus? We can stop her. Lock her in the laundry room."

William shook his head. "All humans have free will, Derek. That is God's gift to them and that is what the Dark Lord wants to take away. The Dark Angels want to make humans slaves. That's what the fight between us is all about. Don't you understand this yet? Rachel has to make this decision herself. You've done your best to help, though you probably did more harm than good. The decision must be up to her now."

Derek didn't understand. He didn't want to argue with William, though. He owed the angel one.

"Anyway, thank you, sir," said Derek contritely. "I would have been on my way to the bad place if you had not come for me."

"If you had faith in Heaven, son, you would've known that I'd come," William said, and, sighing again, he walked away.

Seventeen

For the rest of the night, Derek struggled with the inner demons that were putting up as big a battle as the real ones he'd faced in the alley. Despite what William had said about this being Rachel's decision, Derek longed to go and tell her what to do. He could not sleep. He was frantic to know what decision Rachel would make. One moment, he thought she would defy Zanus and stay home from work. In which case, Zanus would probably come here after her. Derek was hoping that this was what she would choose. He would like nothing better than to tackle the archfiend again—one on one. Not even William could fault him for that, for Derek was obeying orders. He was watching out for Rachel.

Then again, if she did decide to defy Zanus, she

would be putting herself and her friends in danger. Perhaps it would be better if she went along with him. Heaven knew what was going on now. Perhaps they could act to stop things.

He tried calling her, but her phone was turned off. Of course, she wouldn't want to talk to Zanus. Figuring that he might be needed, either by Rachel or William or both, Derek called in his replacement, then told the manager he was taking the day off.

When it was her usual time to go to work, he stayed inside his apartment, keeping the door open, watching for Rachel. She came out of the elevator and he went out to meet her. She was a mess. Her hair was uncombed. She wore no makeup. Her clothes looked as if she'd grabbed them up out of the dirty laundry and flung them on without paying any attention to what she was wearing.

She headed for Derek's desk. "Are you all right? I've been worried sick! I tried to call the police, but for some reason my phone quit working! I tried to convince the cabbie to call nine-one-one, but he didn't speak English." Rachel sighed and ran her hand distractedly through her hair. "I guess I could have called you, but I've been afraid to even turn the phone on. I don't want to hear his voice . . ."

"Uh, everything worked out okay," said Derek soothingly. "As you can see. I managed to get away."

"But he saw you!" Rachel said. "You blew your cover!"

"Actually, my bosses think it may have helped.

Pushed him to act before he is ready. The important thing is that he didn't see you."

Derek was about to ask her what she'd decided to do, when he saw the car that normally picked her up in the morning pull up in front of the building.

"I've got to go, Derek," she said hurriedly. "I'm glad you're safe. I was . . . worried."

"Where are you going?" he asked, following her to the door.

"To work," she said. "I need some normalcy in my life."

"Are you going to do the trades?" he asked tensely.

She didn't look at him. "I don't know," she said. "I haven't made up my mind."

She paused, then said softly, "I know what I should do, Derek. I should go to Mr. Freeman and confess everything. But . . . I'm afraid. When I heard Zanus say those terrible things . . ."

She lifted her gaze, met his. "Can this organization of yours help me?"

Derek didn't know what to tell her. He wanted more than anything on Earth or in Heaven to reassure her, to say yes, they would help, but had no idea what William was doing behind the scenes and he didn't want to make promises he couldn't keep.

She sighed. "I didn't think so. Don't feel bad. I did this to myself. I've got to go."

She hurried out the door, jumped into the car, and it drove off.

* * *

Derek went back to his apartment to get dressed. He had done some research on the Merc, as Rachel called it. He knew they didn't allow unauthorized personnel to go onto the trading floor, but they did offer tours and there was a place where tourists could look down into the pit and see the action. He could keep an eye on Rachel today.

When he was dressed, Derek dashed upstairs to talk to Sampson.

"She laid down, but she didn't sleep after she got back," Sampson reported. "She kept rolling around in bed and squishing me. Her house phone rang and she pulled the cord out of the wall."

"I am going after her," said Derek. "I will be late for our walk today."

"That's all right, sir. I don't suppose you could take me with you?" Sampson asked.

"No," said Derek firmly.

"I guess not. You don't know how hard it is, sir. Having to sit around and do nothing all day while Rachel might be in danger."

Derek was halfway out the door when he paused, looked back at the cherub. Sampson looked very forlorn. He was all scruffy and the cat food, clearly dumped hurriedly in the general direction of a bowl, was untouched.

"I do know," said Derek. "You have done a really good job, Sampson. I am proud of you."

"Are you, sir?" Sampson perked up. "Thank you! That means a lot. I don't suppose before you leave . . . the liver treats . . . They're in that bag on the counter . . ."

Derek took a cab to the Chicago Mercantile Exchange. The structure was imposing—two glass-and-steel towers rising up on either side of the building that housed the pits. He joined the tour, ignoring the guide and making his way immediately to the glass-partitioned balcony overlooking the volatile pits. He looked down into a sea of people. According to the guide, there were over six thousand traders on the floor, all of them wearing various color jackets. How was he going to find Rachel?

Searching the crowd, he listened to the guide in the background and he began at last to have some understanding of why Zanus had chosen Rachel as his target. One year alone, contracts with an underlying value of $333.7 *trillion* changed hands here. Derek couldn't even begin to wrap his mind around such an astounding figure.

Fortunately, there weren't all that many women on the floor and Derek soon spotted Rachel in the heaving mass of bodies. She wore a red jacket and she was standing on a stool on one of the risers that framed the pit. She was surrounded by men, all of them pressed shoulder to shoulder. Derek watched her shouting and moving her hands with incredible speed. Every once in awhile, she'd speak into a headset while still making signs with her hands.

According to the guide, the hand signals meant a variety of things and were used because they were fast and, in the melee of the pits, with everyone shouting to draw attention to themselves, no one could hear themselves think, much less try to perform transactions at the same time. It was incredible to watch.

Two hands held up, palms facing the body, meant buy. Two hands held up, palms away, meant sell. They had come up with a way of signaling numbers with one hand—seven, for example, was a closed fist with the index and second fingers extended. A closed fist pressed against the forehead was one hundred. There were lots more signals: months of the year, market signals, and so on.

Sometimes, the entire mass of bodies swung one direction, then they would shift another, like a great swelling wave of bright-colored jackets. The red-jacketed traders were throwing wads of paper into the air and the runners, in gold jackets, were dashing back and forth, yelling at the traders. Some traders wore bright, splashy-colored jackets to try to stand out in the crowd.

Derek watched with his face pressed against the glass. Rachel stood in the middle of the chaos. She would get pushed one way, then pulled another, and then pushed again. Bodies were writhing around her, their faces red and sweating, their arms flailing wildly in the closeness and heat of the pit.

For the love of God, how does this work? he wondered. How does anyone know who's shouting at whom? How does anyone hear anything? How can you possibly figure out what all the hand gestures mean? How can she stand the din and the noise? It was like the seething pits of Hell . . .

Then Derek remembered what it was like to be in the midst of a battle, fighting for your life and the lives of your comrades. The din of swords clashing and men shouting and crying out and the fear and the exhilarating adrenaline rush . . .

Then it dawned on him. This is what Rachel did on a daily basis. This was her life and it meant everything to her. And she was good at it. William had said so. That was why Zanus had targeted her. Derek's respect for Rachel grew tenfold that moment. This was what Rachel chose to do five days a week. This was a battle that never ended. Sometimes she won. Sometimes she lost.

"As you can see," some guy next to Derek was explaining to a friend, "working in the pit is grueling. It is both physically and emotionally draining. Most traders don't make it through their first year on the floor. They go broke and are never seen or heard from again."

The guy shrugged. "The rest will burn out, eventually. Some even crash and burn, they go broke and commit suicide."

Derek remembered what Zanus had said last night. About how he'd make it look like Rachel would commit suicide. He shuddered. No one would think to question it.

At least, he thought, Zanus can't get to her here. Talk about going where angels fear to tread. The pit might be the one place where even demons might think a second time before entering. Derek headed back to the apartment building.

Rachel returned home again just after the market closed. She looked exhausted, but she held her head up, walked with her shoulders back. She came up to Derek, who had been loitering about the sidewalk, waiting for her.

"I told Zanus I'm not going to make the trades for him," she said and her voice was even, calm.

"How did he take it?" Derek asked worriedly.

"He was furious. He said he would tell Freeman. I told him not to bother. I'd tell Freeman myself tomorrow, turn myself over to the authorities." Rachel grew pale, but she remained resolute. Her chin lifted. "I told Zanus he could rot in Hell."

Derek couldn't help but think that Zanus had been rotting in Hell for quite sometime now and that this was just the next stop on his tour. He smiled at her. He was proud of her. She'd made the right decision.

"Maybe you won't have to turn yourself in," he said. "Maybe something will happen—"

Rachel shook her head and gave him a wan smile. "Thank you for all your help, Derek. I could never have found the strength to do this if it wasn't for you."

He moved close to her, took hold of her hand. She looked up at him. Her lips parted slightly. He bent near her. Suddenly, she snatched her hand away and turned and almost ran up the stairs, through the door, and into the building.

Sighing deeply, Derek went to his apartment.

Minutes later his phone rang. Hoping it was William with news, Derek grabbed it. He was astonished to hear Rachel's voice.

"Derek, something's wrong!" she said frantically. "Sampson's missing."

"Do not panic. He's probably just hiding. You know what a brat he can be," said Derek, trying to calm her.

"No, he's not! I looked everywhere! And when I came home my door was unlocked and slightly ajar. I swear I locked it this morning before I left. Did you take him for a walk today? Could you have left the door open?"

"I shut it and locked it." Derek was worried now. "Go look for him in the hall."

"In the hall? But why—"

"In the hall," Derek said firmly. "I'm coming up."

If her door was open, someone could be in her apartment right this moment. He didn't want to scare her by telling her that, but he had to get her out of there. Not waiting for the elevator, he ran up the stairs, taking them two at a time.

Almost out of breath, he found Rachel standing outside her door, staring hopelessly up and down the empty hallway and calling Sampson's name. She had changed out of her work clothes and thrown on jeans and a sweatshirt.

"He's not in the hall," she said, as Derek brushed past her. "He's not anywhere!"

He went through her apartment, checking every closet, the laundry room, peering behind the couch and under the bed.

"I looked everywhere for him," Rachel continued, her voice rising in fear. "He wasn't by the door when I came home. He's always there. He's not in this apartment, I tell you—"

"And neither is anyone else," said Derek.

She stared at him, puzzled, then caught his meaning. "You don't think that someone . . . that Zanus . . . but how could anyone get in without going past you? You would have seen them!"

Derek shook his head. "Service people are in and out of here all day. According to the logbook, some fellow was connecting the cable in Miss Simmons's place. Another was fixing the dishwasher in forty-two."

"You think someone took him?" Rachel's eyes filled with tears. "But why? He's not a show cat, not valuable . . ."

She stopped, stared at Derek. She put her hand to her mouth.

"Oh, God!" she whispered, horror-struck. "I didn't make those trades. I told Zanus to go to Hell. Oh, Derek, what if—"

"Don't jump to conclusions," said Derek. "Maybe I did forget to lock the door and the wind blew it open. Come on. I will help you look for him. He is probably just out taking a stroll. We will find him. He cannot have gone far."

His reassuring words put some color back into Rachel's cheeks. He wished he could reassure himself. An ordinary cat might have decided to take a stroll. A cat who was really a cherub given a duty to guard a human would not have left under any circumstances.

Unless . . .

Maybe Sampson had taken matters into his own hands—or paws, as the case may be. He'd asked Derek to take him with him this morning. Sampson was known to be scatterbrained and unreliable, although he'd done really well on this job. The cherub might have decided to do some investigating on his own. Derek hoped that was the answer.

They hurried out of the building, searching up and down the sidewalk and out in the street, peering under bushes and beneath parked cars. No sign of an orange striped cat. Rachel and Derek both called Sampson's name. There was no response.

"If he wandered off, he might have gone to the park where we take our walks," Derek suggested.

"I guess that makes sense," said Rachel, though her voice quivered. She brushed her straggling hair out of her face.

"I will go look for him," Derek offered. "You go upstairs and get some rest."

Rachel shook her head. "No, I couldn't possibly sleep. I have to keep searching."

She started off toward the park. Derek had a growing sense of foreboding. Something was wrong. Sampson would have never abandoned his post. Derek had a terrible feeling he knew where to look. He went straight to the bench where he and the cat had often held their discussions. And there, underneath the bench lay Sampson's body, covered in blood.

Derek tried to block Rachel's view, but she was too quick for him. She thrust him aside.

"This can't be him!" she cried. "It's not him. It's another cat! It has to be another cat."

She burst into tears.

Derek looked down at the torn and bloody body. There was no doubt it was Sampson and he appeared to have been mauled by a vicious beast. Long claw marks raked his flesh. One ear was almost torn off, one eye slashed. Blood and saliva dribbled from a broken jaw. His tail was bent at an odd angle. One leg hung by a tendon. His fur matted with blood. Derek drew off his jacket and put it over the cat, wrapped him in it.

Derek's heart stuck in his throat, pain burned inside his chest. He had never thought he would say this, but he had come to like and admire the plucky little cherub.

"Give him to me," said Rachel. "Is he dead?"

"No, but he's hurt pretty badly," said Derek.

Derek picked up the limp body and handed him to Rachel.

"We should take him to a vet!" she said feverishly. "There must be a vet around here somewhere. We should find a phone book—"

"Rachel, wait. Look." Derek didn't want to show

her what he'd found, but he didn't have much choice.

As he had picked up the cat, he caught sight of a piece of paper that had been lying under Sampson. There were three names on the paper, names written in black ink and drenched in blood.

Kim . . . Beth . . . Lana.

Rachel stared at the paper. Her face went deathly pale.

"Oh, my God! If something happens to them, it will be my fault," she whispered. "All my fault."

She began to rock back and forth, holding the injured cat in her arms. Tears streamed down her face.

Derek saw the fear, the despair, the heartbreak in Rachel's eyes, and he had never felt so helpless. He admitted to himself then that he loved her. He never wanted to see her in pain again. He never wanted to be without her, ever.

Damn his orders! Damn William and damn Archangel Michael! Derek knelt beside Rachel. He gathered her and Sampson in his arms and held them both. Rachel leaned against him and wept. He glanced swiftly around the park to see if anyone was nearby. Not that it would matter if there was a rock concert going on. He would do what he had to do. Let the whole world see him.

Let heaven see him.

Gently he took Sampson, away from Rachel. "Go get some water for him," he told her. "There's a drinking fountain over there by the hot dog stand."

Rachel didn't question him. She was too upset, too shaken. She couldn't think clearly. She did as Derek asked, hurrying over to the drinking fountain. The man at the hot dog stand gave her cup and she filled it with a trembling hand.

After she'd gone, Derek put his hands on Sampson's body. Michael had forbidden him from using his angelic powers. Derek had obeyed those orders, even last night, when the demons were trying to kill him. He would have died obeying his orders. He wasn't willing to let Sampson die. The cherub would not be a casualty of this war. Derek wouldn't let that happen to his friend. He felt the power of Heaven flow through him, filling him with warmth. He sent that warmth into Sampson's body.

From inside the jacket came a muffled and indignant "meow!"

"Shut up!" Derek said in a low voice. "You're supposed to be hurt!"

"But it was Zanus, Commander," said Sampson, hissing the name in fury. "He did this to me!"

"Yeah, I know. Calm down. Rachel's coming back. And play along with me. You're bound to get lots of treats out of this."

"You're right, sir," said Sampson. "I hadn't thought of that." The cat closed his eyes and gave a pitiful sounding whimper.

"Derek?" said Rachel, and she sounded dazed.

He looked up, saw her standing there, staring at him, her eyes wide. She held a half-empty cup. Water dripped from her hand.

"Who are you?" she breathed.

"Derek," he said with an attempt at a smile. "You know that. Why?"

She blinked at him, and looked confused. "I thought I saw . . . I had the strangest impression . . . Nothing. Never mind." She shook her head.

"I looked the cat over while you were gone," said Derek. "I think he's going to be all right. His injuries were mostly superficial."

Sampson gave another meow, this one pitiful sounding.

"Superficial? He was almost dead—" Rachel thrust aside the jacket.

The cat's head emerged, green eyes blinking at the sunshine. His fur was covered with blood, and he looked very weak, but he managed to swipe at her hand with his tongue.

"He's okay," said Rachel, amazed. "He doesn't appear to be hurt much, after all. But . . . where did all this blood come from?"

"Scalp wounds," said Derek. "They bleed a lot."

Rachel dribbled some of the water into Sampson's mouth. "I'm so glad he's going to be okay!"

She was silent a moment, petting the cat, who purred loudly, adding in a little cough now and then.

"Zanus did this," she said. "He hurt Sampson and left that . . . that horrible note. He's going to hurt my friends if I don't go along with him. How did he get into my apartment? You weren't on duty today, were you?"

Derek shook his head. He couldn't be in two places at once and even if he had been on duty and not guarding her, he might not have been able to stop the archfiend, who could have entered her place any number of ways from changing himself into a spider and crawling in through the window to turning himself into a puff of smoke and gliding through the key hole.

"I wish I had been there, but I don't think it would have mattered," said Derek. "He wouldn't have come in the front anyway, Rachel. He would have found some other way inside."

"I guess you're right." Rachel sighed. "I don't have any choice," she said in despair. "I'm going to have to do what he wants. I don't care what happens to me. I can't let him hurt my friends."

"Do not let him win, Rachel," said Derek. "Hold out. Be strong. I will talk to my people. They will do something to help. They *have* to do something!"

He reached down to pet Sampson.

Rachel gazed at Derek intently. "You really love him, don't you?"

Sampson winked at Derek.

"I would not go that far," said Derek gruffly. He reached out his hand to ruffle the cat's ears. "But he's a good cat. I am glad he is going to be all right."

"You have been sweet and kind to me and I've been a coward, leaving you at that club. I'm sorry."

She leaned near him, kissed him on the cheek. "Thank you, Derek."

She gathered the cat, still wrapped in Derek's jacket, into her arms. Derek grabbed the note, crumpled it up, and tossed it in a trash can. His hand reached gingerly to touch his cheek—he could still feel the touch of her lips. He wished he could heal her pain, but he couldn't. He could only watch over her and love her.

But at least he had helped Sampson. He'd defied Heaven *and* Hell.

He and Rachel walked back to the apartment in silence. Derek could almost see the shadows of dark wings closing in around her. He put his arm around, held her close as they walked. He had to talk to William, but first he would see to it that Rachel and Sampson made it safely home.

"Do not let anyone inside," he warned from the doorway of her apartment.

"I'll be safe enough," said Rachel, with a wan smile. "Zanus won't hurt me. He needs me." Her lips quivered. "It's my friends I'm worried about."

"He will not hurt them. He will have nothing to hold over you if he does," said Derek. "And, like you said, Zanus needs you. I will go talk to my people."

When he left, Rachel's mind was in turmoil, and, surprisingly, she wasn't thinking about Zanus or the danger she was in. Her thoughts were on Derek.

Sampson had been near death. Rachel had caught a glimpse of him before Derek had wrapped him in the jacket and the little body had been badly torn up, much worse than the few superficial scratches she was treating now.

Sending her off for water had been a ruse. She'd known that. He wanted her to leave so she wouldn't have to watch her cat die, at least that's what she thought at the time. But when she was coming back, she had looked at Derek holding Sampson, and suddenly he wasn't Derek. He was a radiant being, strong and powerful, clothed in white, bathed in a beautiful light that enveloped the dying cat. Then she blinked, the image vanished, and he was Derek again.

"It's lack of sleep," she told Sampson, as she gave the cat a bath in the kitchen sink. "People start to hallucinate when they haven't slept."

Sampson meowed and nudged her hand with his head, wanting her to pet him. She stroked his wet fur. Picking him up, she looked him in the green eyes.

"Why is it I have the feeling you know things I don't? I wish you could talk. I wish you could tell me what was going on with Derek. Who is he really?"

Derek. Strong and powerful. She remembered thinking, when he was holding her in his arms, that she wanted to stay there forever, safe, protected. He loved her. She knew he loved her. And she was starting to think that she loved him.

Too bad, she screwed it up. She screwed everything up.

Rachel reached for the phone, hit the number on her speed dial.

"Zanus," she said quietly. "I'll make those trades tomorrow."

"Good girl," he said. "I knew you'd come around."

"I'll bet you did," she said, as she snapped the phone shut.

Derek hastened to the Fullerton Street bridge to have a talk with William. Derek went over in his mind everything he was going to say. Big picture or no big picture, Heaven would have to act to protect not only Rachel but her friends, as well. He would insist on it. Either they would listen to him or he'd raise a ruckus that split Heaven wide open.

But when he got there, William wasn't around.

"Have you seen my friend?" Derek asked one of the men who had been with William the night they had saved him from the demons.

"The old dude with the hat? Yeah. Some guy came looking for him. Said someone wanted to have a talk with him. Someone named . . . let me see . . . Michael. That was it." The man shook his head. "The dude who came to get him seemed right put out. If you ask me, I think your friend William's in all kinds of trouble."

Derek hung around the bridge until well after dark, but William never returned, and eventually, fearful of leaving Rachel alone and unguarded for too long, Derek went disconsolately back to his post.

William was in trouble. And Derek had the feeling he knew why. . . .

Eighteen

The next day was hell for Rachel.

She had nursed a glimmer of hope during the night that Derek might be able to find a way to help her, but when she didn't hear from him, her last hope was dashed. She knew what she had to do.

Rachel couldn't risk letting Zanus harm anyone else. She would make the trades and then she would live with the consequences. She should have known that Zanus was a fake. Perhaps some part of her knew all along. She'd felt used and manipulated the night she'd slept with him. She'd been stupid to fall for his flattery.

"You can't cheat an honest man." That's what the con artists always said.

If she'd been honest, she would have never gone along with him in the first place. She'd known it was wrong, but she had let her driving ambition, and her single-minded focus on making money, blind her to the truth. Now she deserved whatever happened to her.

She made the trades using the computer, remaining anonymous. That evening, as she was leaving, pandemonium erupted in the pit. Voices screeched and screamed; people pushed and shoved and fights broke out. The reporter for Bloomberg was shouting into his mike, trying to make himself heard. The president of the United States was said to be huddled with his advisers. The EU was in emergency session. The world was in crisis, hovering on the brink of a global economic disaster.

Rachel thought she would feel consumed with guilt, but she didn't feel anything. She was empty, drained.

"Don't pick me up tomorrow," Rachel told her driver in a toneless voice when he dropped her off. "I won't be going in to work."

He nodded and drove away.

Rachel dragged herself up the steps of her apartment building. The door opened for her. She looked up, hoping to see Derek, but it wasn't. It was Mike.

"Where's Derek?" she asked.

"I don't know," Mike answered. "He didn't show up for work today. Fraym's hopping mad."

Rachel wasn't sure she wanted to see Derek anyway. She was too ashamed. Probably he'd found out about what she'd done and left in anger, she thought as she changed out of her work clothes. Derek hadn't wanted her to make the trades. He'd told her to be strong, but she was too afraid. Derek wouldn't have given in. He was not that type of person. It would seem she *was* that kind of person. Not that it mattered. Her life was ruined. There was nothing ahead but shame and degradation. Nothing.

Oh, right. She'd forgotten. Suicide. Zanus had said she'd take that way out and, if she didn't do it on her own, he'd be there to provide a little help.

Maybe that was the best way after all . . .

She started to open the door to her apartment but stopped when she heard a voice coming from inside.

Rachel's hand holding the key shook. All she could think of was that Zanus was inside, waiting for her. She was about to turn and run when she recognized the voice. It was Derek.

Rachel began to tremble all over. Her nerves were shot. She fumbled with the key, but couldn't manage it. Hearing her outside, Derek opened the door. She practically fell into his arms.

"I thought you'd left me," Rachel gasped, clinging to him. "I thought I'd never see you again."

Rachel wasn't going to cry. She didn't have any tears left. Derek's touch was warm and his grip was firm. She looked up into his face and saw concern and caring in his eyes. Her strength gave way. She almost fell. Derek caught her. He was holding her now, holding her tightly.

"It will be all right, Rachel. Everything will be all right. I'm here now. I came to check on Sampson. You're not alone."

She felt a warm feeling of peace and calm come over her. Her despair eased. His words were like soft light that drifted on the air toward her body. Rachel had never felt such security and comfort in a man's arms before. She wanted to stay here always.

She felt his chest moving, felt his breathing strong and measured. She felt his heart pumping, its rhythm comforting. Rachel could feel her own heartbeat quickening to match his.

She opened her eyes and saw, from the shelter of his arms, that he'd done more than walk Sampson. He'd picked up her clothes. He'd washed the dishes. He'd raised the blinds and opened a window a crack to let some fresh air inside the room.

His kindness and thoughtfulness overwhelmed her. What a fool she'd been! Blinded by Zanus's wealth, enthralled by his air of power, taken in by his cunning manipulations. He had used her and he would continue to use her until she was used up. And then she would have no where to go but the top of her building and, from there, take one last step into brief, horrible pain and then blessed nothingness.

Either that, or she could live with what she had done, face the consequences.

Thank God! She'd found the courage to do it.

"Derek, you have to listen to me. I wasn't strong like you told me to be. I was too scared. I made the illegal trades for Zanus. He wants me to do even more, but if I do, even worse things are going to happen. The only way to stop this is to confess and turn myself in to the authorities."

Derek didn't say a word. His grip on her tightened. He pressed her close. That made her feel worse than anything else had yet.

"I'll be barred from the industry." She was surprised at how calm she was, now that she'd made her decision. "I'll lose my license. I will go to jail. And that's not to mention the fines that will be levied against me. I'll be broke. Dead broke and disgraced. No one will hire me. I've ruined my life. But . . . it's funny. I feel better now that I've made up my mind. I think I can get through this."

She took a breath and continued. "Derek, I want you to take Sampson and keep him safe. Zanus will be furious when he finds out. He'll try to stop me, but he won't succeed." Rachel's jaw set. "I'm not afraid of him. Not anymore."

"He will not hurt you. I will not let him—"

Rachel shook her head. "This isn't your problem. I was the one who got myself into this—"

He stopped her with a kiss, a kiss so sweet and sensual that it took her breath away. She never wanted that kiss to end. He smelled so good, like a sweet mixture of leather, salt, and warmth.

Derek hugged her so close that Rachel felt she would soon lose herself in him. They would be fused together never to be apart again. The idea was wonderful.

Derek ended his kiss, but only to move his lips

to her eyes, her cheeks, her neck. Rachel sighed and moaned and sought out his lips again. He kissed her with rising passion, his lips devouring hers.

He moved his hands to hold her face and pulled back for a moment to look into Rachel's eyes, as though he wanted to remember her always. She couldn't believe this was happening.

Derek kissed her again, this time, with abandon. Rachel's passion caught fire. She'd never felt so overcome with emotion. She kissed Derek forcefully. She could feel his driving desire for her in his kisses. He moved from her mouth to her neck, her collarbone, her shoulder.

Rachel moved her hands over Derek's back, reaching to hug him to her. His shirt was in the way. She couldn't feel him, his skin, his muscle. Rachel stopped kissing. Gasping for breath, she fumbled at the buttons on the front of Derek's shirt. He let her unbutton them, one by one, his eyes, burning with desire, fixed on her, his breath coming fast.

When she was finished, she slid her hands around his bare shoulders and shoved the shirt off his arms. It fell to the floor, leaving his undershirt. She reached to pull him close, but he caught hold of her hand, crushing her fingers, and began walking toward the bedroom.

She held back a moment. This was all happening to fast.

"Derek," she said, "this is wrong."

"No," he said, smiling and drawing her into the bedroom. "This is right."

Rachel relaxed. This *was* right, perfect and right. She'd dreamed of this moment, a moment where everything came easily for both of them, and simply being together was joy. This was him. And he was right.

Derek flung her on the bed. She expected, hoped he would jump on her, but he stood before her in his jeans, his desire clearly visible in the afternoon light.

And then, outside the door, came a meow.

"Go into the laundry room, Sampson," said Derek, and he smiled as shut he the door.

Rachel laughed. Fear and tension eased away. Tomorrow and every day after would be dark and painful, but she had this moment of love and she was going to treasure it, knowing that it would forever light her way.

He lay down on the bed next to her, moving slowly, taking his time. She started to undress, but he stopped her.

"What's the rush?" he said. "We have all night together."

At first, he didn't even touch her. Derek gazed at her, seemed to be marveling at her. And then he reached for her, but only to stroke her hair and her face, her arms. He massaged her hands and fingers, and placed a long and lingering kiss in the palm of her hand.

A streak of fire coursed through Rachel's veins

and up her arm at the feel of his lips. She had never felt so aroused with any man. She tried to speak, but desire cut off her breath. She could only gasp and quiver and moan.

Derek continued to explore Rachel's body. He ran his fingers down her neck to her breasts. He reached up under her sweatshirt to place his hand on her stomach. His hand was warm and his touch reassuring. Rachel reached out to him, to unzip his jeans, urge him to go faster, give her what she wanted.

He caught hold of her hand, shook his head.

"No, Rachel, I have been waiting a very long time for this. Be patient. I'll make it worth your while."

Rachel relented. She was used to being in control, and part of her was uncomfortable. Another part was excited, ecstatic.

Derek quickly pulled his undershirt over his head, and Rachel studied him. There were scars on his chest and arms, fresh scars. She reached to touch them.

"How did this happen?" she asked him.

"I was in a fight." He took her hand and held it pressed to his chest.

"What fight?" she asked.

"We're not going to talk about it now. It doesn't matter."

Rachel could see the sinew beneath his skin. He was a born fighter. His leanness kept him quick and agile. He pulled her sweatshirt over her head and then moved to take off her slacks. When she was naked, he gazed at her again, as though he could never grow tired of looking at her.

She thought she should be embarrassed, lying naked in the sunlight with a man's eyes going over every inch of her. Instead, she felt beautiful. Rachel reached to touch the scars on his chest.

"You're right. It doesn't matter. Nothing matters but us."

Derek lowered himself on top of Rachel's body. Feeling his skin burning on hers made her ache with longing. Rachel concentrated on him, on his touch, allowing herself time to experience every delicious sensation. He cupped her breasts and kissed them. He kissed her stomach, and moved his mouth to the soft warmth beneath her thighs. Rachel sucked in a sharp breath. She felt very vulnerable, and very excited. He kissed her there and caressed her and brought her to a frenzy.

He stopped, moved his kisses back up her stomach to her breasts and neck.

"Your turn," he said, rolling off her.

Rachel tugged off his jeans and underwear and threw them aside, releasing his erect manhood. She reached out to run her hand over his flat stomach, and now it was Derek's turn to gasp. She felt the ripple of muscle that grew softer as her hand neared the base of his shaft. She encircled it with her fingers and then her whole hand. Derek let out a low moan and pushed himself on top of her. He began to move himself against her body. Rachel arched her back as Derek grabbed her hips and thrust himself forcefully into her. Rachel gasped a little.

"I am sorry," he said huskily. "I could not control myself. Am I hurting you?"

"No!" Rachel whispered. "You're wonderful!"

She writhed beneath him, urging him on. Derek began to move with her, slowly at first, then he increased his motions with his intensity. Rachel let her legs relax, and grabbed his firm buttocks to force him deeper inside of her. Derek's pace increased, bringing Rachel nearly to her peak. Then he backed off again. He brought her to the edge again and again, but didn't allow her release until finally both lost control.

Rachel saw a flash of white before her eyes. Her body grew very hot and she had to hold her breath to keep from bursting into flame. The warmth in her stomach grew more intense, as her whole body spasmed tightly, then suddenly sweet release came in a rush.

Derek gave a sharp cry and shuddered and then relaxed.

They were both sweating profusely and trying to catch their breath.

Derek rolled onto his side and pulled Rachel to him, holding on to her.

"I never want to let you go, Rachel. I will never let you go," he said softly.

Rachel felt the tears come, the tears that were not of sorrow, but of joy. The tears they said were

Cupid's tears, brought on by the wounds of his arrows.

And then the phone on her nightstand rang.

Rachel jerked up and stared at it. A feeling of dread washed over her. Her only thought was that it was Zanus. He tried to reach her on her cell and when she didn't answer, he'd called her home. She didn't recognize the number on the caller ID, but he might be calling from anywhere.

"Leave it," said Derek harshly, reading her mind.

"No. If I don't answer, he might come up here!" Trembling, Rachel picked up the phone. "Hello? Oh, yes!" She gave a sigh of relief. "He's here."

She handed the phone to Derek. "It's for you. It's your friend William." Rachel was puzzled. Why would he be calling Derek on her phone?

Derek took the phone from her. "Hello?"

The man was talking so loudly, she could hear his voice over the receiver, though she couldn't understand what he was saying.

Derek's face darkened. His eyes narrowed. "You cannot do that!" he said angrily. "Not now!" He glanced at Rachel and his brow furrowed. "I cannot go into it . . ."

Another pause. Derek listened just a moment, then cut the man off, saying impatiently, "Meet me in the park. Let me explain. Please . . . you owe me that much."

He handed her back the phone and then slid off the bed. He grabbed his jeans. "I have to go."

"What? Why? I don't understand. Who was that? What's wrong!" She sat up, frightened. She didn't like the stern, set look on his face.

He managed a smile. "An old friend is making a very bad decision. I have to go talk him out of it."

He put on his shirt, then bent over to kiss her on the lips.

"Don't worry. I will not be gone long. Stay here and get some rest. You're exhausted."

Derek put gentle pressure on her shoulders, urged her to lie down. She obeyed his touch. She was tired. So very tired. He drew the sheets up around her, tucked her under the blanket.

"I will come right back. We will have dinner together."

Yawning, she murmured, "That would be good. I'm hungry. Maybe we could do . . . Chinese . . ."

Rachel drifted off to sleep.

Nineteen

Rachel was fast asleep when she heard a sound coming from her living room.

"Derek," she called out, sitting up. "Is that you?"

"Sorry to disappoint, darling." Zanus walked into her bedroom.

Shocked and terrified, Rachel grabbed up the bedsheets and clutched them around her naked body.

"What do you want? I've done what you asked," she said in a shaky voice.

"Yes, you have, my dear, but there is more you need to do, and word has come to me that you've decided you're not going to finish the job, that you're considering turning yourself in to the authorities."

"I wouldn't do that," Rachel said with an attempt at a smile. "I'm too big a coward. I don't want to go to prison."

"You may be many things, Rachel, but you're not a coward. Anyway, I'm not taking chances. We're going to go to my office together and finish the job there."

"I'm not going anywhere with you!" Rachel tried to sound defiant to mask her fear. "Get out! I'm calling the police."

She grabbed the phone.

Zanus smiled and shrugged. "They won't arrive in time. You saw what I did to your cat. I can do the same to you and then to your friends." His voice hardened. "I'm not playing games, Rachel. Get dressed and let's go. I'll wait for you in the living room."

He walked out, shutting the door behind him. Rachel thought a moment, then put the phone down. He was right. By the time the police came, all they would find would be her corpse.

Rachel's hands were shaking so she could barely put her clothes on. She looked around her bedroom for something, anything that would help her. Unfortunately jewelry, photographs, candles, and knickknacks were not going to save the day. Her only hope was to stall long enough for Derek to come back.

She walked out of the bedroom and said meekly, "I'll do what you want. Just don't hurt me."

Zanus smiled. "That's the girl I've come to know and love."

Rachel's stomach turned, but she had to remain calm.

"I'll need my paperwork and log-in information. I take it you have a Globex machine that I can trade on?"

She began to search around the living room. Too bad Derek had cleaned up. Otherwise the mess would have been the perfect excuse to stall him.

"Find whatever you need and let's go. I'm on a schedule," he said.

Rachel pretended to look for her things, wishing Derek would come. Zanus was growing impatient. She knelt down by her bag on the floor and began to slowly sort through some random papers, muttering something about passwords. As she was pulling things together, she suddenly saw Sampson poke his head out from underneath the couch. The cat looked at her with his bright green eyes and before she had a chance to think, Rachel scooped him up and popped him into her bag.

"If you're waiting for your lover, he's not coming," Zanus said suddenly.

Rachel's heart stopped. "What have you done to him?"

"Me? Nothing. I didn't need to. I've left that to a friend of mine." Zanus reached down and grabbed hold of her by her hair. "Time's up."

Rachel cried out in pain and grabbed hold of his wrists, trying to break his grip on her. He was too strong and only grunted in annoyance when she dug her sharp nails into his flesh. He jerked her to her feet and pushed her toward the door.

She fell against an end table, knocking it over. A lamp crashed to the floor.

"Pick up your bag and let's go."

Rachel had no choice but to obey. She couldn't fight him. He was too strong. But maybe when they got to his office, she'd have a chance. At least he couldn't kill her until she'd finished making the trades for him. Rachel picked up her bag and slung it over her shoulder. She put her hand inside, stroked Sampson's head. The cat was quivering, but he, too, seemed to sense the danger and was keeping quiet.

"Go to hell, you son of a bitch," Rachel told Zanus.

"I'm already there, my dear," he said, as he led her to the service elevator and out the door to his car, waiting in the alley.

Derek walked to the park at a rapid pace. The sky had grown dark, leaden with storm clouds rising rapidly from the west. He saw lightning flicker on the edges of the clouds, heard thunder rumble. As he reached the park, rain began to fall. He found William pacing back and forth near the bench where the demons had dumped Sampson's body. When William caught sight of Derek, he stopped pacing and began yelling.

"What the hell have you done?" William cried, waving his arms in exasperation. "Archangel Michael is furious with you. And with me, for that matter. I *have* to send you back to Purgatory. Right now."

"William, I cannot leave. Rachel is in trouble—"

William shook his head. "You've broken one too many rules, Derek. I warned you not to get personally involved and you let yourself fall in love with her and now she's in love with you."

William glared at him. "In love with you, an angel! Have you thought of the consequences of that? And then you used your power to heal the cherub."

"He is my comrade. I couldn't let him die!"

"His soul was in our keeping—"

"Like my soul was in your keeping when you let me die?" Derek demanded savagely.

"You interfered with the natural order of things," William said grimly. "And, what's worse, a mortal saw you use angelic powers! You've placed us all in jeopardy, Derek. The entire operation is in peril."

"At least let me try to make things right," Derek pleaded.

"No. You're going back," William said. "I have my orders. Archangel Michael . . ."

"Michael be damned!" Derek fumed. He was so angry he wasn't certain what he was saying.

William cast him a swift, penetrating glance and suddenly light burst on Derek, almost like a bolt from heaven.

"Michael!" he gasped. "He is the traitor! Michael was the one who sent me into that trap at the jazz bar. Michael refuses to let me use my powers. He said I was just supposed to spy on Rachel, not try to help her. And now Michael wants to send me away, just when she is in danger. I am right about him, William. And you know it!"

William heaved a sigh. "I *don't* know it. Not yet. I'm working to try to prove it." He glared at Derek. "And you're not helping."

"How long have you suspected him?" Derek asked grimly.

"A long time. Truth be told"—William gave a wry smile—"my suspicions began when Michael chose me for this job. And he didn't argue that much when I suggested you. We're neither of us 'angels' if you take my meaning. I couldn't help but wonder why he picked the two of us."

"Because he thought we'd screw it up. This changes things," said Derek. "You have to let me stay now."

"No, I don't," said William sternly. "You *have* almost screwed this up! You broke the rules. You can't be trusted, Derek. Now I'm sending you back and that's that. If you continue to defy Heaven, you're going to lose your chance to return."

"I do not care. I am not going back," Derek said angrily. "I'd rather live my life out here and take my chances. Your heaven is not my heaven, William. It never was."

William raised his hand, reached out for Derek. "I'm going to send you back now—"

Derek clenched his fist and gave William a sock on the jaw that knocked the angel to the ground.

"I am sorry, old friend," Derek said remorsefully, checking to make sure William was all right. He hadn't hit him hard, just enough to knock him out for awhile. "But I cannot go back. Not now. I won't leave her."

A streak of lightning blasted across the sky. Thunder cracked. The ground shook beneath his feet. Rain poured down on him. He glanced up at heaven. "Yeah, I guess that clinches it, doesn't it?"

He started to pick William up, intending to carry him to a bench, but this didn't turn out to be that easy. William was unaccountably heavy. Derek struggled to pick up the unconscious angel and lug him onto a bench. He didn't think much about it at the time; nor did he think about the fact that he felt a sudden twinge in his back. He was too worried about Rachel. Derek carefully put William's hat on his head to protect him from the rain.

Everything was falling into place. Michael was the traitor and that was why he'd picked Derek and William for this mission. They'd been sent here to fail. They weren't supposed to succeed in stopping Zanus.

A sudden, terrible thought stopped Derek dead in his tracks. Michael had outwitted him *and* William. Michael had known Derek wouldn't go quietly. He had known Derek would argue with William. He'd known Derek would refuse to go back.

His heart constricted. He'd left Rachel alone . . .

Derek raced back to the building, running through the pouring rain, his fear nearly suffocating him.

He bounded up the stairs and reached for the

door handle. Mr. Fraym, the building manager, stood blocking his entry.

"You're not coming back in here, Derek. Ms. Duncan filed a complaint. She says you tried to assault her. You're fired."

"She would not say that!" Derek said through clenched teeth.

"She didn't have to. Her friend, Mr. Zanus, left a message on my voice mail. He said she was too distraught to talk."

Blood pounded in Derek's ears. "Zanus! . . . Mr. Fraym, you have to let me in!"

"The owners don't want you on the property—"

"Then call the cops!" Derek gave Fraym a shove that sent the man reeling backward.

Derek ran for the elevator and jumped in. The doors closed before Fraym could catch up to him.

Of course, Fraym would call the police. Derek would have to deal with that later. Right now he had to find out about Rachel.

He reached her door and banged on it.

No answer.

Maybe Zanus was in there, holding her hostage.

Derek had her spare key, but it was in his room and he didn't dare go back down there in case the police had arrived. He raised his hands, pointed at the door, and summoned his angelic powers. He would blast the door to Hell and back . . .

He waited expectantly for the rush of warmth. It didn't come. Instead, he felt a rush of fear, a terrible emptiness, and the weight of his flesh and his bones. He was human, just plain human.

He stared grimly at the door.

"So be it," Derek said.

Turning his shoulder, he flung himself at the door and smashed into it. The pain brought tears to his eyes. He grit his teeth and hit the door again, with all his strength. This time, it burst open.

He ran inside. The apartment was in shambles. A table had been overturned. A lamp lay broken on the floor.

Rachel and Sampson were both gone. He had no doubt that Zanus had taken them.

And Derek had been stripped of his powers.

Twenty

Derek tried hard not to give way to despair, but he found it hard to think, hard to let go of blame and guilt. "This is all my fault," he muttered. "I should never have left her alone."

Then he lifted his head, a tiny spark of hope flaring inside him.

Rachel wasn't alone! Sampson was with her!

Derek had searched the apartment, but he'd found no trace of the cat. Of course, there was always the possibility that Zanus had gotten rid of the cherub for good this time, but Derek didn't think so. He would have found blood, a body.

Derek started for the door. William was always urging him to have faith. Well, he would. He would have faith that Sampson and Rachel were together. He had some doubt as to what use the cherub might be to her, but he had no doubt at all about Sampson's loyalty and courage.

Derek ran down the stairs. Reaching the lobby floor, he paused in the stairwell, opened the door a crack, and looked out. He wouldn't have been surprised to see the lobby filled with policemen, but it was empty, except for Mike sitting at his desk—Mike, the new doorman.

Derek smoothed his hair, opened the door, and walked out. He moved purposefully, with resolution, as if he belonged here.

"Where is Mr. Fraym?" Derek asked curtly.

"In his office," said Mike, looking up. Of course, he was clueless, as usual. "What are you doing here? Didn't you get fired?"

"I was upstairs returning a key. I think there has been a break-in in one of the apartments. Rachel Duncan's. The door is smashed in and she is not there. I thought I heard screams—"

"My God!" Mike bounced to his feet. "I'll go tell Mr. Fraym!"

He dashed off. Derek looked at the log but Zanus's name wasn't there. He made a bolt for the door and clattered down the wet stairs to the sidewalk. A white limo was waiting there, its driver sitting in the car, a bored expression on his face.

Derek pounded on the window and the driver rolled it down.

"Did you see a large black limousine pull up? Maybe you saw a woman getting into that limousine?" Derek asked.

The driver shook his head. He rolled the window up and went back to looking bored.

Derek was baffled. It had to be Zanus! Unless he'd sent some of his minions. Derek headed to the back entrance of the building. A couple of women on the housekeeping staff were there, having a smoke under an awning to keep out of the rain. The women smiled when they saw Derek. He was something of a favorite. One shook her head as she tossed her cigarette butt to the pavement.

"Hey, kid, I heard about you getting fired. Too bad."

"What are you going to do?" asked the other one.

"I will manage," Derek said, pleased and touched by their concern. "Say, did either of you see a black limousine pull in back here?"

The women both nodded. "Yeah! What's with that?" asked one.

"We thought it was strange," added the other, "but the driver said there was no place to park out front. That Ms. Duncan and her rich boyfriend got inside."

"She's a nice lady," said the other. "Always smiles and says hello and thank you. Not like some of them."

"Did you hear him give the driver directions?" Derek asked urgently.

The women shook their heads.

"How did she look?" Derek asked, his heart pounding. "Was she . . . all right?"

The women exchanged glances. "She looked

pretty upset, but she wasn't hurt, if that's what you mean. Why, is something wrong?"

"Maybe. I am not sure. Did she have anything with her?"

The women thought back.

"Her purse," said one, and the other nodded in agreement. "A big purse."

"She wasn't carrying . . . uh . . . a cat?"

The women stared at him. "What would she be doing with a cat?"

Derek sighed in frustration. Zanus had taken Rachel away, probably by force. But Derek still had no idea where they'd gone.

"Well, thanks," he said disconsolately.

"Sure, any time. I hope things work out," one of the women told him.

Derek nodded. He thrust his hands in his pockets, turned around, and walked headlong into William.

The angel had water dripping from his hat. His clothes were soaked through. He was regarding Derek with a stern frown.

"You can't do anything to me now," Derek said bitterly. "Michael has taken away my powers. I am human. Flesh and blood and bone. So you cannot send me back. The only way I am going back to Purgatory is the standard way—death. Now, if you will excuse me, I have to find Rachel."

Derek started to walk past the angel. Then he paused. He didn't turn around, he felt unable to face him. "You have been good to me, William.

You have saved my butt more than once. I am sorry I let you down. I am sorry I hit you. I hope I did not hurt you—"

He felt warm pressure on his arm. Astonished, he looked down, saw William's hand resting there. Derek stared at the angel.

William gave a rueful smile. "You didn't hurt me. You knocked some sense into me. After I regained consciousness," he said dryly, rubbing his jaw, "I started thinking about things. I realized I'd become so obsessed with proving that Michael was a traitor that I had lost sight of our real goal, which is to protect humanity. I gave way to my own feelings, Derek. Just like you gave way to yours. Only yours are at least worthy feelings. Mine, I'm afraid, are feelings of outrage, and the desire to wring Michael's neck."

"So what do we do?" Derek asked eagerly. "How can we prove Michael is the traitor? He has to be removed, William. He will stop us if he can, and we have to save Rachel."

"I have an idea on how to catch Michael, but I must return to Heaven to do it. You'll have to carry out your part down here."

"I will," said Derek. "Just tell me what to do."

William fished around in his pocket, brought out a crumpled bit of paper. "Here's the address where Zanus took Rachel. His office is near the Merc on South Wacker Drive."

Derek seized it thankfully. "How did you get this?"

"Michael gave it to me."

Derek looked at him.

"Yes," said William. "It's another trap."

"I don't care." Derek thrust the paper into his jacket pocket. "I do not suppose you could give me back my heavenly powers?"

William shook his head. "No," he said sadly. "I'm afraid not. Only God can do that."

Derek reached out, shook William's hand. "Thank you again—for everything."

He went racing down the alley at a dead run. He'd have to find a cab and that wouldn't be easy in the rain . . .

"Derek!" William called.

Derek skidded to a halt, turned around.

"You need to get Zanus to cross over, to take his true form. Like those demons at the jazz club."

"What good will that do, besides get me killed," Derek demanded. "In his true form, he can unleash his full power."

"Faith, Derek," William said testily. "You've got to have faith. Remember, son, humans have powers of their own. As strong as angels," he shouted as Derek was running off, "because it's all the same power—the power of love."

As Derek ran, he thought about what William had said. He loved Rachel with all his heart. He only hoped that William was right, that love would give him strength.

He was going to need it if he was going to go up against an archfiend.

Derek had not prayed in a long time. He had not prayed to God since those futile prayers in that dungeon. He prayed now and he realized, ashamed, that praying with love in your heart is much different than praying with a heart filled with anger, as had been the case when he thought God had abandoned him.

"I am not asking for anything for myself, Father," Derek said, the wind catching his words and whisking them out of his mouth. "Please watch over Rachel and guard her and keep her safe."

He felt better after the prayer, as if he had found another comrade to join him in battle.

And, there, at the end of the alley, defying all odds and expectation, was a taxi.

Twenty-one

Seated in the limo, which she had once thought so cool and elegant and which now she hated with a passion, Rachel looked out the window into the rain-smeared night. She was trying to avoid touching Zanus, who was sitting close beside her. She wondered where he was taking her. She knew Zanus had an office somewhere. He'd mentioned it before, but she had no idea where it was located.

She kept her bag close to her. Every so often, she put her hand inside and stroked Sampson's fur, feeling the comforting warmth of his body that lay curled up at the bottom of the bag. She had been afraid that Sampson would meow or start purring, but the cat seemed to know that he had to keep silent. She wondered fleetingly if Louis Vuitton had ever guessed anyone would be using one of his expensive bags to secretly transport a cat.

Rachel's thoughts turned to Derek. She loved him. She knew that now. She had been falling in love with him for a long time, maybe ever since that night he'd followed her into the ladies' restroom. She had no idea who he was or where he'd come from or why he was here. None of that mattered. What did matter was that he loved her and cared about her and that she loved him. Not because he took her to Paris for champagne or to Rome for spaghetti. Not because he bought her expensive bracelets.

She loved him because he had followed her into the ladies' room.

Because he had told her that she wore silly shoes.

Because he threw a grape at her.

Because he laughed with his entire body.

Because he had offered to stay with her when she faced ruin, disgrace, prison.

That was why she loved him.

He is ennobled by love and so is she, Rachel thought, remembering what he had told her on the day of their picnic. *Their love for each other makes them better people.*

She would probably never see Derek again, but she was determined that if she died tonight, as she was certain she would, at least she would die with courage. Derek would be proud of her.

* * *

The limo stopped in front of an empty office building. Rachel looked about frantically, but could see no signs of life—no lights in any of the windows of adjacent buildings, no friendly tavern on the corner. Across the street was a warehouse. The building next door was under construction. This neighborhood would have been bustling with people during the day, but it was deserted at night and Rachel's last hope flickered out. She had been counting on the fact that there would be people around—people returning from restaurants or out late walking their dogs. There might even be a policeman on his beat or a squad car patrolling the street.

But the sidewalk was deserted. The building was not only empty, there was a large "For Sale" sign in front of it. The driver opened her door. Rachel tensed, ready to leap out and make a run for it.

As if he could read her mind, Zanus clamped his hand over her arm, digging his fingers into her flesh.

"You're hurting me," she cried, flinching.

"Get used to it," he said harshly, and shoved her out the door.

He stopped to confer with the driver. "Go back to headquarters. Tell everyone to be ready."

The driver nodded, and, getting into the car, he drove off.

Keeping his hand like a vise on her arm, Zanus propelled Rachel up to the front door of the empty office building. He drew out keys, unlocked the door, and pulled her inside.

The place was pitch dark. He turned on a flashlight and shoved her across the floor and toward a bank of elevators. She didn't speak to him, nor did he speak to her. She tried desperately to think of some way to escape, but there didn't seem to be any way out.

She had no illusions. Once she'd done what he wanted, Zanus would kill her. He couldn't let her live. She began to shake with fear. Her heart thudded. Blood pounded in her ears. But she refused to crumple in front of Zanus, to let him see her fear. She was determined to keep fighting until the very end.

The elevator jolted to a stop on the sixth floor. Zanus stepped off, pulling Rachel with him. As they walked down the dark and deserted hall, Rachel realized suddenly that while she was still afraid, she was also mad as hell. She was mad at him for betraying her. She was mad at herself for falling for his lies, his wealth, his charm. He had seduced her, betrayed her.

She turned her anger on Zanus. He had undoubtedly been plotting to use her for some time. She had been duped, that was true, but he had targeted her. He knew a lot about her. He knew her faults and how to play on them. She had succumbed to temptation, that was true. She had let him ensnare her with visions of wealth and independence. She could admit that and she would accept her punishment.

She felt a little surge of pride.

He no longer had any power over her. He could no longer dangle money and prestige in front of her like a pretty diamond and emerald bracelet. She was her own person now and she would fight him to the very end.

She resolved she would not place the trades for him tonight. She would suffer whatever torment he planned to dole out to her. She would fight him until her last breath.

Rachel had given up hope that Derek or anyone would come to her aid. Derek had no idea where she was, and she had no way of reaching him. There was no one in this building. No cleaning crew. No night watchman. No one to hear her if she screamed for help.

It was up to her to save herself.

Zanus unlocked the door to an office and shoved Rachel inside. He flipped on a light that was nothing but a bare bulb in a socket. The office was devoid of any amenities. The walls were empty. There was hardly any furniture—only a desk, a Globex trading computer, a phone and headset, and several chairs. Papers and pens lay scattered on the desk and there were some empty coffee mugs and an ash tray filled with cigar butts.

A second door was probably a closet. There were heavy curtains and blinds over the windows so that no one would see light in what was supposed to be a deserted building.

Rachel looked around, but she couldn't find anything she could use as a weapon, not even a letter opener. Zanus was a big guy, muscular and strong. She doubted if she could club him to death with a Swingline stapler.

Zanus thrust her into the chair in front of the computer.

"The European markets are open now. You're going to finish what we've started. Keep bidding up the Euros until I tell you to stop."

Rachel lowered her bag with Sampson inside to the floor, keeping it by her feet, underneath the desk.

"I'll do what you want," she said, and she sniveled a little, as though she was beat down, terror-stricken. "Just . . . just give me a moment to acclimate myself. I'm used to working on the computers at the Merc. This one is different."

She eyed the phone. Perhaps she could figure out some way to distract Zanus so she could call 911, alert them that she was in trouble.

Zanus took off the overcoat he was wearing and opened the closet door to hang it up. Rachel was tapping on the keys, logging in, but she managed to sneak a peek inside the closet. As Zanus reached for a hanger, Rachel caught a glimpse of a golf bag filled with golf clubs.

She almost laughed out loud. The golf bag looked so ridiculous and out of place in this secret office that had been set up to be used for illegal transactions. But, of course, Zanus would play golf. More business was transacted on the golf course these days than inside fancy office buildings. Rachel wondered, suddenly, how many crooked deals Zanus and his cronies had going. A lot, seemingly, to support him in the style to which he was accustomed.

He shut the door, but not all the way, and cast a nasty glance at her.

"What's taking you so long?"

"I told you," she said in a quavering voice. "I'm not used to this system. And . . . and you're not helping any. You're scaring me."

"I don't think you're scared," he said. "I think you're stalling."

A nine iron would make a good weapon, Rachel thought, clacking on the keys. If she could distract him long enough to get to his golf clubs, she might be able to knock him out.

"Damn, it's stuffy in here," Zanus muttered. He pulled off his tie. "And hot."

He was red in the face and sweating. Rachel hadn't noticed the heat particularly, but fear had messed up her internal temperature. She was chilled one moment, feverish the next. Now that he spoke of it, she did notice that it was hot in the room. A heat vent was blowing out hot air. Zanus walked over to peer at the thermostat.

"Some idiot left it on!" he said. He gave it a flick and the heat shut off.

"Open a window," Rachel suggested.

"So you can scream for help." He gave a snort. "I don't think so."

Maybe he's nervous about being caught, she thought. The body always betrays the mind.

As if he were reading her thoughts, he muttered in a low voice, "I hate this weak body. I detest being human."

He walked over and flung open the door to the office. Cool air wafted into the room.

"You're *not* human," Rachel retorted. "You're a monster!"

"Shut up and keep working," he told her.

All the while she had been tapping on the keys as if to be working on logging in. Rachel was already logged in, however. She was trying to lock his account. Rachel knew it could be done. She just had to find the right file. She hoped the information she needed was on some of the papers she'd grabbed before they left the apartment.

Rachel reached down to her purse and opened it. Before she could stop him, Sampson leaped out of the bag and streaked across the room, making a run for the open door.

Rachel's heart jumped into her throat. If Zanus spotted the cat, there was no doubt he'd kill him.

Rachel dropped the paper and began to cough loudly, drawing attention to herself.

"Now what's wrong?" Zanus demanded, looking at her and away from the door.

"My throat is dry. Could I have some water?" she asked hoarsely.

"You're wasting time." Zanus leaned over the desk and smacked her across the face with the flat of his hand. "Get back to work!"

Rachel cried out, as much from shock as from pain. Her cheek stung from the blow and she tasted blood. Out of the corner of her eye, she saw Sampson dash out the door and disappear into the darkness.

Rachel went back to her work. The blow left her

trembling. She knew it was silly, but she felt suddenly bereft and forlorn without Sampson. He was probably terrified at the sight of Zanus. After all, the man had nearly killed him. Sampson had taken the first opportunity to run away. Rachel couldn't blame him. She was glad he was safe.

But now she was truly alone.

The taxi seemed to crawl through the city and Derek cursed the traffic, sure that Satan himself was behind it. Every light was red and the one time the light was green, the driver had to screech to a stop to avoid hitting a pedestrian who thought he would try to beat it.

"Rain," said the driver, shaking his head. "It makes people stupid."

At last, the taxi driver pulled up in front of the building.

"You sure this is the place?" he said, gazing at the dark and deserted office building. He twisted around to look at Derek. "This is the address you gave me. Is this where you want to be dropped off or not?"

"This is fine." Derek fished out some money, all he had, and handed it to the guy. He flung open the door and jumped out. "Keep the change," he said.

"Hey, thanks, man!" said the cabby. He tucked the crisp one hundred dollar bill into his pocket, and said to himself, marveling, as he drove off, "I knew there had to be a reason I pulled into that alley. Some good angel must've led me there tonight . . ."

Derek ran up to the door. He gave the handle a yank and nearly tore his arm out of the socket. The door was locked. He eyed the glass on the door, thinking he could break in, but it was heavy security glass in a metal frame.

Derek looked up at the building and doubt crept into his mind. *Was* this the right place? It was dark, deserted. No sign of a light. No sign of life.

He looked up and down the empty street. Maybe William had deliberately sent him off on a wild goose chase. After all, how did he know he could trust William? Maybe William was in on this with Michael!

His doubt, like a demon's sharp claws, tore at him inside. He stood in front of the locked door, a prey to despair, wondering if he should waste time trying to break inside or if he should go back and confront William.

"Faith, have faith . . ." he heard William's words.

But that was Derek's problem. He had lost his faith and now he was groping in the night, seeking to find it again. He wanted to trust William. More importantly, he wanted to trust God. He wanted to believe that he'd been brought here for a reason.

Derek thought of William and all he had done for him. He thought of what William had said, how Michael had deliberately chosen Derek because he was rebellious, because he was angry, because he had no faith in anything. Michael was counting on Derek's doubt to destroy him. And here was Derek, doing just what the powers of darkness wanted—doubting William, doubting Heaven.

But what if Heaven had known what it was doing all along?

William had sent him here. And he believed in William. He believed that God had given him this opportunity to set things right.

"Just help me find a way inside," Derek prayed. "I'll do the rest."

And, suddenly, an orange face with wide green eyes appeared at the door.

"Sampson!" Derek cried. Right now, he could have hugged that cherub.

The cat reared up on his hind legs and began to beat frantically on the glass with his front paws.

"Commander! Rachel's in danger! You have to come help her!" The cherub's words almost exploded inside Derek's head. Certain now that he had Derek's attention, the cat dashed off, heading to Derek's right.

"How do I get in?" Derek shouted.

Sampson came dashing back. He glared through the glass at Derek, then inclined his head toward his left, which was Derek's right.

"I'm trying to show you, sir. What are you standing there waiting for? Come this way. Hurry!" Sampson dashed off again.

Derek ran back down the steps and hurried along the front of the building.

And there was an office with a broken window. Derek wrapped his hand in his jacket, knocked out the rest of the glass, and hoisted himself inside.

Sampson was there to meet him.

"You took your sweet time, sir!" The cat hissed

at him. Sampson leaped around Derek's feet, nearly tripping him. "He hit her, Commander! I wanted to rip his throat out, but I had to find you."

"Is Rachel all right?" Derek asked worriedly.

"She's tough, Derek. She's going to fight him. I know it. And then he'll kill her. We have to hurry. This way, sir. Don't take the elevator, he'll hear it. Use the stairs."

"Wait a minute," Derek called after the cat, who had dashed away. "I can't see a thing. It's pitch dark in here!"

"Begging your pardon, sir, but this is no time to go all regulation on me," Sampson said angrily. "You could flood this whole building with light if you wanted. Use your powers, Commander."

"I cannot," said Derek. "I've lost them. I'm human now. Mortal. And I can't see my nose in front of my face."

"You're still going to stop Zanus, aren't you, sir?" Sampson asked.

"What do you think?" Derek said grimly. "You go on ahead. Talk me through this. I can hear your claws click on the floor. I will follow you."

"I'll be your seeing-eye cat," said Sampson and off he went. "Put your faith in me, sir."

Faith in a craps-shooting angel. Faith in a green-eyed, orange furry cherub. Faith in himself—an angry, rebellious angel.

Derek smiled as he followed Sampson into the darkness that suddenly didn't seem so dark anymore.

Twenty-two

Zanus stood over Rachel's shoulder, watching her bring up the trading screens. Luckily he didn't know much about this. He'd never been present when she was doing her trades on the Globex machine, and he didn't seem to be catching on to the fact that she was attempting to sabotage his plans.

"There," she told him. "I'm in."

"It's taken you all this time just to log on? I think you're stalling. If you're hoping your angelic boyfriend is going to come to save you, forget it. He's lost his powers. He has no idea where you are. So quit fooling around and make those trades!"

Rachel had no idea what he was talking about as far as Derek was concerned. She barely heard him, in fact. The strain she'd been under the past few days, the hurt and anger at his betrayal, the guilt over what she'd done—all of it had been pulling and twisting her so that she was stretched thin.

And, suddenly, it broke.

"I'm not going to do it," Rachel said, and she was amazed at how calm she felt after she said those words.

Zanus's face twisted in rage. His eyes bulged, his lip curled. She couldn't imagine how she ever thought him handsome. He was ugly, hideous.

She stood up and turned to face him. "You're right. No one knows where I am. No one is going to save me. It doesn't matter. I'm not going to place these trades for you. You can do whatever you want to me. I won't do it."

"Oh, I'll do what I want with you. You'll be begging for death before I'm finished," he snarled. "But you'll have to be patient. I have business to transact first."

He grabbed Rachel, twisting her arm, and flung her to the floor.

"I don't need you anymore. All I needed was for you to get me inside . . ."

Rachel gave a little laugh. "Don't be a fool! You barely have any idea what you're doing. The other traders will know you're an amateur. No one will take you seriously—"

"Shut up!" Zanus whipped around and struck her across the face with the back of his hand.

Pain burst in her head and the world went

white as snow for a moment. Rachel slumped to the floor, dizzy and sick and hurting. Her head throbbed and her vision blurred. She gulped in air and dug her nails into her palms to keep herself from passing out.

Her head hurt horribly. She was groggy, but awake. She lay on the floor, keeping quiet, hoping he would think he had knocked her out.

Zanus was smart and he knew his way around the market but not the computers. What she had said about the traders refusing to take him seriously had been a bluff. He might well succeed. She had to stop him. She watched him focus his attention on the screen. Unfortunately, she hadn't been able to sabotage his files. She needed more time. She couldn't fight him and win, she knew that. If she could only stun him or hurt him enough to get to the computer . . .

Zanus's attention was fixed on what he was doing. He was muttering to himself, talking to the screen. He had forgotten her. Probably he figured he'd knocked her unconscious.

Moving slowly, inch by inch, scarcely daring to breathe lest he hear her, Rachel gathered herself to make a desperate lunge. If she could reach the closet, grab a club . . .

At that moment, there was a blur of orange and an ear-splitting howl. Sampson burst into the room and suddenly the cat was airborne, hurling himself at Zanus, speeding straight for him like a ground-to-air missile. The cat landed on Zanus's head, dug his claws into the man's scalp.

And right behind Sampson was Derek.

Rachel didn't know how or why. She didn't have time to ask. She could only breathe a grateful prayer and feel her love for him flow through her, easing her pain, giving her strength. She and Derek exchanged one swift, glad look in which they each told the other all the secrets of their hearts. Then Derek jumped at Zanus.

"Run!" he shouted to Rachel. "Get out of here!"

She ran, but she wasn't about to leave. She dashed for the closet, wrenched open the door, and made a dive for the golf bag.

Zanus had seized hold of Sampson and dragged the cat off him. He flung the cat, still spitting and yowling, across the room. Sampson slammed up against the wall, then slid down it, and lay still.

Zanus cast a baleful glance at Derek, then, smiling as though he hadn't a care in the world, he turned his attention back to the computer screen.

"You have to stop him!" Rachel cried, hauling a club out of the golf bag.

Derek ran at Zanus, prepared to drag him out of the chair.

Zanus didn't even look over his shoulder. He held up his hand, pointed his finger.

A blast of air, hot and stinking as the breath of Hell's foul master, struck Derek full in the chest. The force of the blow lifted him off his feet, sent him crashing painfully into a metal folding chair.

Zanus didn't even look around. He continued with his work.

Rachel heard the crash, heard Derek groan in

pain. Swinging the golf club just as she'd practiced at the batting cages, she aimed it at the back of Zanus's skull and struck.

She had put all her hatred and pain and fury into that blow. It should have smashed his head like a rotten melon. It would have, if it had connected. Zanus waved his hand. The club vanished in a puff of black smoke.

Rachel stared at her empty hands. She was baffled and dazed. She didn't believe what she had just seen.

Zanus cast her an evil glance. "You stupid, stupid mortal," he said. "Stand in the corner and be quiet until I am finished. Then I'll deal with you, make you pay for the trouble you've caused me."

Rachel suddenly found herself in a corner on the other side of the room with no idea how she came to be here. She stood there, shivering, and wondering if she was going insane.

Derek was picking himself up slowly from the floor. His hand pressed against his chest; he seemed to be having trouble breathing. Yet, he looked at her; his eyes dark with concern. His love reached out to her, took hold of her, soothed and comforted her.

She slumped to the floor, pretending to faint but she kept her eyes open a slit. She watched as Derek straightened. He picked up the twisted metal of the broken chair and, lifting it like a shield, ran at Zanus.

Zanus fired another blast of hellish breath at Derek.

He lifted the chair, deflected the blast upward. The fiery breath exploded on the ceiling, scorching the tiles.

Derek flung aside the chair. Reaching Zanus, he put his arm around the man's neck, got him in a headlock, and began to squeeze the life out of him.

Zanus had to pay attention now. He seized Derek's arms and pulled, trying to break his hold.

Rachel began to crawl across the floor, keeping low, staying out of Zanus's line of sight. She heard what sounded like the crunch of breaking bones and Derek cried out in agony. And then there was a crash, as Derek kicked Zanus's chair out from under him. The two men rolled to the floor.

Rachel grit her teeth and kept going. She could hear the sounds of a desperate struggle and she wished she could see what was happening. She had her own task to do first. Then she could help Derek. And here was the desk! Finally! Rachel rose swiftly to her knees. Reaching up, she began to unscrew the cords in the back of the computer.

The thought had come to her that she could simply unplug it, shut off the juice, but then all Zanus would have to do would be to plug it back in. This way, he'd have to figure out which cords went where and that would take time; time he didn't have. She concentrated on her task that was taking longer than it should have because her hands were shaking. Then she heard Derek give a terrible cry. And then silence.

Rachel was in agony, but she didn't dare say a word or go to him. She hadn't finished yet.

Zanus stood up. He was a little mussed and disheveled. His tie was crooked and he had a cut on his head. He started to walk back to the computer.

And then Rachel saw Derek. His face was battered and bloody. One arm was mangled, the flesh shredded, as though it had been in a meat grinder. His shirt was half torn from his body. His breathing was labored. He could barely stand. He wasn't down yet. He saw what she was doing, knew he had to distract Zanus.

"Hey!" Derek called. "We're not finished here, you and me."

Zanus turned away. Derek took a swing at the fiend with his one remaining good hand.

Zanus calmly sidestepped the feeble blow. Doubling his fist, he smashed it into Derek's face. Blood gushed and Derek toppled over backward.

"Now we are," Zanus sneered.

He turned around, just as Rachel yanked out the last cord. The computer screen went dark.

"What the—" Zanus breathed. He looked up and saw Rachel.

His black eyes began to glow red, lit from within by an unholy fire. He opened his mouth in a scream of rage and she saw to her horror that his teeth were fangs, dripping saliva. Enormous black wings sprouted from his back. Sharp talons thrust out of his fingers. One flap of his wings carried him up and over the desk. He seized hold of Rachel, claws piercing her flesh.

She screamed and writhed as the fiery pain coursed through her body.

"Sampson!" Derek shouted. "He's crossed over! We can take him now. Quickly!"

Lights, bright and beautiful, blazed in Rachel's fading vision. She heard Zanus—or rather, the demonic thing he had become—gibber in fury and rage. He released her, flinging her down, and turned to face this new threat.

Rachel lay on the floor, dazzled by the brilliant light, mesmerized, unable to move.

"I'm hallucinating," she whispered to herself. "I'm dying and this is all a strange and terrible dream."

Sampson jumped to his feet, four feet, that were suddenly two feet. The cat's body morphed, changing shape, losing its orange fur, growing and shifting into the form of a young man, a beautiful young man, with skin like polished ebony, and dark curly hair, and a cherubic smile. The light emanated from his hands.

"I call upon the heavenly host to hear me!" Sampson cried. "Open the gates of Purgatory!"

Sampson spread his hands wide and, as he did so, a gate made of gold and silver appeared before him. It swung open, revealing a landscape that was bleak and blasted, with stunted trees and charred plants; a landscape that looked as though battles had raged across it for centuries.

Derek rose from the floor. With his last strength,

he seized hold of the archfiend. It was like grabbing hold of a lightning bolt. Jolts of fire shot through him as Zanus fought to free himself from Derek's grip.

Derek endured the pain and kept hold of the demon. Black wings beat in his face. Talons shredded his flesh. He grit his teeth against the torment and dragged Zanus, shrieking and flailing, toward the gate.

Once there, Derek drew in a breath and let it out in a battle cry.

"Knights of the Lion, to me!"

Warriors, tall and stalwart, clad in shining silver armor, bearing swords that flamed with blessed light, came running at Derek's cry.

"Commander!" one shouted. "We come at your call!"

"Take this thing back to Hell where it belongs," Derek ordered. "I'm sure its master will be glad to see it."

Zanus broke free of Derek's weakening grip and tried to flee, but the silver-clad knights ran through the Gate, caught him and held him fast. He writhed and howled in their grip and tried to bite them.

"Take the fiend away," ordered one of the knights and the other two dragged Zanus off.

Derek slumped to the floor. Blood dribbled from his mouth.

"Commander, let me help you," said the knight, kneeling down. He started to touch Derek, then he drew back his hand. "Heaven forefend! You're . . ."

"Human," said Derek. He collapsed, rolled over on his back. "Go back to the battle, Wilhelm. That's an . . . order. And take Sampson with you. He's . . . been promoted."

"Yes, Commander," said the knight and he raised his sword in salute.

"Thank you, Commander," Sampson said in a choked voice. Kneeling down, he took hold of Derek's hand. "I hope you have your wish, Sir. I hope you will be promoted, as well."

Derek smiled and squeezed the cherub's hand.

Sampson turned his gaze to Rachel.

"Goodbye, Rachel. I'll always remember you," Sampson said.

"Goodbye, Sampson," Rachel whispered, bewildered. "I'll miss you."

"I'll miss you!" Sampson said. A tear rolled down his cheek. "And the liver treats."

"Stop sniveling, warrior," said the knight sternly. "You are a holy knight now. Come with us. The battle awaits."

Sampson gave Rachel a swift kiss and then, waving his hand, he accompanied the knight through the Gate.

White light flashed, blinding Rachel.

When she could see again, the Gate was gone.

"Rachel . . ." Derek's voice was very weak.

"Derek!" she cried. She tried to stand, but she was too weak. She crawled over to him. "Oh, my God!"

He was covered in blood. His breath came in gasps. His eyes were shadowed with pain. Yet, when Derek looked at Rachel's face, they seemed to clear.

"Are you all right?" he asked anxiously.

"I have a . . . fat lip," she said, trying to smile.

"Your lips are beautiful," he said. "You're beautiful. I want to . . . say goodbye myself." Blood frothed on his lips. He coughed. "Though I never got . . . any of those liver treats . . ."

Rachel gathered him in her arms, and held him fast. "No, Derek," she cried brokenly. "You can't die. You can't leave me. I love you too much!"

"I love you," he whispered. "And I will not leave you. I have been . . . promoted . . . You need a guardian . . ."

"Here now!" said a voice. "You can't be telling this mortal our secrets."

Rachel looked around wildly to see the last person she would have ever expected. The homeless guy, in his shapeless and battered hat, walked into the room.

William squatted down beside Derek. Taking off his hat, he began to fan him with it.

"You did good, son," William said, then he sighed. "The war isn't won, not by a long shot, but you dealt them a blow. It will take them some time to recover. The fiends are still here on Earth, though. They still mean to enslave humanity, plunge the world into darkness. But they won't have any ally in Heaven any more. Michael's been cast out, sent off to serve his evil master. Who probably won't be too happy to see him."

Derek smiled. His eyes closed. "God did not fail me this time," he said softly.

"He didn't fail you the last time, did He, son?" William asked gently.

Derek shook his head. "I failed Him. I was consumed by hatred. I had forgotten how to love." He opened his eyes, looked into Rachel's.

She sobbed and kissed his battered face, over and over.

"When I think of the centuries it's taken to beat that into your thick skull . . ." William eyed Derek.

"Thank you, sir, for having faith in me," said Derek weakly.

He looked at Rachel. "There won't be anything in Heaven quite so lovely . . ."

He sighed, softly. His eyes closed. His body went limp in Rachel's arms.

"No, no, no. You can't leave me." She was sobbing now. "I just found you! I can't go on without you."

She slumped over Derek's lifeless body.

"Yes, you can, Rachel. You must, for his sake." William raised his hands to Heaven. "Blessed be the name of Lord. Amen."

William's prayer was soft, barely heard, but it resonated like a throbbing drumbeat inside Rachel. She could see the holy words glowing as they passed William's lips and shower down on her body like glittering stars. She looked at him and she did not see a homeless man in a tattered raincoat and beat-up hat. She saw a radiant being clad in snowy white robes, enveloped in an ethereal white light. She remembered the vision of Derek she'd seen, kneeling over the dying cat, who hadn't been a cat at all.

"An organization," she said softly. "Derek said he worked for an organization . . . You're angels!"

"Derek never could keep a secret." William smiled. "Neither can I, though. Yes, he is an angel. So is Sampson. So am I. You're not supposed to know, though. Heaven has a reason for keeping its secrets. And so, I've been authorized to make you forget all this, Rachel. I can take away the grief, the pain . . ."

"You mean, you can make it so that I never loved Derek?"

"Yes, if that is what you want."

Rachel shook her head. She leaned over, kissed Derek gently, and spoke softly, talking to him. No matter that he was far from her, she knew he could hear her.

"You told me once that love 'should make you feel as though you want to do great deeds, be brave and heroic. You want to strive for perfection, for the sake of the one you love, not your own. That way, if anything happened, and you lost the person you loved, you would feel pain, but you would also feel pride and gratitude, for you would know that because of the loved one, you are better, wiser, stronger . . . ' "

Her voice broke, choked with tears, but she managed to smile through her sorrow.

"God help me," she said. "I will be."

She turned to William. "I don't want to forget. What you told Derek about the battle, about the evil powers trying to plunge the world into darkness. I'd like to help you in that fight if I can. "

William was shaking his head. "That would be too dangerous—"

"I know. I'm not afraid. Not anymore," said Rachel. "I want to do something with my life. Something good to make up for all the bad. After I get out of prison, of course."

William gave her an intense look, as though he could see right through her to her very soul. Which, she realized, he probably could.

"That might be arranged," he said in thoughtful tones. "I'll talk to my superiors, see what I can do. Here, now. What am I doing? You're hurt and you're exhausted."

William put his arm around her and Rachel had the sensation of being enveloped in soft, white, feathery wings.

"It's time to go home," said William.

Twenty-three

Rachel woke the next morning to find that she'd slept so deeply, her arm had gone numb. She'd fallen asleep with her arm over her eyes and now she couldn't move it. She drew her arm away from her face and felt the stinging-nettle sensation that foretold the blood rushing back to her fingers.

She felt numb as her arm and she waited, tensely, for the stinging sensation to come back to her. It did not take long. The pain of Derek's death rolled over her like a tank, seeming to crush the life out of her.

She felt empty and lost and alone. So very alone. She'd even lost Sampson. He wasn't there to lick her tears away. Rachel let the tears and sobs come and she wept until she couldn't cry anymore.

The memory of last night was vivid. She recalled

how William had told her he could make that memory go away and how she had refused. She recalled her brave words to William last night, but she didn't feel very brave this morning.

She rolled over on her back and lay there on the bed thinking for a long time. Derek had given her a gift—her life. Rachel was lying here sobbing and breathing, because Derek had sacrificed himself so that she could continue to do those things.

You are alive, so now what do you do? Keep feeling sorry for yourself? Throw yourself off the roof like Zanus wanted? No, you're weak and you need help, and William's not here to pray for you and spread his wings over you.

Rachel wiped her face free of the tears. She closed her eyes and she slowed her breathing and she prayed.

"Dear Father, please hear me. I'm one of your charges and I need to ask for your forgiveness. I've been weak. No, I *am* weak and I need your help to get through today. I let myself become seduced by greed and power. I was afraid and I stumbled. I lost faith. Please forgive me. Oh, and please watch over Derek. I love him. Keep him near to you. And tell Sampson I said hello and I miss him. Thank you. Amen."

Rachel opened her eyes. Resolved to feel something, anything, she climbed out of bed and went into the bathroom. Her face was red and puffy. Her eyes bloodshot. Remarkably, though, she felt fine physically, despite the beating that Zanus had given her. Her lip was still fat, though. Rachel took a long, hot shower, and then dressed to go to the office.

She went down the elevator and emerged into the lobby. It looked foreign to her. She stared at it as though she'd never seen it before. This wasn't her lobby. Something were missing.

"Derek is missing," she whispered.

A stranger—a new doorman—looked up at her. He rose, walked toward her.

"Good morning. I'm Sean . . ."

Rachel ran past him, not saying a word. She pushed open the door before he could manage to reach it and hurried down the stairs. She'd told the car not to pick her up this morning. She'd have to take a cab and she wasn't about to ask the new doorman to call one for her.

Given what she planned to do this morning, she'd have to move out of this expensive building anyway. She found herself feeling almost grateful. She walked down to the end of the block to catch a cab.

Rachel stood outside Mr. Freeman's door. She hesitated just a moment, just long enough to steel her nerves.

"Love makes you strong," she said to herself and she knocked.

"Hello, Rachel, please come in." Freeman looked very grave. Maybe he already knew everything.

Rachel seated herself in the chair opposite Freeman's desk. She clasped her hands tightly, drew in a deep breath. She'd gone through the scenario of what she would say to him in her head a thousand times today already. That didn't make this any easier.

"Mr. Freeman . . ."

"How did you hurt your lip?" he asked.

"I . . . uh, bumped into a door. Listen, I'm not going to make this any more difficult for both of us than it has to be. I'm just going to rip off the bandage, so to speak." Rachel cleared her throat. "I made some illegal trades recently for a client of ours."

Rachel watched the color drain from Freeman's face. He stared at her. A nerve in his jaw twitched. He was seeing the ruin of his company come crashing down around him.

"I want to assure you," said Rachel, "I'll take all the blame. You won't be implicated. No one here will."

"Which client? How many trades?"

"The client was Mr. Zanus. You can view the trades in his account on your computer."

Freeman blinked.

"Zanus! What Mr. Zanus? We don't have a client named Zanus."

Rachel sighed. "You're in denial, Mr. Freeman. Mr. Andreas Zanus is in the system. Go ahead and look him up and you'll see." Rachel gestured toward Freeman's computer.

Freeman started tapping in the name. "Zanus. Z-A-N-U-S. Is that the correct spelling?"

"Yes, that's it."

Freeman shook his head. "I'm not finding him."

He looked back at Rachel, who was staring at the computer screen.

He was right. There was no Zanus there.

Freeman looked back at her. "Why don't you sit down, Rachel," he said gently. "Here, let me pour you a glass of water."

Rachel sat down. She lifted the glass to her lips, but she couldn't take a drink. Her head was spinning.

"But what about the Euro? The markets? Yesterday . . . the disaster . . ."

"Disaster?" Freeman was staring at her in perplexity that soon changed to concern. "Rachel, you've been working awfully hard lately. I'm afraid you're suffering from burnout. I've seen it before. Not enough sleep. Not enough to eat. Maybe you should take some vacation time and rest up. Please don't take offense, but you don't look well."

Rachel set the glass on the desk. "Maybe you're right, Mr. Freeman. I haven't been sleeping."

Now looking very worried, he dismissed her from his office. "Take a month off! You've earned it."

Rachel walked out of the room, dazed. How could there be no record of the trades she made? No record of Zanus? Was she going crazy? She went back to her office and opened her computer files.

The folder on the desktop labeled ZANUS was not there anymore.

Rachel looked at her cell phone. Zanus *was* still listed there. She stared at his name. Rachel had seen him dragged off to Hell the night before. Or rather, she thought that's what she'd seen. Trembling, she pushed the button to dial his number. There was an ear-splitting tone and a mechanical voice said dispassionately, "The number you have dialed is no longer in service. Should you believe this message is an error, please hang up and dial again."

"No, it's not an error," said Rachel, shuddering in relief. "Thank God!"

She took a cab back home, wondering what she was going to do with the rest of her life.

The angel had said he might be able to arrange things . . .

The cab pulled up in front of her building. Rachel stepped out. She walked toward the door, keeping her gaze on her shoes—sensible shoes.

She couldn't look up to see that strange doorman standing there. This was silly. She knew it was silly. Derek was gone and she'd have to get used to going through the lobby.

She didn't know what to do with herself. Her apartment was empty. There would be nothing but silence waiting for her up there. No cheerful meows. No cat to walk in circles around her legs, getting under her feet. What would she do now?

She could go back to the Merc, but the thought of all the commotion, the pushing, the shoving, made her almost sick. She thought of calling her girlfriends. They would remember Zanus. Or maybe not. If not, how could she explain what had happened to her?

"I can't," she realized bleakly.

Maybe she would call Kim just to talk, just to hear her voice. But Kim hated to be bothered at work. And anyway she'd probably be in a meeting, Lana wouldn't be awake yet. She was working the nightly news. Beth would be in the middle of three different things at once. They would be living their lives.

Rachel needed to find a way to live hers.

She sighed and, bracing her shoulders, prepared to grit her teeth as the strange doorman held the door open for her.

"Good morning, Ms. Duncan."

At the sound of the voice, Rachel's heart stopped beating. She looked up.

And fainted dead away.

"Rachel, darling, Rachel, come back to me."

Rachel came to herself. She looked into Derek's eyes. He had carried her to a bench in the lobby and lain her down on it. Now he knelt beside her, stroking her cheek with his hand.

Rachel reached out to touch his face. His skin was warm. His eyes were warm. He was breathing, alive.

"I'm sorry, Rachel," he said ruefully. "I wanted to surprise you, not scare you to death."

"Speaking of death," Rachel said shakily. "You were dead. I saw you die!" She clutched at him, held on to him tightly.

"Shh, shh. I know. It is okay. I am okay." Derek hugged her, stroking her hair, soothing her. "William says to tell you that they've accepted your offer to help us fight. But you need a partner."

Derek shrugged. "And he says I have still got a lot to learn before Heaven is ready for me."

He looked at her and smiled. "But you will help me with that, will you not, Rachel?"

In answer, she pulled him close and kissed him, long and lingering.

"Oh, before I forget, I have a present for you."

Derek unzipped his backpack and pulled out a gold-and-black tortoiseshell kitten. He handed the kitten to Rachel.

Disturbed from his nap, the kitten mewed loudly.

Rachel hesitated for a moment. She looked at the kitten, then at Derek.

"Oh, no, it's really a kitten. Just the ordinary kind." Derek smiled. "And I'm Derek. Just the ordinary kind. An ordinary man who loves you with all his heart and soul."

Rachel smiled and took the kitten and cuddled him close, rubbing his head with her chin as she and Derek walked toward the elevator that would take them upstairs to her new life.

Celebrate the new year and get started on a fresh batch of romance novels to rejuvenate the soul and rekindle the passion!

Want unforgettable romances and amazing authors? Then look no further than these four Romance Superleaders.

Not Another New Year's

Christie Ridgway
Coming January 2007

USA Today bestselling author Christie Ridgway taps into all that New Year's pressure in her fun and sexy new book. Hannah Davis has made a resolution—she's going to have a memorable New Year's Eve! At a bar on December 31, she picks up ex-Secret Service Agent Tanner Hart, a gloomy good-looker, and lets him take her to bed. She was feeling great until the next morning, when a woman bursts in on them and a bleary-eyed Hannah realizes that the man she's in bed with is more complicated than she bargained for.

♡

Women had always been a weakness of his, Tanner Hart admitted to himself, looking down at the flushed, long-legged beauty in his lap. When he'd spied her careening toward him out of the crowd, he'd had a gut-churning moment of foreboding when he thought she was his bad luck charm, Desirée, but one breath of her scent, one second of her resting in the cradle of his body, and he'd known she was someone else entirely.

Funny, though. The foreboding wasn't fully gone.

And because of that, and because he'd given his vow, he knew he should set her back on her feet.

But hell, it was New Year's Eve and how could one little kiss hurt? He was just drunk enough to forget that it was one little kiss that had fried his ass in hellfire to begin with.

So Tanner bent his head toward her, his gaze on her lips, flushed such a pretty red. He smiled a little, appreciating the passionate color. In his experience, a woman's mouth reddened to the exact same shade as her ni—

"Here's your drinks," a no-nonsense voice grated out.

Tanner's head jerked up. His eyes met those of his brother, Troy, as the other man clacked down another beer and some girly drink on the table.

"I was this close to tossing her butt out," Troy said, nodding toward the figure in his arms.

That was Troy, all right, out to save Tanner, his Marine medals always invisibly pinned to his T-shirt.

"But now I realize . . ." His brother's voice trailed off.

"Yeah," Tanner agreed, reading Troy's mind. His arms tightened possessively on the flushed beauty, even though he figured the other man's presence had ruined the moment.

Now that most of the midnight kissing in the bar was complete, his chance of getting a second shot at the dark-haired female he held was probably remote. Too bad, he thought, but it was probably for the best. After all, he *was* sworn off the opposite sex until he got his career problems straightened out and his life back under his control.

"She's not her," he told Troy. "She's . . ." He tilted his head to study the woman in his arms. While her hair was silky darkness like his bad luck charm's, and what he could tell of her body claimed the same stellar curves, instead of possessing the slight exotic cast of the big D's features, this woman's were of the apple-cheeked, cute-nosed variety.

Lovely in the extreme, but one hundred percent American rose. Long-stemmed. Dewy. Velvety. Sweet.

In that paper crown, she looked like a princess who should be reigning over the American Legion's parade float on the Fourth of July.

". . . definitely not Desirée," he finished.

The girl's face flushed deeper and the inside points of her arched brows slammed together. Her big brown eyes went from soft to stone. "Why is everyone saying that?" she hissed.

Tanner glanced at Troy for help. "Uh . . ."

The strange woman scooped up the girly drink and jerked straight in his lap.

Tanner bit back a yelp as her offended tailbone connected with the bone on his body that had reacted like a pointer's tail on the opening day of duck hunting season the instant the American rose had landed against him. And okay, so the dog metaphor fit, because yes, he was already hard. Horny.

Sue him. He'd been celibate for eleven months and counting. It was supposed to make him a better person, maybe not a bona fide white hat like the other men in his famous family, but at least someone who could be known for something other than screwing up.

The girl tossed back the booze, slammed the glass to the table again, and glared at him. Then she grabbed the sides of his hair and yanked his face close.

Kissed him.

Desirée had done that once too.

Except American Rose didn't taste like Desirée. Well, he couldn't remember *what* damn Desirée had tasted like. But certainly not tangy-sweet like this, with a little bite of mint. Mojito, he thought. Mojito and her own unique flavor.

He liked it. He liked it a hell of a lot.

Now she really went after the kiss, mashing her lips against his, more function than form, and he drew back, not just because he could sense her desperation, but because it was surging weirdly through him too.

"Whoa," he said, fighting her pull on the ends of his hair and trying to sound amused and casual and not hornier than ever. "Whoa whoa whoa. Where's the fire, sweetheart?"

Troy snickered and walked off, while American Rose froze. Then her hands dropped, her shoulders slumped, and a long sigh fluttered the ends of his hair. He thought she might cry.

"God," she moaned instead. "I read *this* all wrong too, didn't I? You don't want me either, do you?"

Maybe they were both a little tipsy, because she continued to sit on his thighs, though wilted now. "I haven't looked at a man in four years," she continued. "And then I have to be attracted to one who doesn't find me—"

She broke off, brightened a little. "Are you by any chance gay?"

Definitely both tipsy, he decided, not just because she'd asked such a question, but because he felt so instantly compelled to answer it.

With his mouth against hers.

Bending to her again, he licked his tongue across her pillowy bottom lip. Once. Twice. Felt her startled sip of air and the way her belly tensed against his inner forearm.

"Sweetheart, does that seem like gay to you?" he whispered, letting the words play across her wet mouth.

Bite Me If You Can

Lynsay Sands
Coming February 2007

USA Today bestselling author Lynsay Sands continues with her popular vampire series starring the Argeneau family. Lucian Argeneau may be a vampire, but he's also a bit of a grump. Hundreds of years spent hunting rogue immortals will do that to a man. The last thing he expects to find is a reluctant vampire who's having a bit of a tough time adjusting to her new life. Lucian hasn't had to interact with a woman this closely for thousands of years, and he has no intention of starting now. But the best laid plans . . .

Lucian jerked his hand back and waited. The door only opened halfway before the brunette named Leigh slid through and took a cautious step into the kitchen.

As he stared in amazement, her head slowly turned and she blinked at the sight of him. Lucian saw fear leap into her eyes and moved quickly, clasping one hand over her mouth and drawing her silently away from the door so that her back was pressed hard to his chest.

Her body briefly tensed, as if preparing to struggle, then she suddenly went still. When Lucian glanced down, he saw that her wide eyes were on Mortimer and Bricker on the other side of the door.

Both men were giving her what he supposed were reassuring smiles. They just looked like a pair of idiots to him, but it apparently worked on Leigh. As he watched, Bricker placed one finger to his mouth to warn her to be quiet, while Mortimer stared at her with a concentration that suggested he was sending her reassuring thoughts and perhaps the silent warning to stay quiet. The brunette relaxed against Lucian and he found himself responding as her body molded to his, her bottom unintentionally nestling his groin.

"I had just fallen asleep, Donald. I don't appreciate being woken up for this."

Lucian stiffened as that voice floated up the stairs, aware that Leigh had gone still. She was actually holding her breath, he realized, and found he disliked that she was so afraid.

"I'm sorry, sire," someone—presumably Donald—responded, but in truth he sounded more resentful than apologetic. "But I've searched the basement and she—"

"Because she's not going to hide in the basement. She's going to run, you idiot!" Morgan's angry voice snapped back.

"But why? Why isn't she willing?" Donald's voice had turned frustrated and even whiney.

"Not everyone wants to be a child of the night. I warned you of that. I told you, you couldn't turn your back on her for a moment until we have control over her. Not for a damned moment! I *told* you that! She isn't a willing turn. Until she accepts me as master, she'll try to run."

"I just left her alone for a minute. I—"

"You shouldn't have left her alone at all. Get her back and—"

"But what if she's outside? The sun's coming up!"

"You wanted her. She's—"

The words stopped short and Lucian felt himself stiffen further. The voices had drawn closer with each passing moment and by his guess the speakers were at the bottom of the steps now. The sudden silence seemed to suggest something had given away their presence.

Lucian glanced at Mortimer and Bricker, but he was sure neither man could be seen from below. He let his gaze drop over the woman before him, and spotted the problem at once. Lucian hadn't pulled Leigh far enough back. She was short, the top of her head barely reaching his throat, but she was generously proportioned, and part of her generous proportions were protruding past the edge of the door in her bright white blouse.

"Is that a boob?" Donald's voice suddenly asked and Lucian closed his eyes.

The ensuing silence was so long, he just knew that Morgan was seeking out Leigh's mind and searching for information on the situation at the top of the stairs. Lucian supposed it would have been too much to hope the man would just assume she was a bimbo bartender too stupid to leave the house, and she was standing up here contemplating her navel. No. Morgan suspected something was up.

Knowing their surprise approach was now over, Lucian shifted Leigh so that he could lean forward and peer around the edge of the door. On the other side, Mortimer did the same thing, and they found themselves staring at two men frozen at the bottom of the wooden steps. Then all hell broke loose.

Morgan and Donald suddenly spun and sped up the dark hall below, breaking into a run as they slipped out of sight. Bricker and Mortimer charged after them, and Lucian pulled Leigh away from the door, pushing her into a chair at the kitchen table.

"Stay," he hissed, then paused briefly, his gaze sliding over her face as he got his first close-up of her. She was a beautiful woman, with glossy chestnut waves of hair framing large, almond-shaped eyes, a straight nose, and high cheekbones in an oval face. She was also terribly pale and swaying in the seat he'd placed her in, so that he wondered just how much blood she'd lost.

Lucian would have asked, but a burst of gunfire from below reminded him of more urgent matters and, instead, he left her there and turned away to hurry downstairs after his comrades.

Warrior Angel

Margaret and Lizz Weis
Coming March 2007

New York Times bestselling author Margaret Weis teams up with her daughter for a paranormal romance series featuring good but flawed Guardian Angels striving to protect their mortal charges, never expecting to fall in love. Derek is a fallen angel, formerly of the Knights Templar. Disillusioned with God and His grand plan, he chooses to remain forever in Limbo, fighting against the Dark Angels, rather than enter into Heaven. But then news of impending war between the forces of good and evil sends Derek to save mankind—and a tempting woman named Rachel Duncan.

♡

Rachel left her apartment and rode the elevator down to the lobby. A car usually picked her up for work. She owned her own car—a Volkswagen Passat—and she drove it around town. But the parking fees at the Merc were insanely high and it was cheaper for her to hire a car service. Only the car wasn't there yet.

She looked at her watch. She was on time. Mildly irritated that the car was late, Rachel stood tapping her foot impatiently inside the entrance, keeping out of the wind that came roaring off Lake Michigan. She suddenly felt the hair on the back of her neck prickle, like she was standing beneath an air-conditioner blowing cold air on her. Only there was no air-conditioner. Someone was staring at her.

Rachel turned to say, "Good morning, Alex—"

She stopped mid-sentence. The man wearing the livery of the doorman was definitely not Alex. This man was handsome—really, really handsome—devastatingly handsome. He was maybe thirty, with a body that went to the gym, yet didn't brag about it. He had blond hair, crystal blue eyes, and a strong, take-it-on-the-chin jaw. And this handsome man was scowling at her like she'd done something to offend him.

"Oh, I'm sorry. You're obviously not Alex," said Rachel, taken aback. "You must be new. I'm not quite awake yet, I guess. . . . I'm Rachel Duncan. I'm in apartment 2215. I guess maybe Alex's wife had the baby . . ." She realized she was babbling like a schoolgirl and she made herself shut up.

The new guy didn't say anything. He stood there glaring at her in complete and utter silence. Was he mad that she'd mistaken him for someone else? If so, he could let it go, for heaven's sake! Rachel felt her neck prickle again, this time in hot embarrassment. She was suddenly annoyed that he wouldn't say a word to ease her obvious discomfort.

What a jerk!

Fortunately her car pulled up in front of the building. She turned and gave the doorman The Look. Then she shifted her gaze to the door and stood there, waiting. He didn't seem to get it at first. He just stood there like a bump on a log.

She looked back at him. "You're a doorman," she said coldly. "You're paid to open doors. Right?"

He grudgingly walked over to the glass door and held it open. She breezed past him without a glance. She hoped he froze to death in the backlash of the arctic chill she sent his direction as she walked by.

The nerve of some people. She'd at least tried to apologize for calling him by the wrong name. But what was his right name? Damn, she hadn't thought to look at his name tag. And why was he giving her that awful look, as if he resented her for something she'd done to him, and she'd never even seen him before? She was sure of that much, at least. She would have remembered him.

Damn! Was he ever good-looking, she thought as she settled back into the black leather seat of the car. Six foot three, she guessed. Sandy blond hair that just kissed the collar at the back of his uniform. And icy-blue eyes. Cold and hard on the surface, though. They weren't the eyes of a nice man. No, that look and those eyes weren't nice at all. But there was something underneath the ice, something smoldering. Fire and ice . . .

And he had to be one of the best-looking men Rachel Duncan had ever seen in her life.

The Secret Passion of Simon Blackwell

Samantha James
Coming April 2007

From *New York Times* Extended and *USA Today* bestselling author Samantha James comes a powerful and sweeping romance in which a tortured hero has a second chance at love. Simon Blackwell tragically lost his wife and sons six years earlier in a fire and has simply been going through the motions of life, until he meets the alluring Annabel, who soon finds herself falling for the handsome and brooding widower. But for Simon, to love so completely, only to lose everything—is not something he's willing to risk again.

♡

Anne was in the habit of walking daily. Even at Gleneden, when the Scottish winds blustered and squalled, only the fiercest of weather kept her indoors. If she was not walking, she was riding. Admittedly, as she ambled toward Hyde Park, the notion of crossing paths with Simon Blackwell again cropped up in her mind. But that was silly. She wouldn't allow anyone to keep her from her pleasure, certainly not him.

The day was not as hot as previously, but it was still very warm. Anne rested her parasol on her shoulder, quite enjoying her stroll. She passed a man angling in the Serpentine—and then she saw him.

Oh, no. It could not be. It simply could not be.

Their eyes tangled. He stopped short—or was it she?

Anne had the oddest sense he didn't know what to do as well, or what to say. But it appeared there was no help for it.

"Well, well, my lady, I see your dilemma. You are uncertain whether to acknowledge me or ignore me."

His bluntness took her aback, but only for an instant. "And I see you're as eager to see me as I am to see you."

He accorded her a faint bow. "I trust you've quite recovered from your headache?"

His tone was politeness itself. He knew, damn him, he knew it had been a lie!

They eyed each other. The oddest thought shot through Anne's mind. He was dressed entirely in severe black. No one would ever accuse him of being a peacock, that was for certain. And just as last night, she sensed power and strength beneath the clothing.

Her heart was pounding oddly as well. Anne swallowed. "There is no one present," she said. "We need not stand on pretense as we did last night."

"Pretense? Is that what it was?"

His gaze had sharpened along with his tone.

"The truth is, I didn't expect that you would come to supper last night." The confession emerged before she could stop it.

"My dear Lady Anne, I was invited."

"So you were."

"And if I hadn't come, would that have made me a coward in your eyes?"

"Of course not," she stated shortly. "It would simply indicate that you've a mind of your own."

There was a sudden glint in his eye. "Some might take that as a challenge, my lady."